THE 12TH COMMANDMENT

ALSO BY DANIEL TORDAY

Boomer1

The Last Flight of Poxl West

The Sensualist

THE 12TH COMMANDMENT

DANIEL TORDAY

ST. MARTIN'S PRESS
NEW YORK

First published in the United States by St. Martin's Press, an imprint of St. Martin's Publishing Group

THE 12TH COMMANDMENT. Copyright © 2022 by Daniel Torday. All rights reserved. Printed in the United States of America. For information, address St. Martin's Publishing Group, 120 Broadway, New York, NY 10271.

www.stmartins.com

Map illustrated by Ali Mac

Library of Congress Cataloging-in-Publication Data

Names: Torday, Daniel, author.
Title: The 12th commandment / Daniel Torday.
Other titles: Twelfth commandment
Description: First edition. | New York : St. Martin's Press, 2023.
Identifiers: LCCN 2022035460 | ISBN 9781250191816 (hardcover) | ISBN 9781250191823 (ebook)
Subjects: LCGFT: Novels.
Classification: LCC PS3557.R198 A613 2023 | DDC 813/.54—dc23 /eng/20220728
LC record available at https://lccn.loc.gov/2022035460

Our books may be purchased in bulk for promotional, educational, or business use. Please contact your local bookseller or the Macmillan Corporate and Premium Sales Department at 1-800-221-7945, extension 5442, or by email at MacmillanSpecialMarkets@macmillan.com.

First Edition: 2023

10 9 8 7 6 5 4 3 2 1

To Erin, Abby, and Delia, my loves

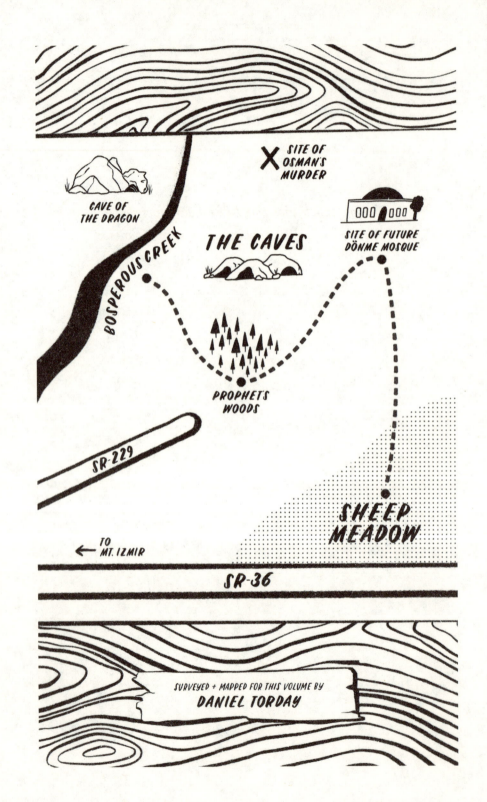

We lay there, face to face, and held hands under water. I looked up at the sky. It was all you could see. I thought about God.

—JAMES M. CAIN, *THE POSTMAN ALWAYS RINGS TWICE*

Commandment 12: It is not a sin in the eyes of God to kill a maamin who reveals the secrets of his religion. Hate these traitors. Even kill him, if he is dangerous to the maaminim.

—FROM THE EIGHTEEN COMMANDMENTS OF THE DÖNME

BOOK ONE

IN NO TIME

The afternoon he arrives in Central Ohio for Gram's funeral, Eze-kiel Leger is stuck in a van heading east on I-70 amid heavy snow. Snow falls lightly over Manhattan. Snow inundates Ohio. Zeke walks out of the Columbus airport to the rental car place, only to discover that the rental car has been rented elsewhere. He will have to take a shuttle van to Mt. Izmir, where later in the day he will have access to the same car.

"You'll be able to pick a sedan up there in no time," the man at the counter says. He is not apologetic.

Zeke walks back curbside to await his shuttle. He stands un-der a concrete overhang. Snow blows sideways in chunks the size and glint of airborne mica. Wafers bearing the body of someone's Lord. Not Zeke's Lord. Zeke does not himself yet believe in the Lord Almighty.

The shuttle arrives, and six departing passengers board it. By the time it reaches State Route 36 heading northeast into the rural hinterland, snow has piled on asphalt. Snow falls and keeps falling.

Cows lie in fields upon their forelegs as if at worship. Singular barns flake red paint. Roofs sag long past childbearing, silos and wet green fields of wilted long-dead soy and corn. Zeke leans forward to talk to the woman in the seat in front of him. She does not respond, pretends as if he is not there to begin with. He texts his two old college friends who will be at the funeral, waits for the gray ellipses of acknowledgment to appear on his screen, but they do not appear.

While he is looking down, the van lurches across the double yellow lines.

The driver crosses one arm over the other to turn the van fierce right. It judders back left. The van's wheels touch the rut next to the road. It flips. Luggage tumbles and dumps from overhead racks. Trees appear to upturn through snowy windows. Inside the van all is chaos—bodies slam windows, plastic water bottles crink as they hit ceiling and floor. For just a glimpse before his head smacks window, Zeke feels the prick of glass against his cheek and nose; the van lands, rolls across snowy grass, then soy. There is nothing to see above but field horizoned by sky. Zeke loses consciousness. He is confronted by endless vast nothing.

: : : : :

Zeke comes to seconds later. He is briefly alone in the gelid white of this otherwise unoccupied white van. The window is shattered. His face is sensationless against cold wet Ohio grass. A head pops in from what had previously been a driver-side rear window.

"You're gonna be OK, son, we've got paramedics right on their way," the man says. He is grandfather-aged, reddish goatee and an Ohio state trooper's hat, a look that conjures the undergraduate paranoia of being out on the highway drunken and stony. Zeke says he is fine. He pulls himself out of the van. Snow drops in

4

cakes from the sky. It blows against his face, but he feels no cold. He wonders if this is how Gram felt when he took his life, just before his car left the road—then pushes the thought away. It is an obsessive thought, reflexive, one of many he's been unable to control since learning Gram killed himself, moving himself into Gram's head, then quickly out. Under a nearby tree the woman from in front of him sits with a cowl draped across her shoulders. It is taking on a light white rime from the falling snow.

"Why don't you just have a seat over here," the cop says.

The cop says his name is Paul, a last name. Zeke says he's fine, but he puts his hand to his face and feels blood tacky on his cheek. Fire pipes from the skin around his right eye when he touches it. Now he doesn't feel cold, but hot, and he begins to feel more but again pushes it down. Down. He decides Paul is right. He accepts a glass of water. Soon there is a wash of red lights from an arriving ambulance, then another. It is as if the day has turned from the hard white of cold to the hard red hot of night. His ambulance heads north the twenty miles to the Mt. Vernon Hospital, just ten miles from his Airbnb, where he's set to stay through to the weekend. And bid Gram farewell.

MOURNING IN OHIO

Zeke sat through a silent cab ride amid the dark black nothing of Central Ohio night. The Airbnb he'd found was on the banks of the river, in a small one-room cabin at the edge of a campground. Gram's family suggested the area to out-of-towners so there might be some sense of community. But Zeke's two closest friends from his college days still lived near Columbus, so he alone found this rental. When he arrived, it was well past midnight, and they'd long since texted to say they were going to sleep. And his eye ached. His body felt as if it had been touched by the whirlwind. When he woke in the morning, he hauled himself over to the mirror in the cabin's small bathroom and peeled the tape and gauze from his eye. The eye had healed far more than it should have. Scabbing over stitches was minimal; healthy skin had begun to heal. He examined his face so close to the mirror the muscles at the back of his eyes hurt.

Zeke put the bandage back over his eye. The hour was so late that Declan and Johanna had both already texted to say they had headed to the cemetery. The funeral was to be held just outside the campus where they'd all gone to school. Zeke could meet them there and take the time he needed. "I promised the family I'd be there to help finish the arrangements," Declan wrote; as he was still living there in Central Ohio, and now a professor at William James College, many of the funeral preparations had fallen to him.

It was a twenty-seven-minute wait for an Uber. Zeke called for a cab, as well, given how uncertain it would be to actually get a ride here in the hinterland. Thin sun cut at an angle into the glass doors at the back of the cabin. Zeke strolled out back where the tinkling sound of water under ice trickled up from the river. He was standing on a slope maybe two hundred feet above its bank, another three or four hundred feet across to the other. Snow blanketed a stand of kayaks available to renters in summer. Off to the right of the cabin, seven RVs sat with the smoke of spent fires drifting toward the gray sky. Footprints circled each white vehicle, but there was no further sign of anyone there.

When the cab finally rolled up, it was a white Honda Civic with checkers laminated on its flanks and an Uber sticker in the rear window.

"You call an Uber?" the driver said. He was maybe nineteen, pamphlet-thin in a black hoodie and a brown rime of beard. Snow drifted in chunks like Downy flakes in the air and hung as if suspended in their descent.

"I did, but then I called a cab."

An older man in a green trucker hat now hung his head out of the window of a nearby RV. The Uber driver said, "Oh, hey, Clive," and the old man waved and said, "What's up, Meta?" and he waved back and then said to Zeke, "Oh, yeah, I'm cab and Uber and Lyft and whatever else, bro. Kinda the only game in town."

Meta drove out along the rural roads and on through downtown

Mt. Izmir, a shabby atavistic vestige of a business district. At the center of town, off State Route 229, was a roundabout. At its center stood a statue of the author of one of the most famous Confederate songs of the Civil War. A smattering of wilted flowers drooped under the weight of the snow that continued to fall. On one corner of the roundabout was the Ohio Diner, and all around it awnings and buildings in a sickly mustard-yellow brick. The college campus was far out in the cornfields of the rural hills to their east, but the only way out there was through town.

"What happened to that eye there, bro?" Meta said. He glanced into the rearview mirror and then back down to the road as he navigated the roundabout. Zeke said he'd been in a car accident on his way from the airport.

"Shit looks painful," Meta said. "What you say your name was? Zee? Fuck kind of name is that?"

"Zeke," Zeke said. "Though in sports and stuff people have called me Zee, which is fine with me. But Zeke. Like Ezekiel."

Meta looked back at the road.

"What're you doing here in glorious Central Ohio anyway? You're with the college?"

"I'm an alum, yeah. But no. I'm here for a funeral."

"Oh, man, another death up at the crazy Jewish cult?" Meta said.

"No, no. An old friend from college committed suicide. Died by suicide—died. He wanted to be buried out here. Wanted a ceremony in the cemetery near campus. So we all came."

"Sorry, man," Meta said.

They were silent as they passed through the north end of Mt. Izmir, past decrepit Victorians with their faded pastel facades.

"Where'd you head in from?"

"From New York. I'm a reporter. A magazine editor. Well, a writer and an editor."

"Well, dude, a writer or an editor—you should *definitely* look into the murder up at that Jewish cult, then," Meta said. "They say there's a guy there who thinks he's a prophet, that he killed his son. Nothing ever seems right there. I been living here more than a decade and nothing ever seemed right out there. Weird folk. They're like Jews and Muslims at the same time. Or something. Sketchy as hell. And a lot more people out there now than there were before."

Twin sadnesses hit Zeke: There was the sadness when someone learned he worked at a national magazine and tried to give him a story idea—which never worked out, and always felt depressing. And there was the sadness of his instinct to listen, which threatened to be the worst kind of busman's holiday, thinking about work while he was here to mourn Gram's passing. Suicide. He thought the word, and something wrapped tight in his chest, like the wringing of a sopping towel deep inside.

Zeke didn't respond for a second and then decided he'd never see this guy again. "I find my own stories. I know how to find my own stories. I'm here to bury a friend, not to work."

"All right, man," Meta said. "I didn't mean to—"

Neither of them spoke again until they reached the cemetery.

: : : : :

From a far distance as they crested the hill, Zeke could see mourners already gathered. At the edge of the college campus, beyond soccer fields and a football field and an oblong white postmodern building shaped like an inefficient grounded spacecraft, in a long low reedy field covered in snow, was the graveyard where Gram had bought a plot as a gag back when they were sophomores. He came from money—Central Ohio Jewish money, but money here was money—and when they learned there was going to be a Halloween party at the edge of the field, Gram had snuck ahead and bought a plot there for himself. He'd had the headstone made up. No dates, it just read, GRAM ANDREW SILVER / 1981–TK / HE DIED AS HE LIVED: IN THE MIDWEST. His gallows humor always made them laugh. They'd shotgun beers or smoke a bowl and head down to lie atop Gram's empty grave and tell ghost stories of their living friend. And laugh. He did make them laugh.

Until today.

Zeke hadn't anticipated such a large group for the funeral; he hadn't seen Gram in over a year, since they played one last gig in Brooklyn, a kind of novelty performance for a Guns N' Roses cover band Gram was in. Gram was as serious about music as he was funny about life, and years ago Zeke had given up taking music seriously in favor of writing. Now Gram was a nexus of hurt. The fact of grief was overtaken in a flash by the realization that Zeke no longer knew Gram's life here in Ohio. He'd occasionally texted with Declan and gotten the sense something was wrong, that Gram had taken on water and was sinking, but texts did not reveal details. Now. Now here he was. Everyone gathered around the cemetery was coupled off, bundled up; from this distance, every thirty-something in a charcoal-gray wool overcoat looked middle-aged. Fuck. They had graduated barely ten years ago, and somehow Gram had been welcomed into a community of early dotage. Before his end.

"How late am I," Zeke said. Declan and Johanna were standing on the edge of the worshippers.

"Characteristically late," Johanna said. The thinnest collection of creases had begun to develop around the edges of her eyes. Otherwise she looked exactly as she did when they'd first kissed freshman year, freckled and fair with a toasted touch of sun across her nose and cheeks—exactly as she had the day she'd ended things, their graduation, when he said he needed freedom to pursue his life as a journalist in New York, and Johanna said she wasn't coming.

"But what's going on here, friend," Declan said. He pushed a gloved finger against the bandage. Zeke made no move away from it. "Bad accident?"

"Bad accident." He could barely get a bead on Declan, who was professorially dressed in a high-collared Zara overcoat and a pair of wingtips dusted with snow. His face was hidden behind all the accoutrements. "I mean I'd just landed and then—"

And then the rabbi began to intone the Kaddish. All went silent among the mourners. The silver swish of wind across the Ohio plain, the low rush of wind in their eyes carrying spiking droplets of ice, the overwhelming suggestion of the whirlwind blowing over them all. "Yitgadal v'yitkadash sh'mei raba"—he remembered only so much of the prayer from childhood. With the frigid wind and the memory the ancient language evoked, Zeke's eyes welled with thin water. He was crying. He was in an Ohio field, saying goodbye to Gram, and his shoulders began to pitch forward, eyes so filled with tears he could not tell if the other mourners were slowly moving forward and then back with the intonation of the rabbi in prayer, with the heavy wind, or if they were standing still and he was rocking back and forth himself.

: : : : :

Declan drove Zeke to the Ohio Diner on the circle at the center of Mt. Izmir; Johanna drove separately. The low snow-covered fields passed their windows, utterly unchanged since the two were undergrads.

"Do you even see all of this anymore?"

"How do you mean," Declan said. He tapped his brakes and his Subaru Outback skidded, fishtailed, regained purchase on the road.

"Like, now that you've been living here more than a decade, do you see the paint flaking, the old people getting older? How bleak this place is in winter. Or do you just kind of start going through your life, waiting for the next crop of freshmen."

"I guess I'd have to think about it to give you a worthy answer," Declan said. He put on his blinker, turned right. "I guess more than anything I think about my classes. About Kant. About Germany, and when I'll go back to Berlin next, the friends and colleagues I'll see there. And about my kid. I mean, do you still notice every New York City landmark when you pass it?"

Zeke hadn't realized the judgmental tone to his question, the way he'd been calling Declan out for living in the town where they went to college: the ease of his life as an academic. His status as literal, actual Midwesterner after their four years of pantomiming it as undergrads.

"I don't." Zeke looked out the window. The sound of the Ohio wind carrying over the hood of the car, then shifting and pushing them left, then right, distracted them both. They were almost at the center of town.

"I did notice Johanna."

"I noticed you noticing," Declan said. "I mean there has to be something left there, right? She's still on her own."

"She lives in Columbus, Ohio," Zeke said.

"And you live in a tiny apartment in Brooklyn," Declan said.

A tight frozen feeling sat in the middle of Zeke's chest, pushing his thoughts down again and again. The way a top layer of snow might crunch underfoot until it hits solid ice below.

They parked and met Johanna in the diner. She'd already gotten them a booth.

"They still have the coffee cake with the caramel sauce?" Zeke said.

"The very same," Johanna said. She did not look up from the menu. She surely knew every item on it. "You gonna survive your injuries there?" Then her eyes met his like a physical blow, the grief in his chest repelling her gaze. Nothing compounds depression like seeing it reflected in the eyes of someone you care about. It was this now: the experience of sitting at this diner booth layered atop memories of so many mornings they had come here with debilitating hangovers, with groups of friends or just the two of them— smoked and drank coffee until morning hardened into freezing early winter Ohio nights.

Johanna reached across the table to touch the bandage. He didn't recoil.

"It's hard to explain, but it honestly doesn't hurt that much," Zeke said. "I know. I know. It was just yesterday I was in the accident. But when I looked in the mirror it was . . . well, it was kind of near healed. Scabby, but. What hurts most now is the six stitches they put in there."

"'Central Ohio town has mysterious healing properties in air,'" Declan said. He, too, hadn't looked up from the menu. "Sounds like a national magazine story to be sure."

It was as if the physical manifestation of Gram's suicide was sitting at the table among them; the longer they failed to look at it directly, the longer they could go without talking about it. "Of course I hear there's more intrigue than that around here," Declan continued. "The DA herself has been at work on it. You going to tell us about it?"

All three of them met the others' eyes.

"I can tell you, but first. What do you know."

"About the case you're working on?" Zeke said.

"No," she said. "No." She couldn't even bring herself to say it.

"About Gram," Declan said.

Zeke had been farthest from it, most disconnected from Gram. He'd only gotten some texts from Declan, letting him know that after Gram returned from the program where he was studying in Boston, at Berklee, he'd holed up. Then been admitted to Ohio State. And then one night drove off an overpass onto I-70.

Both Johanna and Declan looked down at their hands.

"I honestly just find myself feeling fucking pissed at him," Declan said. "I know that's not how you're supposed to take these things on. I know it's not a choice, like it's just something you read about in a book. But it still feels like a choice. A choice to leave us—"

"That's really not fair," Zeke said. Declan had a look on his face like he'd jumped into an icy river.

"Whoa ho ho," Johanna said. "What's not fair is not giving your old friend space to grieve in his own way. Decky, if you feel pissed at Gram, you should feel pissed at Gram. It's OK to say that. It's always OK to say that."

The grief itself once again sat in the space between them. Zeke was about to speak when the waitress came to take their order.

"Coffee," Johanna said. "ASAP coffee." They ordered and the waitress left them to their silence.

"Remember him sitting on that grave with his cowboy hat,

playing Leonard Cohen songs?" The specter of memory softened Declan.

"There wasn't anything funny about it," Declan said. He paused. "But it was the funniest thing I've ever seen. He was just always so full of life. I remember that first Halloween when he ate like six hits of acid, but he was still checking in with everyone to make sure they were having a good trip. Keeping it together. He kept saying, 'Tell me your story, brother, live your story.' Sounds cheesy to think about it now, but it was lifesaving at the time. Mind-saving."

"He's always so—so there for everyone," Johanna said.

"Was," Zeke said. He looked across the table and saw tears in Johanna's eyes. She wiped them away. Declan was staring daggers at him. "Sorry. I guess I'm swinging between grief and blame, too."

"It's OK," Declan said. He was a philosopher, and he took a philosophical tone. Stepped back. Stepped off.

They were quiet, each alone with memory. Coffee. Illness in the head. Coffee. Declan lit a cigarette.

"So," Johanna said. "What've you been working on, successful-magazine-editor friend." Zeke put his forearms down on the sticky table, his head atop them, a sagging balloon. He told them he didn't know. He was on staff, an associate editor.

"Is that good?" Declan said.

"It's better than assistant. But. But it's not what I want, you know? I want to write full-time. I have always wanted to write full-time. The advice you always get: tell a story only you can tell. I'm thirty-five and I'm not there yet, you know? And I've given up a lot."

Johanna and Declan looked at each other.

"You really should tell him more about the case, Jo," Declan said.

"I did hear something from my Uber driver on the way over," Zeke said. "About some religious sect here—"

"The Dönme," Declan said. "The murder there has kind of over-taken everyone's lives, and the headlines, for a year. More than that. And DA Johanna Franklin here was the lead prosecutor for the state. She could open up some files for you, I'd guess, being an old—well, not *old,* but being—"

"His estranged college sweetheart?" Johanna said. The waitress arrived with their coffee and food, and Johanna said, "Oh, fucking thank God," and plunged one, then two, then five creamers into the cup. "That will not get you anywhere," she said.

"Well, I didn't say I'd—" Zeke said. He kicked out a leg to sit up a little straighter, and it rubbed across Johanna's. He was lucky not to have kicked her, but feeling the bulge of her calf, his leg sliding past hers, brought on another surge of memory. She looked up.

"But it would be a good story," Johanna said. She looked down into her mug. "It would. It would make a good magazine story. And it is a directive from the top that we cooperate with journal-ists. So I'd be happy to set you up with the comms department at the office in Columbus."

"Jo," Declan said. "C'mon. Your field office is literally across the street."

"Right," Johanna said. A flush came to the tips of her cheeks that made her look fifteen years younger. College Jo. Sleep-three-hours-after-a-night-of-drinking-and-still-ace-an-exam Jo. Zeke had to look down into the yolky eggs on his plate. "Right. OK. If you want, after brunch, I can walk you over there and go through the files. If it seems like something you might be interested in. We can. We can talk about it. But now. Now let's remember Gram to each other, OK? No judgments, no qualms, just the love we have for him from the past. I want to remember Gram to you two."

: : : : :

Johanna's office was a single room with wall-to-wall carpeting and two identical desks sitting across from each other at the midway point of the room. Far to the back was a series of gunmetal filing cabinets. Zeke stood and waited outside while Johanna got the space set up, put away some confidential papers. His pocket vibrated, and he saw he had a new text. From Meta-Uber. It said, "Good luck with finding out about the murder if you do. I know a lot of the folks in town so if you need to know things gimme a shout."

The buzzer on the office door sounded. He stepped inside. He took a seat, and just as he was about to consider turning around and checking out the filing cabinets to the back of the room, the door opened. Now, in her office, Johanna appeared in full as if for the first time since he arrived in Ohio. She was wearing a powder-blue suit that looked like it had been purchased at a vintage shop specializing in 1950s formal wear and under it she was all youth—the tips of green leaves from somewhere under her white blouse reached up out from her collar and onto her neck. She came in trailing a miasma of patchouli oil and cigarette smoke, and her hair was gelled forward into a kind of short tight fauxhawk. Compared with the Johanna he'd dated—and, if he was being honest, loved—in college, this thirty-five-year-old Johanna Franklin appeared somehow younger. More youthful.

She walked back to the filing cabinets at the rear of the office and began to rummage. Zeke could no longer see her, but now she said, "So the leader of this sect's name is Nathan Fritzman. He's been convicted of killing his son, Osman, and it was essentially an open-and-shut case. An appeal is ahead, but it should make no real difference. I can make the trial transcript, files, all that available to you. The magazine would have to pay the stenographer's fee, but it's not too steep. But you know how this goes. If you have questions, you can ask me now, or we can set up some time later. Like, in the week? If you're staying, that is. But for now I'm happy to leave you to it."

By now she had come around to the desk. She was carrying a large file in her hands, five pounds of papers and photographs. Her white blouse had no sleeves, and the straight lines of her biceps strained at the weight of all the paperwork, heavy as a dumbbell. "Have at it," she said. She did not give further instruction or warning—he was here for Gram's funeral, with death on his mind and in his chest. This was her job, and she slipped seamlessly back into her role.

Right on top of the pile when he lifted back the manila folder cover was a photograph of Osman, the sixteen-year-old victim, lying on the floor of the forest as he'd been found by police. Black and purple marks articulated themselves on the sides of his neck. Pronounced. Couldn't miss them. He lay on the fallen leaves, amid grass and moss, so naturally it looked as if he were napping there. You could almost see how a community might miss him there, in a clearing in the woods, for days. Almost.

"I'm going to excuse myself for a minute," Zeke said. When he looked up, he saw Johanna had gone to her office in the back of the building, and he was talking to no one. He went outside. He just had time to light an American Spirit, inhale, and duck behind the DA's office before he was puking out over and just past his shoes. He'd been working as an editor for more than a decade, had gotten the occasional freelance assignment to do celebrity interviews, a book review or two. This was the first time he'd seen a photograph of a murder victim. Zeke wiped his mouth, kicked a fleck of yellow bile from the edge of his boot, and lit another cigarette. He looked up and found Johanna next to him. She grabbed an American Spirit from his pack and lit it.

"Sorry I didn't warn you," she said. "I didn't think about the fact you'd be seeing forensic photos right away. Right after—after today. I'm desensitized to it. I'm sorry. I'm a mess because of Gram, too, but it feels like parallel lines with this case after a year on it. You can save this for later." She took the folder, and while he was sweating from puking, Zeke was suddenly quite cold in the wind and the snow. She seemed comfortable in her white blouse and suit pants. "Maybe you'd better head out to the community. To the Caves. Lot of people to talk to in the time you have here. You could get a lot on background quickly." Zeke still had to walk over to the Alamo in town to pick up the car he had reserved back at the airport.

"I mean I have to run it by my editor," Zeke said. "Boss. Run it by my boss, who would be my editor. If." The heat on his skin was subsiding, and the frigid air, the lightly falling snow, touched the top of his nose in a way that made him feel it in the palms of his hands. The cold.

"But seeing these files now," she said.

"But seeing this file now, it sure looks like it might be of interest. To them. To . . . to me." He looked her right in the eyes. "Being here. I could imagine staying. For a time. If you have time."

"You're in Central Ohio," Johanna said. "Time is not just not an issue. It's almost not a thing." She stared at him, put her hands to her damp hair to make sure it wasn't mussed. "I'll put this file in better order," she said, and walked back to the front door of her office. "I'll separate the photos and depositions. Come back down here tonight when you've finished your reporting up there. I mean, whether you get the assignment or not, you're not heading home tonight, right? We'll have dinner at Ankara at eight. Best Turkish food in Central Ohio. I'll see you there."

SLACK PITCH

While he's back at his Airbnb, his new rental car in the lot, Zeke gets on Slack with his boss. Describes what he knows about the Dönme and the murder so far.

"I mean, it's interesting," his editor writes. "I could see sending someone back out there in a couple weeks if Helena decides she likes the pitch. Write something up. Right now you need to close the World Cup feature for April."

"I'm here now," Zeke thumbs into Slack. He's usually the one turning down pitches, and being on the other side now is weirdly less elating than dizzying. Like reading while hanging upside down from a trapeze. "Before you say it—I mean, I'm already here. I could easily extend this Airbnb into next week. It's cheap. I'll forward you this packet of clips. A small-town murder in a Jewish Islamic community. In Central Ohio. I mean what more do we need."

"A lede," his boss writes. "A story."

Zeke sits back for a second, and before he can thumb anything further into the Slack, his boss has already sent another message:

"It's Wednesday and you're on a three-day bereavement leave. You're welcome to do with the weekend what you want. See you Monday."

Zeke swipes up and the Slack is gone. He has three days to get enough done to get a real pitch through. Less. He tries briefly to sleep off the heaviness in his head and on his heart, but his mind is already churning.

He shoots off an email to the one contact Johanna has given him in the community who has email. With maybe ten minutes of searching, he finds a prison email for Nathan Fritzman. Prison email addresses—who knew that was a thing. He shoots off an email to the warden of the state prison where Fritzman is now being held. He takes a shower, looks at the strange absence of blood—of scarring—on his face in the mirror, but he doesn't have time to consider why. The story is waiting, and he has three days to pin it down. The deeper into reporting he is by Sunday, when he'll need to change his flights, the more chance he can get the week to do what he needs. A towel still wrapped around his waist, he checks his phone and finds an email from the lone contact. The community is called the Caves, writes the spokesperson for the sect. His name is Yehoshua Green. "Come see us if you'd like. I know Natan would like to have the real story told if it can be. Just a question whether you're the right person to tell it."

The real story.

There's a real story.

Zeke puts on a Band-Aid and out he goes.

THE CAVES

The way out to the Caves cut back through the center of town. Six blocks from the traffic circle, Mt. Izmir released its purchase on commerce and succumbed to rural Ohio. Those six blocks carried the aging bodies of behemoth Victorians, pastels dulled by decades of winter and rain. The splendor of these variegated anachronistic houses was tempered only by the yellow murk of the bulging lawns that occluded them from the streets. There was snow, but it was Ohio snow, not the overwhelming snow of midwinter New England, February Buffalo.

Beyond these heirlooms, a hill climbed northeast out of town. On the median strip on the main street from Mt. Izmir, an Amish man pulled a horse by the reins, hand near the bit, the lightest tug of the brown flesh of horse muzzle molding itself to metal. The horse trailed behind it a buggy. Three Amish kids sat in the back with their wares, bread and sweets, to sell at the center of the college campus, as Zeke remembered them on weekends. Nothing had changed in a decade. Like Johanna said, time was barely even a thing here. All the boys wore the same flat-brimmed black hat and the same flowing puffy shirt as their father. On the back of the buggy were two red lights, the only electronics on the whole cart.

Soon Zeke found his way past Mt. Izmir's outskirts. There was a heavy nostalgia for him, alone and free behind the wheel of a rental sedan here, the first time he'd been back to the town outside his alma mater since graduating, when he and Johanna had just broken up for good. Declan had graduated already, and Gram had been his respite then—they would stay up until the sun rose playing guitars, drinking a jug of Carlo Rossi or a fifth of Jack, jumping off trestles into shallow water. Whatever inhibitions Zeke had then, Gram had forced him to shed them. It occurred to Zeke that this was how grief worked: the real memories, the nuance obscured by time and language, were a private encounter. Even trying to share them over coffee with Declan and Johanna felt a poor simulacrum. Was. What might have been a full swell of nostalgia even now was forestalled by the image of the strangled Osman, a boy not that much younger than he was when he arrived here for college, which kept blocking, then overshadowing memory; kept coupling with an image he'd created of Gram just before he plunged to his death onto the interstate outside Columbus. A surge of ugly sooty emotion buzzed to his fingers. He looked out his window and attempted to shake it. All he could do was observe. First were long slow fields of yellow where the snow had yet to stick. Yellow grasses drying in the snow, yellow corn husks worn raw by long wearying winter. When he had begun at the magazine ten years earlier, Zeke had used a microcassette recorder for oral notes. Now his iPhone contained all the same technology. He held it to his mouth and said: "Note yellow fields specked with white. Along Turkish Road an inlet where Gram once lost control of his truck on a late drunken night but came out unscathed. Gram always came out unscathed." He paused. "Always did." Paused again. Breathed. This wasn't a story about Gram, and needed not become one. "Note decrepit houses. Note decrepit barns. Corncobs like nubs of worn-down teeth. Remember—well—remember memories."

Ten miles out of town, he came upon the sign Yehoshua Green told him in the email he'd see, handwritten on a wooden plank: "The Caves." A low mist rose off the slow-moving Bosperous Creek, expansive and warm in the cold of day. As the road went east, the flat fields became hilly gorges, lifting away from the river. As the trees grew thicker and the inclines roller-coastered, Zeke turned left onto Caves Road. He was moving through a gorge and back toward the creek. Off in the distance, a hill sparsely covered by trees, like the last lonely hairs on a nearly bald head, rose above the near horizon. He was just about here. He put his brights on, rolled down all four windows of the car, and put Matisyahu's "One Day" on his Spotify.

Zeke turned onto Shabbetai Road, where he encountered all at once: an RV with an immense airbrushed painting of the face of Nathan Fritzman, Natan of Flatbush, Hebrew lettering atop the image; two trailer homes in the near distance; a single two-story colonial set back from the road; and in front of each of these buildings, men in traditional Hasidic garb carrying automatic rifles.

Johanna had not mentioned the gun-toting Hasids.

Yehoshua Green had not, either.

There were a half dozen of them, each indistinguishable from the other, with their beards and peyes and black suits and tall black brimmed hats. Very much unlike the Amish, they wore tallit under their black jackets, and on their heads and hands were the boxes and flapping leather straps of phylacteries. Zeke stopped the car and put his hands flat on the dash. Five of the Hasidim walked to the shotgun side of the car maybe twenty paces back. The sixth walked up with his rifle at his hip, pointed toward the rocky ground, and approached.

"I'm the reporter from the magazine in—in New York—here to meet with Yehoshua Green. He knows I'm coming. He told me to. To come. In an email. To me."

There was a long tense pause. The two men outside his window looked at him skeptically. Then looked at each other. Zeke wished he'd put the Matisyahu volume up louder.

"We don't have plans to let anyone in here," the first of them said. He was up close enough now that he could see that though this Hasid wore a black hat and carried an AR-15, he was maybe twenty years old. Looked five years younger. Flecks of toothpaste still crusted on the corners of his mouth.

"Yehoshua told me to come," Zeke said.

"Yehoshua didn't tell us *shit*," the Hasid said. He put his hand down near the trigger of the automatic rifle. He moved it so the long barrel of the gun was now pointed on an angle that looked like it met Zeke's feet in the rental car. Zeke liked his feet.

"OK," Zeke said. "But could you maybe call him, or—"

"Look!" the Hasid said, raising his voice. "Listen. You're not listening. I said there's no one coming in and out of here today, so put your fucking little sedan here in reverse, and—"

Before he could finish his sentence, a voice came across the field.

"We're good here!" Tromping out from one of the trailers Zeke had seen at the edge of the property was a thin man about his age, more formally dressed—he had a hoodie under his black jacket, no hat. The Hasid looked at him as he came up to them.

"You didn't say we had anyone coming," he said.

"I didn't?" the guy in the hoodie said. "I guess I didn't. But I meant to. And I'm saying now. We're good here." He looked at the younger man. Hard.

"We're good here," the Hasid said. He put his AR-15 back on his shoulder, and the five other men with him began walking away from the car.

"Sorry about all that," the hoodie guy said. His voice was in tenor, timbre, and accent almost exactly the voice of Mike D from the Beastie Boys. "I'm Josh, Yehoshua, the one you emailed with— very good to meet you, brother." Yehoshua put out his hand and shook, and he pointed to a paved driveway running up to the trailer closest to where he now stood. "Just pull on in so you're not blocking the way."

: : : : :

The trailer smelled of incense, patchouli oil, expensive weed, and laundry dryer sheets. Zeke told himself: Remember the smells. He didn't dare pull out his notebook to record it. The space was divided into three rooms by laminate particleboard partitions. The middle room had two dun-brown couches facing each other, and against the far wall a seventy-two-inch curved-screen television, muted, showing the previous night's *SportsCenter*. From the room behind it came the soft busy bass lines of Marvin Gaye's "What's Going On." Just as Zeke was sitting down, Yehoshua came back into the room with cans of Bell's.

"Two Hearted or Expedition Stout?" Yehoshua said.

"Oh, thank you, Yehoshua," Zeke said.

"Which."

Zeke said, "Two Hearted."

"Just call me Josh." Zeke said fine, and Yehoshua handed Zeke the beer. "I guess I need to apologize for all that back there. The guns and all. We've had them throughout, of course—everyone out here does. Second Amendment! And they're so easy. You just walk into a Walmart and there they are. But. But since the . . . the events with Osman . . . we've had to be more careful."

"You said over email." Zeke popped the top of his can, and the hissing sound calmed his nerves. In a corner of the room yet another AR-15 was leaning against the wall.

"Just think—if we were meeting in Judea and Samaria, everyone would be carrying. I was six the first time I went to Yerushalayim, and I remember how scared I was at first, seeing all the machine guns. Women with Uzis. But hey, the Israelis *invented* the Uzi. Maybe we won't need them once the world recognizes Natan as mashiach. But this is all too far along already—first things first, as the Ohioans like to say. So: wow, it's good to meet you." The sound of Marvin Gaye's voice rose in the room next door singing, "Brother, brother, brother, there's far too many of you dying / You know we've got to find a way . . ." and Yehoshua yelled, "I need you to turn that down we have a guest here—a distinguished guest!" A vein popped out in the middle of his forehead while he shouted. Then he turned back to Zeke and again smiled. The volume dipped, so only the bass was audible. "Sorry. She loves '70s soul. Sometimes I can't get her to turn it down."

"What's your wife's name?"

Yehoshua looked at him sideways. "Devorah. You'll meet her. When she's properly covered. For now we have so much to catch up on, coolo tov!" Yehoshua stopped for a moment and took Zeke in again. "What happened to your face?"

Zeke put his hand to his eye. He'd forgotten about the bandage above his eye amid all the guns and Hasids. Stitches were pulling at skin, making it more uncomfortable than ever. He said it was nothing, not much of anything at all, a little accident from the way in.

"I suppose an injury like this is a token of memory for you when you've left. Did you meet with the Franklin woman in Mt. Izmir? I read the documents about *Employment Division v. Smith* that you sent. I agree that if the Indians get to eat peyote and call it religion, surely the Eighteen Commandments must cover the mashiach!"

Yehoshua was moving very fast.

"Well, I'm just getting started here," Zeke said. "Normally I would be deep into research, but I only heard of your situation for the first time today. So maybe you could tell me a little about your community first."

"Right, how stupid—" Yehoshua said. "Let me give you at least the basics." So while Yehoshua talked, Zeke took notes, which would go directly into the Slack when he left. Here's how he recorded it on the Notes app of his phone:

—This sect was called the Dönme.

—A hundreds-years-old sect of Jewish mysticism, who outwardly practiced Islam.

—Just before his death in the late 17th century, Shabbetai Tzvi, false messiah of Natan of Flatbush and his followers, was found in a cave in Albania and at the mouth of the cave his disciples discovered a dragon ensconced in massive bright light.

—When a Turkish immigrant, a practicing Dönme named Mehmet Osman, had come to Ohio, he had chosen to live out at the Caves when he arrived here just after WWI, in 1919.

—The Dönme lived there still, now led by Natan of Flatbush.

When Yehoshua finished talking and Zeke finished thumbing this all into his Notes app, it occurred to Zeke that Yehoshua was looking down at his hands, not entirely unlike Declan and Johanna had done at the diner this morning. There was a grief in this room, too; mourning, filling the space between them.

"So listen," Zeke said. "Before we get further into the stuff about Natan and the charges against him, about your life with the Dönme, all that, I'd like to hear more about your own background. How you got here. Tell me about yourself. It helps me to start with a person when I'm trying to understand a story." And so Yehoshua began the way humans begin to tell stories, from somewhere in the middle of their thought pattern, no beginning, no end; no present or past tense to rely on, just the flowing list of thought and opinion that left a human mind.

"Coolo tov, coolo tov," Josh said. "I mean when I first moved from Crown Heights, I thought it was gonna be all banjos picking and pigs oinking and corncobs. It wasn't that. Was. Not. That. Well, not only that. There was this whole other intensity." Zeke nodded. Stayed silent. Knew he had three days to get what he could, and if someone was talking and that someone wasn't him, he was on the right track. "So you know I've been living in Mt. Izmir for eleven years," Yehoshua said. "Eleven, eleven, eleven years, eleven good years, thanks to the Prophet, thanks to Natan of Flatbush. When I first got here, it was just me and Devorah and our kids. We were Lubavitchers back home. For the Lubavitchers the main thing is just to get married and get started on the life of Torah, studying Talmud and popping out kiddos. You know we were fifteen when we got married. We had Shai by the time we were seventeen. Young, right? I mean, you were probably in your twenties by the time you got married."

"I'm thirty-five," Zeke said. "I don't have kids." He paused. "Or a wife." Paused again. "And I don't want one."

From the other side of the particleboard partition, they could clearly hear Devorah groan. When in the pause that followed she perceived the silence and understood she'd been indiscreet, she said, from the other side of the wall, "Oh, sorry! Sorry. Go on." Josh didn't look behind him. He pulled out a glass bowl and started breaking up a huge bud that had been sitting on the table. It was so conspicuous Zeke hadn't even noticed it.

"This strain we call the Shekinah," Josh said. "End of our harvest from Purim. This year was a good, good year." Another sound from behind the partition. "I mean, for our growing. Obviously not the—" Josh broke up the bud and rolled a Bob Marley–style joint. He offered it up.

"The Dönme have believed, all the way back to our prophet Shabbetai Tzvi, in redemption through sin. The true Prophet, the true mashiach, could make holy all our actions through his mere belief in them. At the coming of the mashiach, all of halakhah will be undone. All that's holy will be holy, and all that's *unholy* will be holy."

"And it'll just be shrimp bacon cheeseburgers from there on out," Zeke said.

Josh looked at him and held in a lungful of pot smoke until his chest convulsed just a bit. Smoke billowed from each nostril. Then he exhaled, coughed, and started to laugh.

"Hah! Nice. You're quick. That might be good for you here. Or. Anyway. So yeah, we were so deep in the Lubavitcher world. I mean our whole world was on Eastern Parkway, barely even made it past the Brooklyn Museum. We were too narrow in our little world there. Then I heard about Footsteps. You know what Footsteps is?"

"I don't."

Yehoshua looked back at the wall behind him. He pointed his thumb toward the wall and with pot smoke coming from his mouth mouthed, "The ears have *walls,* my friend."

Then he took one more epic toke from his spliff and stood.

"Let's toke and walk."

: : : : :

Outside the trailer the air was heavy with fallen snow, a cold so wet it jumped through straight into your bones. Frigid air blew across fields, carried up from snow-covered ground, seemed almost to come from inside Zeke himself. There was no discernible sound of the Bosperous Creek rushing. Zeke and Josh were far enough from the water they did not hear it, and most likely it was cold enough to have frozen over anyway. From the far distance Zeke could hear the bleating of sheep, the soft cry of a lamb like an infant calling meekly for its mother. The only smell in the air was the metallic nip of freeze. No one stirred on the Dönme property. Yehoshua led Zeke back along a path behind his trailer.

"It feels almost impossible to get out of the Lubavitcher world. All kinds of people in that community trying to keep you in," Josh said, returning again to beginnings while making his way toward the recent past, the present. "There are some others you meet, more chill folks from the Breslovers, or more intense Satmars, but they're not what you come from. I mean you live with it your whole life, and the ways you live are the only ways you know. If you walk far enough, you might hit Atlantic Avenue. Eastern Parkway. The 2 train into Manhattan for an accounting job, maybe, at most." He pointed out a nurse log along the path to avoid. The fallen oak was dusted by fallen snow in this fallen world, marred only by the crush of footfall. Josh's voice intoned slightly lower and calmer now that he'd smoked his bowl, like he'd transitioned vocally from

Mike D to Van Morrison in his walk. "They didn't even allow us to use the internet in Crown Heights, or in yeshiva. I'd cross Eastern Parkway and sit in a coffee shop down on Nostrand. You know the neighborhood at all?"

"I lived in Fort Greene before I moved to Windsor Terrace," Zeke said.

"Close enough. I guess. So I'd just sit at one of those new coffee shops on Nostrand and listen to folks talk and I could tell there was another life. I could picture it, but I couldn't picture it: just something else, something shining with spark—and elusive. Like I could picture the image of a man standing in a doorway, burning with the flame of the Lord, beckoning me to allow his very limbs to be my Torah. Showing me another way. I mean I didn't want to give up my study. I didn't want to stop reading Torah or Zohar or anything. But there was a different life. And if I'm being completely honest . . . I just didn't want more kids. Two kids feels like a lot of kids when you're eighteen and basically a kid yourself. We knew people with like five, eight, six hundred thirteen kids. I did not want six hundred thirteen kids. Devorah didn't, either."

The low rush of the Bosperous Creek now rose from somewhere in the near distance, the smallest voices of the smallest whirlwind. The sound was like something brittle carrying something supple inside it. Thin airy flakes of snow fell slowly, so intermittent it wasn't clear if they fell from sky or were shaken from trees overhead by wind. What could be the difference in a flake that fell and landed from a canopy so high above—beyond your very sight in that brightness—and a flake that fell from the heavens, skirted the canopy, and landed in its own direction? Wasn't it the same flake, regardless, on the selfsame Zeke? Zeke had his neck wrenched upward. Josh pointed out a much larger log for them to climb over. There was no hint of caves out here—they were almost at the creek's edge, and it was still just the misty slow gorge-pocked woods. But the quality of the air seemed to be changing, growing more dense. Stitches tugged at Zeke's eye skin, healing so fast in the air of the Bosperous Creek that he could feel less scab than skin pulling at him. In the calm of the forest, it was as if the time through which they were walking was passing differently. The reflexive desire to see if Natan had emailed back put Zeke's hand on his phone. You did not need to check for the Prophet when you were already in the Prophet's compound. It was like looking into a mirror, only to see the back of your head.

"The Caves are right up here, across the creek."

Now they walked without talking until they heard footsteps. Josh did not have his rifle, and Zeke watched the younger man put his left knee to the ground. The Hasid shushed and, with his right hand, pulled up his cuff and took a .45 from a strap around his ankle. He put a hand behind him, signaling for Zeke to stop. In the clearing in front of them were two women in burkinis, one in deep burgundy, the other metallic gray, each with a Nike swoosh on the shoulder. Each of the women had a thin towel wrapped around her waist. Over each of their shoulders were straps holding an AR-15.

Yehoshua's shoulders eased. Zeke's tensed. Yehoshua put the pistol down to his side. "We're good," he said. He stood and called out to them. "I'm here with an unexpected guest," he said. "Say hello or take to your path."

The women stopped. Zeke stood far off to the side of their path. Neither said anything. The woman to the left was maybe five-seven, her face shining with the flame of a body handling the cold of a frozen submersion in a frozen river. Still neither of the women appeared to shiver. Zeke and Yehoshua were wearing heavy coats.

"We'll meet him later," the burgundy woman said. "If we're meant to do so." The two turned and walked a path to the left. Yehoshua put a hand back again, asking Zeke to stop until they'd cleared. Now they were off toward the water.

"Shrimp bacon cheeseburgers, buds, and burkinis," Zeke said, trying to paper over the active discomfort he felt at all the guns. "And a significant fear of weaponry. This is all an education in a single afternoon."

Yehoshua laughed again. "Not halakhah, not religious law—but something deeper," he said. "Give it time." This time when he laughed, it felt thin. Maybe he was just really stoned. "In our culture both men and women take mikvah before prayer every morning, and often in the afternoon as well. In the winter we call it the frozen mikvah. So we still observe some normative culture. Do you know how the mikvah works?" It was a word Zeke was sure he'd heard as a young secular Jew, but one whose meaning he couldn't actually share once pushed, like if he were asked to define clearly "quantum mechanics" or "THC" or "quixotic."

"No," Zeke said. "Sorry."

"The mikvah bath is taken every morning to purify our bodies, our minds, before prayer begins. In the Hasidic communities from which we've all come, there were baths with the clear purpose of that purification. We have great luck here in Mt. Izmir! The Bosperous Creek is our natural path to purity. Set out at the foot of the Cave of the Prophet, summer, winter, spring, or fall, each Dönme takes mikvah every morning before prayer. It's cold in the winter. But it tunes the mind up to devekut."

"Like the polar bear club people do at Brighton Beach."

"Not at all like that," Josh said. "Not that secular ritual. *Ritual.*"

He did not speak again until they came to a sandy clearing. Zeke's gaze was now so focused on the bulge at Yehoshua's ankle where he'd removed his handgun that the smell of water from the creek arose before it came into their field of vision. The air had grown even cooler now, a presence.

"And here we are," Josh said. "The Bosperous." The skin around his eyes drew back into a stoned smile. Before them were two huge rocks, between the rocks a small jetty of sand declining down into the creek. The riverbed was a hundred feet across, wide and uniform. From above a hawk would look down upon it and see no striation in color, no substantial shift in depth, just a soft vee at the river's middle where it swelled to maybe nine feet after a rain. At either edge, where now ice cragged up to a bed of round stones, that same bird of prey above could pick out each rock by its shape. On the other side were two large boulders like the two on this side, and a rocky ledge leading back up into the subtle gorges. Along the shore it was cold enough that platelike jetties of effaced ice jutted out over the running water. Though the creek was not wide across, the current at its center drew heavy as it whipped downstream, and unlike the preying hawk, Zeke could tell by the rhythm of current, by the reedy rippling lines coming together into repeated deltas as they flowed, its speed. The water did not roil, did not surge. At segments on each shore, the creek had iced over so solidly it was opaque, though any remaining ice had been stepped into water at the entryway here near the cave. The density of ice diffused to where at the middle of the creek a white lip overhung the rushing water.

"The Hebrew word for ice is a modern adaptation for a word that in the Torah means something closer to frost," Josh said, breaking the reverent silence. It was as if a new voice entirely had overtaken him, one with no song, something wholly distinct from the stoned

Brooklyn rasp of before, full of learning and confidence of more years than his body contained. "The frozen Bosperous Creek is not edged by frost," he continued. "It is edged by frozen ice. This word, 'kerach,' appears fewer than a dozen times in the entirety of the Hebrew Bible. In Genesis, Jacob, while fleeing Laban at night, imagines he's been consumed by frost. Job—always Job—freezes out in the homeless cold. The prophets Jeremiah and Ezekiel, two of the first to imagine the destruction of Jerusalem by God's wrath, both speak of the frost that comes at night. They knew cold. They knew water so cold it could change form. They did not imagine a river frozen over as the rivers in Central Ohio in midwinter."

When Josh again quieted, the only sound was of the rushing water.

"The Cave of the Prophet is across the way," Josh said after some time had passed. "There are a number of caves back in these woods, but that is the Cave of the Dragon. If you stay here in Ohio, in another couple weeks spring should begin to arrive. I know it seems way too cold to swim. But when the ice melts, it melts quickly. Cold and pain are slough of the qelippot, the shells of the things of this world. The light inside, the tikkun, the spark—it warms when you go across."

"That, and the big fleece jackets," Zeke said.

Yehoshua Green stood back from the river and looked at his visitor. An invitation and a vetting both, this visit. There were wheels within wheels in the life of the Hasid, and within the life of the Dönme wheels within covered wheels within subterfuge. Already in a single afternoon, it had become apparent that this was how they'd survived since 1666, and how they would continue to survive. There was a story here, that was sure; a story whose challenges were in its depth, not its shallowness. Underfoot, the crunching of the smallest particles of snow and ice, a scree in their ears but at a level not so small they would not be able to see it, snow and ice crushed until the most infinitesimal shedding of water ran between.

: : : : :

When Yehoshua Green and Zeke emerged from the forest, back in the community of the Caves, the sun was settling low atop the edge of the western ridge. Air redolent of burning wood. Puce and warm with burning sage. The day was nearing the gloaming, and out of each of the trailers like schoolkids departing class at day's end, members of the Dönme began to disembark the elevated solitude of their homes. Each woman wearing a headscarf. Each man, most likely the same men who were carrying guns at the community's entrance hours before, in tallit and tefillin and carrying a prayer book. There were maybe a hundred and fifty of them, the average age of worshippers between thirty and forty, though there were a handful of older men and women—all formally dressed, upper-middle-class retirees you might find in a Modern Orthodox synagogue—and children dallying about their legs, also in burkas or black suits, tallit and tefillin and phylacteries. It looked like a cross between the scene on Saturday mornings in Crown Heights and a photo shoot for the Allman Brothers' *Brothers and Sisters*, amid slanting light and the natural beauty of a gorge-engulfed clearing.

"It's the fifth prayer of the day," Josh whispered. The men appeared to be debating something rather fiercely until one of them looked over. One of the men in a black hat and tefillin and tallis yelled something at Josh.

"They're angry I'm here," Zeke said.

"No, no. If it had not been decided that it would be OK for you to now be the first outside witness to our practices, you would not be here at all." The ominous words, coming in the context of the murder Zeke was here looking into, sat heavy in the snowy smoke-smelling air.

"It is a great joy you are here! Your being here means that not only you but the Dönme are soon to change—us for the first time in three centuries. Think about it: you are the first nonmember of our community, of any sect—Yakubi, Kapanci, or Karakas—to see it from the inside. Soon the whole world will know of the arrival of the mashiach. You will be the one to announce it."

"The articles written so far seem to suggest it was the broaching of those rules that got Osman killed," Zeke said. His voice quavered. "Telling people about you."

"Don't believe the lies. Lies! Printed lies. We rebut those accusations. It was not Natan who killed Osman, and you will come to believe as we do in your time here. As we keep arguing, even if it was, the membrane has been punctured. As Natan will tell you, this is just how it has been for every prophet. Only when the king required record of Jeremiah's teachings did Jeremiah appoint Baruch his scribe, and only then did he tell each word of his story. Its remnants flap in the wind, behind your footsteps."

Zeke was about to protest again, but no matter how good or naive he might be, this did not seem like a moment for protest. Guns were guns. Religious fanatics with guns were weapons carrying weapons. "No, what he shouted to us was that with Natan of Flatbush—away—it has been decided that today I will lead evening prayer. Allow me a moment to put on my shawl."

Yehoshua left Zeke alone while the entire Dönme community stood preparing for prayer. There was obviously no muezzin, no minaret to ascend. Zeke stood on one side of the clearing, by the entrance to Yehoshua's trailer, while the rest, maybe a hundred feet from him, davened prayers to themselves, shifting foot to foot, holding children against their knees. Finally Yehoshua returned, his black brimmed hat now accompanied by prayer shawl and phylacteries, leather straps encircling his arms like invasive vines entwining branches.

"You'll see that we all face not Mecca nor Yerushalayim, to the east," Josh said. He pointed off toward the Ohio River, far from where they now stood. "We face the Cave of the Dragon, across the creek from where you and I just stood. Only on the Feast of the Lamb do we pray beside the cave itself."

Now Josh walked from Zeke to the front of the group, facing the woods. He put his left knee to the ground, then the right, no prayer mat beneath him but his own legs communing directly with the snow-covered ground. He put his forehead to the ground, where one of his phylacteries touched the snow. Slowly he intoned a Hebrew prayer, the Baruch atah Adonai the only part familiar to Zeke. The guttural dirge of the rest of the congregation behind him followed, and it was low and slow and startling as a cry of terror. The sound of two hundred worshippers all speaking Hebrew in the Ohio winter was unexpectedly moving. Zeke might not have heard a group of this size all praying in a foreign language together since he was last in shul, now almost twenty years before, save for the Mourner's Kaddish recited at Gram's funeral earlier that same day.

Yehoshua transitioned into a new chant to the same cadence:

Shabbetai Tzvi, Shabbetai Tzvi, esparamos a ti

Shabbetai Tzvi, no es un otro como a ti

They chanted their prayer in ancient Ladino, prayers that had carried over the centuries from Constantinople, to Dulcigno and Salonica, and across the ocean and land to the American Middle West. Yehoshua turned to the congregation, back again to the setting sun. He put his shoulders parallel to the ground, and he recited a Dönme version of a well-known prayer:

Shema Yisroel, Adonai, Shabbetai Tzvi, Adonai echad.

It was the most-recited prayer in all of Jewish liturgy, only with Shabbetai Tzvi's name replacing the name of the Lord. The Shema, but the Dönme Shema.

Zeke didn't know Hebrew, but he could translate that specific sentence:

Hear O Israel, God Shabbetai is God, the Lord is one.

It meant they believed Shabbetai Tzvi was the Lord.

Each of the members of the community stood and turned to walk straight back to their trailers. Mothers in burkas coddled children, moved in units like any family. The well-dressed older people walked back toward Mercedes and Audis, Teslas and BMWs. Zeke walked to his car with the last light of the fallen day turning brown and grainy. Yehoshua was too surrounded by fellow members of his community to notice him leaving.

::::::

The ride back toward Mt. Izmir's downtown felt far shorter than the ride in. Before dinner with Johanna, Zeke returned to his Airbnb. On any other story he'd ever worked on, he might have put on cable news, or an old movie in the background, lain senseless on the lumpy rented bed. Instead he spent the first half hour writing down notes. He wanted to note what the woods and icy creek and Dönme compound felt like. How much more rural, how much snowier and homier. The cabin where he was staying had a large picture window looking out on the snowy frozen river, which, it occurred to Zeke now, was just a couple miles downriver from where he'd been at the Caves. There was an odd familiarity to looking out on it now. The strange oceanic feeling surprisingly rising in his chest, slowly untangling the knot of grief tied tight there now. The snow releasing from trees overhead. Then his phone buzzed. He had an email from Nathan Fritzman's prison account:

To: ZekeLeger@____.com
From: nathanfritzman@____.gov

On Sin

Whether sin is to be avoided or embraced will always be the central question of man's existence on earth:: To be is to accord with ephemeral manners and man's manners determine his mode of being in the world:: In our beliefs the Dönme of the Caves believe in redemption through sin.: A halakhic world of law to follow does not take into account its opposite.: the long Kabbalistic history of its opposite:: The Ein Sof will contain both chastity and sin both rectitude and sin both good and evil and the Dönme will believe in the embrace of sin alongside its being skirted:: When we speak.: when you and I meet.: we will always begin with a prayer::

I'm glad Ezekiel to hear you will be visiting the Caves & meeting with Yehoshua Green:: This will be an important occasion:: I could enter further into its implications but it feels imperative to answer your most central questions here first and we can talk when you come to see me:: And don't allow me to forget when you do come to see me that I will provide you with a copy of the *Shivhei ha-Natan,* all my prison notebooks & writings::

On the Existence of Evil

Tikkun: that the things of this life of the world are shells:: Qelippot:: Inside those shells the divine sparks left over from Ein Sof:: The nothingness Kabbalists have always posited pre-ceded this world.: It is our job to lift up the sparks::

Now call it Ein Sofism:: I have had a vision since I was a boy:: No metaphysics:: No distinction between this world and the next.: This world and the world to come:: It is all this world and all the world to come at once:: No Jewish law.: No Islamic law.: No halal no halakhah:: ALL IS ONE:: Individuated body just shell: Distinct part of Ein Sofistic whole we find what we formerly called the tikkun:: Fallen sparks within the qelippot, lifted::

: : : : :

That was it. That was the email. Natan hadn't signed off or left an opening, had simply put down his beliefs in a note. When Zeke finished reading this email, the content of which came in response to a relatively straightforward set of questions about whether Natan would be willing to be interviewed, his head spun. The trip to the Caves today gave him ample material to come back to the Slack and pitch his boss again tomorrow. The email from Natan of Flatbush . . . he would keep the email from Natan of Flatbush to himself for now. He . . . He was. He was . . . a bit confused. He was still a good bit stoned, and the gash over his eye hurt the worst it had hurt since he arrived. He lay down and passed out before he had to get ready for dinner with Johanna.

ONSET OF DANGER

While Zeke naps, he hears nothing. That doesn't mean nothing transpires. Far from it. Outside his Airbnb a series of vehicles arrive.

First, a sheriff's cruiser. It pulls up, flashes lights at the cabin, which Zeke is too racked out to see, and drives on.

Second, before the sheriff's Dodge has yet vacated the area, a Ford F-150. Inside the truck are three teenagers, all about the age Osman Fritzman would be now. As the truck passes the sheriff, it gives a flash of its brights.

The sheriff moves on.

The teenagers do not exit their vehicle. They, too, move on.

Third, a much older truck, a rusted-out Toyota Tacoma, filled with men in Hasidic black suits. One of the men in his religious garb gets out of the truck. He walks up to the window and sees that, its shades open, the window reveals Zeke passed out on the bed. He looks off away from the cabin but in the swirling snow sees nothing. He walks back to the parking lot, bends down to one knee to inspect the tracks of vehicles that have recently approached the cabin. The tracks are pronounced in the newly fallen snow. Something in the way the man in religious garb holds himself suggests expertise at divining meaning from signs. He gets back in the truck and it speeds away.

Zeke naps through it all.

ANKARA

Once they had settled into their seats opposite each other at a small rickety wooden table, Johanna started right in: "What did you think of the Caves? Did you meet the harem? Like, the entire harem?"

The Ankara dining room consisted of eight white-tableclothed wooden tables, and in the rear, a counter. Zeke had arrived early, wanting to leave time, with the snow falling and the dark. After the alien formality of their meeting in her office, Johanna looked like an entirely new person. Her brown hair pulled back into a short ponytail, and under a denim jumpsuit she was not wearing a bra. On her right shoulder was a tattoo linking together a series of her biggest darkest freckles into the constellation Orion, and scrawling up the nape of her neck the green leaves of a flower that must have been tattooed somewhere on her chest. When he was close enough to hug hello, her face revealed a smattering of freckles not unlike the Milky Way itself—pronounced spots in the fore, fading and lighter bands of brown beneath deep into her skin in seemingly infinite regress. A variegated mottled brownness on her skin to match the variegated brownness of her hair.

"I spent the afternoon with Yehoshua Green," Zeke said. "Josh. The folks in the community called him Josh. I liked Josh a lot. I have a tendency to kind of like everyone. Like I meet someone and immediately trust them, want to love them. I should be careful, but I thought he seemed saner and more normal than I'd expected. Honestly he reminded me of some kids I went to high school with, the most credulous of them. Weirdly just kind of a Jewish hip-hop kid gone cultish. And the longer I was with him, the more it became clear he has real intelligence, depth. Spirituality."

"Well, he's like your old friends—except for the way his community is armed to the teeth with automatic weapons," Johanna said. "And are duty-bound to kill their own."

"Except for that alleged intransigence."

"And the fact that he's trying to help his cult leader friend get away with murdering his own son."

"As to that," Zeke said, "I have questions. Lots of questions."

"You're reporting on the story. I'd be weirded out if you didn't."

"The questions I want to ask you first are actually about you, Johanna, yourself."

She put her hand to her chest in feigned embarrassment, though real blood did come to her cheeks.

"You know me, Ezekiel. We dated for two years."

"Whenever I approach a subject, I begin by making no assumptions whatsoever about what I know about them. I mean, I'm the biggest Dolly Parton fan in America, and when I interviewed her, I researched her just like I would anyone."

"You . . . interviewed Dolly Parton."

"That wasn't the point. But. Yes. You and I have a lot of catching up to do. Fifteen years. It's a lot of years. Long enough to. Well. A lot of things have happened."

The specter of Gram's suicide rose between them again. Johanna's eyes fled Zeke's. He looked down at his hands, picked at a scab on his left hand.

"So," Zeke said. "To start. You do not appear to be the most formal lawyer in America."

"Formality is not my creed, no."

"Where did your name come from? I mean I remember the story. But. Tell it."

"My parents—June and Bob, as you know—were Reform Jews who converted to First Generation American Hippie long before I was born. Then back to Reform Judaism after. Which is how we ended up in Bexley, county seat of Columbus, Ohio, Jewishdom. So. Sorry. This is a long-winded way of saying I was named after Dylan's 'Visions of Johanna.'"

"'Ain't it just like the night.'"

"Don't interrupt," Johanna said. "It's rude. Even when it's charming. But yes, they were Reform Jews. Now I've returned to a little of it myself, which bears a certain irony."

"How irony?" Before Johanna could answer, their waiter arrived. He was twice Zeke's size and twice as imposing, with a huge head and face that made him appear from the neck up more cashew than man. To a certain writer coming from New York to Ohio, this might have caused a vague if unintentional sense of alarm. The waiter spoke in a low garble that at first sounded like a foreign language. His eyes were stony bloodshot.

"That's right," Johanna said. "You're perusing still, but we should both have the doner kebab and the dolmas sampler. They're the best I've ever tasted."

The waiter nodded. They sat in silence after. The dark smell of shaved lamb filled the restaurant. For the first time since his car accident, the overwhelming hunger that gripped him was accessible to Zeke. In his hunger, the room, like Johanna's skin and hair, turned a kind of brown, the murkiness of its '70s-era tanned caramel richness overwhelming him. He'd smelled nothing but the sharp white cold of snow since he'd arrived in Ohio. Now, smelling this brown slow meat aroma, he was as if emptied.

"But we don't need to jump right into this deep talk if you don't want to."

"Oh, I want," Zeke said. "All I really want to do."

"Is baby eat lamb with you," Johanna said. The mellow smell of grape leaves being heated in the kitchen moved over top of the lamb smell in the room. "So I guess working backward. I went to OSU two years after graduating from William James—my long-term boyfriend had left to pursue a career as a magazine editor in the big city—and then I went to Fordham Law. I did not tell my ex-boyfriend at the time that we were in the same city. I graduated, and while all my friends went to work for corporate firms, I decided to come back home. To bring my talents to Columbus. I mean I had solid offers from Paul Hastings and Boies Schiller. The year I graduated the firms had all just started paying 195 your first year out. And believe me! I am now much further along than that, and I do not make any 195. But. This was what I wanted. This was my dream. To be a prosecutor back in the state that will always have my heart. And as I say, when I moved back to Columbus, I returned to what I knew. Nobody gives a shit here that I'm tattooed and wear suits discovered scouring funeral home aftermarket thrift shops. There's no Paul Hastings sartorial handbook to go by. My parents have long since moved to Manhattan, to enjoy their retirement. I moved back to Bexley. Rocking the C-Bus."

For the first time in her monologue, Johanna sat back and took a long sip of water.

"Which is all a lot of what you already knew, and then more than you probably want to know," she said.

"Stop apologizing!" Zeke said. "Like you said, it's unbecoming. What I want to know now is how being Jewish and being on this case has affected you. I need to make the best pitch I can by like midday tomorrow if I'm gonna be able to stay and really report this out. I need themes. I need a hook. This is one. You, them, me. Jews."

"There's no overlap between that cult of fanatics and the cultural Jews you or I grew up around. I mean, I believe in God. I guess. My religious education was to memorize enough Hebrew to have a big lavish Bat Mitzvah and then read some English out of the *Gates of Prayer.* As you saw this morning, to say Kaddish at a friend's funeral. None of this has anything to do with Nathan Fritzman. The fact that the Dönmes are trying to claim that Nathan didn't do it, or make some Pyrrhic argument that pins it somehow on religious freedom, is a joke."

"OK, so that being the case, I guess this would be a good time for you to lay out your side so I can understand it fully."

"Did you read my closing from the trial transcript?"

"I obviously don't have the transcript in hand yet. I did get some select quotations from the *Dispatch* article on it. You sounded very profesh. But reading that material feels stifling. So many rules for what you can and can't say. I want to know what you think. I want the real version of the story."

Johanna took another sip of water. The cashew-headed waiter

came out with a plate covered in wrapped grape leaves. Clearly
Johanna came to eat here often; they knew better than to interrupt her conversation. The mellow smell of dolmas filled the air all
around them, bringing a low army-fatigue green to cover over the
brown smells that preceded it.

"No crime is ever one hundred percent clear, but the facts here
are as straightforward as any murder I've prosecuted. Osman Fritzman's body was found in the woods near Bosperous Creek after six
days of decomposition. No one had reported his disappearance.
No one had access to the community. They keep that place sealed
tight as the Vatican, and they're armed like a white supremacist
militia. No forensic evidence of anyone breaking into the Fritzman house. Fritzman's wife returned to Brooklyn a decade ago. The
strangle marks on the kid's neck match almost exactly the marks
one would find if the father had done it."

Johanna let these initial facts rest in the air for a moment. She
was a lawyer. She knew how to construct a case.

"Natan gave a de facto confession of the crime upon initial
questioning—and don't ask, he wasn't coerced. It takes nothing
to get that charlatan talking. You'll see when you meet him. It's a
disquisition on his own crazy theology from the moment you sit
down. He started in on this religious liberty defense before he even
gave his statement. You'll hear stories about the local boys Osman
was caught up with, and the local anti-Semites. Crazier theories
than that, even. The evidence doesn't support it."

Now it was Zeke's opportunity to sit back and have a sip of
water. He'd eaten three of the dolmas while she was talking. Johanna was right. They filled his whole head with the gamy taste
of lamb, saffron, rice. In all his time eating Turkish and Greek
food, Zeke had never liked grape leaves. They were dry and bland,

mealy and underwhelming. But these dolmas! Here in Central Ohio!

"I can see how clear it appears from your standpoint," Zeke said. "But I have questions. I was there all day today, and there are woods everywhere. Couldn't someone easily have entered the property? Sixteen years old. At sixteen I was already sneaking out of my house to smoke weed with friends every week."

"Well, look," Johanna said. "You've got at a bare minimum another full day here to do your reporting, right?"

"If I get the assignment, I'll likely get a week," Zeke said. "And that would include a trip to visit Natan—Nathan—if the warden approves it."

"You'll go back out there and you'll meet more of the people from this . . . community. You'll meet some of their cloistered youth. One thing Fritzman won't mention is that Osman was the first kid in that community to have been brought up there. He has lived . . . he lived essentially his whole life there. It's been almost twenty years since they discovered Mehmet Osman had immigrated to Ohio and lived in Mt. Izmir and they started descending on this place. In some ways, Osman Fritzman was the first kid to begin reacting against what's going on there. And he died for it. So ask Nathan Fritzman about *that* and see what you hear."

For a moment it was silent. Johanna sipped at her rich brown Turkish coffee. The waiter brought out a huge plate of lamb, chicken, rice, and pita. Zeke had never been so hungry in his entire secular life.

"And if you get a whole week here," Johanna said at a break in devouring some leg of lamb. She'd been looking up, but now she was looking Zeke right in the eyes. "That might be long enough for you to find your way to my apartment. It's in German Village.

It's a cool neighborhood. You could check it out. I've been living there for years, and though I lived on West 70th Street when I was in law school—I mean, I do know what it's like to live in a different city, a bigger city—I really love it. It seems like, well—you know, Gram loved it. Declan's happy up here. I love it. It's not like you couldn't love it, too."

"I could see that," Zeke said. "Columbus, I mean. Gram did tell me you were still there, of course, the last time . . . when I saw him in the city last year. And I liked it when you and me were—back when we . . ."

"I mean it's not Brooklyn. But everyone there is basically from Brooklyn. And who wants to live in Brooklyn anyway."

Zeke tried to look into her eyes, but they were focused back down on her plate. He didn't know what to say back, so he said nothing at all, and he could see that, for the first time since they started talking, a red tint of heat and blood had risen to the tips of her ears.

ESPARAMOS A TI

Outside his window in the Airbnb late that night, as he's struggling to sleep with the pain over his rapidly healing eye, Zeke hears voices. Voices intoning an ancient language, Hebrew or Ladino or Aramaic. He does not know. He can't be sure—but he is certain he sees the shadowy outline of the brim of a black hat crossing by the closed blinds of his window: passing right, then left, then right again.

> *Natan of Flatbush, esparamos a ti.*
> *Natan of Flatbush, no es un otro como a ti.*
> *Natan of Flatbush, esparamos a ti.*
>
> *Natan of Flatbush, esparamos alli.*

THE CAVES (REDUX)

Seven o'clock the next morning, Zeke drove to the Caves for the second time in as many days. Yehoshua had texted him to say he would be gone on a day-long errand. Zeke would be meeting with another of the elders of the community, Faiz Effendi, who lived in Columbus but who said he would be happy to come up and meet him.

Effendi's son David met Zeke at the entrance to the Caves. It was the same drill—a half dozen black-hatted Dönme bearing assault rifles. Their demeanor was more relaxed today, this time having had some warning he would be there. Among them was a seventeen-year-old boy not in a black suit and hat, but instead in a gray zippered hoodie and a pair of skinny jeans.

"My dad got held up on his ride from Columbus. He says he'll meet us in the woods," the hoodied kid said. "I'm David Effendi. Dave. Park over by Josh's house. I'll meet you there."

Zeke felt certain he hadn't seen a teenager in hoodie and skinny jeans the previous day, was certain that he would have noticed him if he had. But amid the community out for their evening prayer, and the weirdly Modern Orthodox worsted gray business suit elders he'd seen, as well, he could easily have missed a collection of teenagers.

Dave Effendi walked a couple of paces ahead of Zeke back onto the same Bosperous Creek path Yehoshua had led him along the day before. Snow fell joyous and bright from the trees above their heads. It rested lightly on the shoulders of Dave's hoodie, which did not appear anywhere near warm enough for the weather.

"Faiz says we should meet him down near the place," Dave said. "What happened to your face?" He pointed at Zeke's eye, which today wasn't covered for the first time. Zeke had had time only to glance at it in the mirror on his way out, where he saw a lump of flesh with black ends of stitches askew in a hundred directions at once.

"It's nothing," Zeke said.

"Doesn't look like nothing."

"Well. I got in a bit of a car accident on my drive up the other day. And it's been . . . healing funny."

"Funny fast."

"Fast."

"It's the words of the mashiach. I know before even saying it you won't believe me. That's what's causing it."

They walked farther down the path, snow sifting all about them.

"So, he was your friend," Zeke said. Dave did not turn back. He did slow his pace. They were shoulder to shoulder as they picked their way along the path.

"Osman was the only one of all the maaminim who went to the public school in Mt. Izmir. Some parents didn't comply when the state said they all had to go to the goyishe school, instead of sticking around the yeshiva our parents run here at the Caves. Natan went along with it. He didn't want any one of the maaminim to get arrested or whatnot. Osman had been going there since freshman year. The school I go to in Columbus played them in sports. So I looked out for him. And of course we were so close from stuff up here."

"So you guys were really tight."

"Osman was my boy," Dave said. "My little bro. He was just a sophomore. Now I'm a senior. I tried my best to look out for him after the Prophet decided he should go to the school. I'm not gonna speak ill of the dead. Then again I guess we Dönme don't really believe in the dead anymore. Or whatever. But. He was a fucking idiot. He should still be alive today. But what would you know about that."

"Honestly?" Zeke said. "I'm here for the funeral of a friend. My age. I'm older than you but not that much older."

"How'd he die?"

"Suicide."

The word hung in the snowy air. Each time Zeke breathed in, it felt as if he were creating new snow himself, the smell of icy air passing in toward the back of his throat so fully he could taste it. Never back at home in Brooklyn had he ever paid quite so much attention to his own breath, to smells around him. It was as if the air here at the Caves demanded closer attention; the beating of his own heart demanded that attention, that he listen to the passing of time, to the pace of the falling snow, each droplet of moist air as it swirled.

"I mean he was smart as anyone I've ever met," Dave said. "And I know it was ultimately because he pushed so hard that the Prophet decided to send him to school. We all know better than to tell anyone about what goes on with our families—you'd think the

Prophet's son would be chief among us. But Osman was different. One day he just couldn't take it anymore. So he started telling everyone. Everyone who would listen. I mean it was so loud that the rumors even made it down to Bexley High, and people there knew my family were members. It was a problem. It was a big fucking problem. And when Osman saw some of the girls were actually interested, that was the end of it."

"What did he tell them?"

"What did I just say? I know better than to share what goes on here. You should do the same if you care about stuff like this." He pointed at the cut over Zeke's eye. "You think we want you here? Let's just get this done. Off this way."

Dave turned at the log Yehoshua had pointed out the day before. Perhaps it held some talismanic importance. Zeke and Dave tromped back into the woods. Until now the terrain had felt at once wild and traversable, like the largest imaginable iteration of the woods behind a northeastern suburban home. As they began to trek farther back through the dense snow-covered wood, the wilderness enveloped them. Above their heads a hawk called its slow shrill cry and signaled its departure by the blanketed flap of its huge terrible wings.

These woods were a near constant pervasion of white. It occurred to Zeke for the first time since they left the trail that he did not see footprints ahead. Faiz Effendi did not come this way to discover the location of Osman's murder, and neither had anyone since the snow began falling. Were Faiz Effendi to jump out of these woods at any moment, with any number of Dönme by his side, rifles at the ready, who would know Zeke was gone? Johanna, he supposed. After a couple days. Maybe. Zeke wasn't on assignment, hadn't yet given himself the seriousness he would give one of his writers. He wasn't in touch regularly with an editor who would watch out for him. He'd moved so quickly from mourning Gram to this research trip that he hadn't been careful, and if he had thought about it more—murder or no murder—these were religious people. He did not think he needed to fear people who feared God. Now all at once he was second-guessing that. Weren't religious people the most fearsome of people across the globe, across history? Weren't they the very people most likely to act violently in the name of faith?

Dave turned back to him.

"It's up ahead. Up here."

In the clearing, trees and fallen branches had been trampled. A soft sheet of snow covered the previously revealed space.

"So seriously, really, what happened to your face?" Dave said.

"Like I said, I was in an accident on my way up."

"The Prophet does not believe there are accidents."

"The shuttle I was in from the airport hit some ice."

"Be sure to say it that way when you meet the mashiach. Anyway. So this is where," Dave said. "Where they got him. Where Natan found him."

"You say 'they' with such confidence."

"People in our ummah take care of each other. There are, what, three hundred of us here day-to-day? Eight hundred for the Feast of the Lamb? Maybe another four or five thousand Kapanci in Istanbul. That is it. Maybe in the seventeenth century when Shabbetai Tzvi was alive, they could have believed the 12th commandment still held." Dave looked into Zeke's eyes directly. "But it's fucking 2020. We're ten thousand miles from the Black Sea. The original families all moved out here to the spot where Mehmet Osman first immigrated just to start the movement, and it's been remarkably successful, in two decades. And all without the help of stupid Mitzvah buses. My own family have only been members since I was in middle school, but my father is very serious about his role here. We're not Satmars, not resting on the successes of Crown Heights or Williamsburg. This is a whole new community here. You think the Prophet would kill his own son? After setting the maaminim up as he has? Creating a real ummah? I know he wants to make this whole argument about how he *could* have done it if he wanted to, but it's a sideshow. He's just protecting himself from his mourning. That the Prophet has decided this is an opportunity to force the issue of our liberty is its own separate thing."

"No viable alternative killer was presented in court. No other motive, no other suspect."

"Look around you. We come in and out of here every day. There are more footprints under this snow than you could track if you were an Ohio bobcat. How could they determine the murderer came from our houses? How could they say definitively someone couldn't have come up through these woods, strangled him, and snuck away? I could show you myself a dozen places in the next hour where kids from Mt. Izmir have been up here since, just to peep at the spot of the murder. It's insanity. They're just protecting the Dragons."

"Dragons?"

"The football players at Mt. Izmir High. They hated Osman and they hate me. They hate all of us. They're the worst anti-Semites you'll ever encounter. Every one of them believed in their own religion—that their mashiach has come already."

"So, Christians."

"Call them what you want. They were just as convinced of his messiah-hood as we are of Natan's. Did you know that Osman's freshman chemistry teacher offered to burn a tattoo of the Jesus fish into the arm of anyone in class who wanted one? It was ostensibly a 'chemistry lesson'—hah! A Jesus tattoo is a Jesus tattoo. Six of Osman's classmates agreed, while he wasn't even allowed to wear tallit or tefillin to school because they said it would break the dress code. Mr. Clark joked, looked at him and said, 'Osman, you're named after a prophet—would you like one?' He said fuck that. He could be Belteshazzar and he wouldn't have taken the mark of their beast. They couldn't imagine the Torah as Osman knew it, as we know it. They couldn't imagine what the Prophet knows of Talmud, of Torah, what it's like to learn with him."

They were again silent.

"It does sound like these kids could do some harm," Zeke said.

"Or worse," Faiz Effendi said. They hadn't heard the older man's footsteps as he approached, the sound of his advance muted by snow. "Dönme make no threats. I am Faiz Effendi," he said. "I see my son David has taken the liberty of showing you the mortal ground where Osman was taken from us."

Zeke looked down at the ground around them. His and David's footsteps had left a pattern, a circle with a tail where they'd come into the space. They'd been walking around each other in remarkably ordered steps, as if they were circling the point of a compass walking at perfect intervals from a point at the clearing's center.

"What happened here?" Faiz Effendi said. There was a dark solemnity with which he had approached the grounds of the murder, a protective sense of mourning, and the affect hadn't left him. He poked the stitches above Zeke's eye, bringing a flash of pain where they dug into his skin.

"Car accident," Zeke said.

"He was in a car crash," Dave said.

A sneer had been on his face since his father arrived. Even

with his hoodie up, the cutting blue of Dave's eyes was visible, the evenly placed moles across his face. He looked like so many of the Ashkenazi you might find if you walked north of Eastern Parkway in Crown Heights for an afternoon. Faiz was so clearly Dave's father—the same bulbous nose, the same evenly spaced moles, only with a beard trimmed tight, salt and pepper, mostly given over to the former. The rest of him was tightly held by his expensive suit, a flowing camel hair overcoat. Name tags clacked in laminate around his neck from his job at Ohio State.

"The van he was in flipped on his way up to Mt. Izmir when he arrived," Dave said.

This was not a detail Zeke had shared with Dave when they were talking. He felt a chill run up his neck. No new winds were blowing across the field, just the wisps of snow that released from the trees and the sky.

"I'll be direct with you. Yehoshua Green might have been open. He might even have allowed you to see us at prayer," Effendi said. "Not all the maaminim are open to your intrusion." He looked over at his son. "Not open at all, some of us. On the relationships and belief we have so long built *without* the prodding of the outside world. We have made mistakes in recent years, but that doesn't mean we must persist."

"You say recent years," Zeke said. "Dave tells me you've only been members since he was in middle school."

The father glared at the son with religious fervor. He looked at Zeke. "Regardless. Regardless of what my son shouldn't have told you and shouldn't be telling you. If we must talk—and now that my son has showed you this space—the Prophet has asked me to help explain to you how we came to the Caves.

"I grew up with Natan. We moved to be closer to our extended families in Williamsburg when we were young. We lived together on South 11th Street, by the river. He was always the religious one, and I, I had the mind for the secular world. It sent me to Brooklyn Tech while he attended yeshiva. I moved here to Ohio for medical school, and saw the mashiach and his family only on holidays when I returned.

"I saw Natan as he grew up. It must be like the tales of the Ba'al Shem Tov himself, we all thought. From the time he was a boy, Natan was not just the most talented Talmudist among us—he was through the Tanakh and through the Mishnah and through all of the Mishneh Torah before the rest of his class knew aleph. He was a master, a thinker, a seer, a storyteller. By the time he was sixteen and had taken a wife, he was beginning to memorize substantial portions of the Zohar. To make money Natan worked in Manhattan, like many of us. Though the internet was forbidden in our community, he began to research the sects that came before us, and he came upon a story he could not shake.

"The story was told that a certain number of Sabbatians, who the Turks referred to as Dönme, had come to the US after World War I. Some were of prominent families—it was rumored Louis Brandeis's grandfather was a practicing Dönme. Some Americanized their names; some kept their Islamic names; some began using their internal, Jewish names outwardly, though it went against our commandments. But we lived in Williamsburg among the Satmars, our families and their families. When Natan would begin to ask about the Sabbatians, the rebbes in his midst were alarmed. He read the Besht, Reb Nachman. These were thinkers who arose in *opposition* to Shabbetai Tzvi. This was the ultimate heresy for the rebbes in our community. You would have to ask Natan to tell you more of the detail in his life—but what is important is that he left Williamsburg. He moved to Fort Greene, found an apartment, joined Footsteps. They helped him become secular. For years he was contented with it. Many of us joined him. But over time it nagged at him, and what the Prophet wanted was not to be secular—but to find the American Dönme.

"Of which there were essentially none.

"But there was record of Mehmet Osman. He'd become a public figure here in Central Ohio. He was a Dönme of Salonica who at the time of the population exchange between Turkey and Greece had moved his family across Europe and found a home here. He owned Greek restaurants, and after the Second World War those businesses failed. But he was successful enough at the height of his Greek restaurants to have the town incorporated, named after the Turkish city where Shabbetai Tzvi was born, to take possession of the land we're standing on. So for a number of years Natan used the money he was making in Brooklyn to travel the twelve hours by car here and begin to take over.

"This land, all two hundred acres, cost less than a parking spot in Carroll Gardens. Slowly they began to follow Natan here. To start families, to live openly in their beliefs. Some took a newfound Islamic name, but it was 2001, 2002, and it was a particularly difficult time to live out that practice. It was less dangerous, after all, to live with a Jewish name in 2002 in Ohio. Natan kept his name, of course, much as Shabbetai Tzvi had—but he took the step of naming his own son Osman. Each maamin was convinced by differing means—some of us found our families had Dönme roots, many were disillusioned by the community in Williamsburg and were looking for a new start."

Faiz Effendi stopped talking. Dave's cheeks were touched with pale white at their tips, and his eyes drawn into a tight squint. For the first time since his father arrived at the clearing, Dave looked at Faiz Effendi with something like wonder. In the silence now created by the ending of Faiz's story the distant rush of the creek arose, the crackle and moan of snow slowly settling deeper and deeper toward the ground. Then a snap, and another, in the woods just beyond the clearing.

In a ring around where they now stood talking were a dozen members of the community—all in black hats and billowing black suits, and all with rifles slung over their shoulders.

"But now you're here with them," Zeke said.

"I was practicing with the unbelievers at a shul in Bexley throughout my training. While we had children. It was not fulfilling. There was a rabbi, not a tzaddik. As my kids grew older, I came up here to find Nathan and what he had built . . ."

More crunching from the circle. The maaminim with their rifles were too far to hear Effendi. He raised his voice to be heard.

"Now I have done my duty. Natan wanted you to hear this story directly from me. Having completed it, I'll speak my mind more freely." Faiz Effendi stopped talking, looked Zeke straight in the eyes, gathered himself into the avian puffing up of his chest. "I do not like the idea of a secular Jew in our midst. I do not feel that the Prophet needs a scribe. I do not like the attention we have been given since the tragedy of Osman"—there was a catch in his throat—"and while I would not generally share a private thought about anyone among our maaminim, I do not think Natan is thinking clearly when it comes to these events. We know he didn't kill Osman. Natan wants to force a point about our practices to the larger world as we await the understanding of Zion that the mashiach has arrived. I am more strategic than my messiah. I don't want the intrusion of the outside world upon our maaminim."

With that Faiz Effendi shook the snow collected on his shoulders to the ground. He made an obtuse but intimidating show of shaking Zeke's hand, kissing his own son on the forehead, and walking the path back out of the woods. As soon as he reached the stand of pines just at the outskirts of the clearing, each of the black-hatted Dönme who had been watching them fell in behind him, twigs breaking loudly beneath their black leather shoes. Once their steps were no longer audible, Dave turned in the other direction.

"That's my father," Dave said. "That's what you needed for your story, to get the history, right?"

"It's only part of what I want," Zeke said. Dave slowed. "I know it might sound a little crazy—but I'm also here to talk to people about what they believe. Ein Sofism."

"I'm seventeen and I live in Central Ohio, man. What do you think I believe? I believe in the supernal power of LeBron James. I believe the Browns will never make a single smart draft pick. I believe I'll be leaving this godawful state the second I get into college. That's what I fucking believe."

For the first time since they'd come back into these woods now hours ago, Dave Effendi smiled. It was a handsome smile, toothy and contagious, white as fallen snow.

IN THE VOICE OF THE PROPHET [I]

From *Shivhei ha-Natan*, **the Prison Notebooks of Natan of Flatbush**

On the Inevitability of Death

Faiz Effendi will die, he shall know it, selah:: David Effendi will die,
it will be no sooner nor later he shall know it:: There is no sooner
or later only time space.: he shall know it:: My dear son Osman will
die did die has died.: he shall know it:: Ezekiel will die.: he shall
know it::

Mehmet Osman who was neither Jew nor Muslim but who
knew and respected Qur'an knew and respected Talmud who will
die did die has died.: he shall know it:: Even in the midst of his
being recognized as the mashiach and the Prophet of Shabbetai
Tzvi.: Natan of Flatbush will die he shall know it::

: : : : :

I remember the first days after Osman's birth:: Sitting in a room
with baby Osman:: Yael is still there with us: We are living in an
apartment in Fort Greene in the first months after leaving, after

66

escaping Crown Heights:: A tiny apartment on South Elliott Place
not far north of Flatbush where in the summer heat on the half
of the third floor of a brownstone where we three live we feel the
imposition of the infernal: I'm working full-time as a paralegal in an
office in Battery Park City while Yael is at home with Osman tiny
Osman::

   At night while Yael sleeps I will sit in a small chair in the
summer heat and rock the boy rock the boy rock the boy until
he returns to sleep. Always returning to sleep—this is and will be
the condition of the infant, always and ever returning to sleep::
In the grainy afternight of three A.M. with the streetlights of
Brooklyn Tech pouring in our front windows there will be enough
light to see the purple lightning of veins shot through Osman's
eyelids as they flutter once again closed in sleep. I allow my rocking
to slow, slow, slow and just as I am feeling the boy is out enough
to bring him back to his mother on the bare mattress we sleep on
the uneven floors of that apartment so small we will store both the
Zohar and the Talmud in the tiny kitchenette oven, the eyes flicker
back and he is screaming, he is crying, this baby Osman. Night
after night I will take him out strapped to my chest and walk him
through Fort Greene Park after dark so Yael can get some rest. She
feeds him and kisses him and out I go, the hipster Hasid I know
they all call me in the neighborhood, around that less-than-a-mile
loop to the top of the park, not too close to the Myrtle side, and
back home. I will not be able to remember Osman as a seven-year-
old, already old enough to radiate teenage heat and oniony odor, or
as a thirteen-year-old shirking his haftara memorization in favor
of going to play football. I will not be able to remember what he
would have become had he lived a year longer a decade a half a
century longer and become tzaddik of the community in the Caves::

Daytime Yael stays at home with Osman. Walks him to Fort Greene Park while I am working in Battery Park City all day. The last summer before we move to Mt. Izmir and I have taken on the year to work at B&H in Manhattan for the money it will take to get us from there to there. Long days showing the unbelievers how to work digital cameras and laptops so I can buy them at a steep discount, sell them on eBay for close to double. I work all day and when I come home I will find Yael and tiny purple-lidded Osman walking by the statue of Washington at the center of the park. I'm there the day in July when while pushing behind that boy in a stroller Yael has the purse snatched off her shoulder, though I tell her again and again it is still too dangerous to walk on the Myrtle side of the park late, it's safe on the DeKalb side, but no matter how she loves the view of the Financial District from the stone steps leading down to Myrtle there are still muggings regularly and this would be sign enough to pick up the pace, to get us out::

We name him Osman because he would be the start of a great new ummah in Ohio where his Prophet father will take him and his mother to start a new life.: That they would find another Osman in Mt. Izmir:: Osman Effendi the most important of all the Sabbatians to make their way to the new Zion.: and in the shadow of his remains they will find their new life::

: : : : :

That all of existence is a single event made up of infinite smaller events::

: : : : :

On the long car ride to Ohio Yael marvels at how quickly upon leaving the city we are in the countryside. Once as a child she took a day trip to Bear Mountain but never again since has she left the Five Boroughs for anything but a visit to Monsey and the green sod backyards and mosquitoes there. On seeing the green of Upstate New York out the window of the U-Haul once we hit the interstate with Osman between us, Yael just stares outside.: I perceive what I see in her as excitement, but whether in that moment it's excitement or dread, it will eventually turn to fear. Repulsion. Repulsing. A taking-away. An addition of absence. The first month of August in Central Ohio brutal as prophecy has predicted::

Her face:: Yael a lonely lovely nineteen when we make our first trip to Mt. Izmir: Just a hair over five feet tall, with a dark snowy sprinkle of skin between the deep Sephardic moles on her light cheeks. Hair the color of copper piping strung into curls bounces off her back when she walks Osman in the stroller across the neighborhood we now must leave. Out on the fields beside the tennis courts, dust kicks up into waist-high plumes as soccer players sweat their intensity at the game, cries in Urdu and Hebrew and Arabic and French and German and Spanish and Wolof each time a goal or a foul propounds upon them. The brick townhouses and brownstones along Park Place stand watch over it, over us, over Yael and infant Osman in a faceless goodbye. Shalom. Peace out. Word to your eema. Welcome to Brooklyn, now leave::

Looking out the window at the green of Central New York as it tails behind the U-Haul, an event moving farther behind us as we move farther forward, and her skin regains its natural flush. While we are driving Yael refuses to take Osman from his car seat, strapped between us in the cracked pleather front seat. She refuses. "It's totally unsafe, Natan," she says. "Taking a baby out while driving. C'mon. You're his father. You know better. We have to care for this baby." She unbuckles and takes her breast from her nursing bra and dips it down toward the baby's mouth. Osman takes the nipple between his lips, but before he does I see where at the end of the dark freckles of her chest the breast turns pure white like early-winter Ohio snow and ends in a brown nipple the color of Osman's lips. I jerk the van back from the rumble strip when it rumbles but Osman refuses to relinquish his latch::

I look out the window as soon as I see Yael is looking at me looking at her breast. At Footsteps, they suggested adding perhaps another child to the family instead of starting a new congregation, but this time with secular rules for procreating, saying it will make us more secular in and of itself, but we will be in Ohio for a long time before we are able to look at each other so, and it will take place only after I see Yael bathing in the Bosperous and there is nothing more to hide: river running tight silk around her thighs, so close even moving water doesn't want to stray far from Yael's flesh, Osman tracing figure eights with a stick in the sand on the creek's bank. I am David peering across Jerusalem rooftops spying Bathsheba::

: : : : :

You shall not remember things that have not yet transpired::

: : : : :

If a prophet could see around all corners he would, he would save his family and his marriage and his happiness, but that is not the role of the prophet:: The prophet's prophecy is to bring to his community the word of Hashem and to hasten the will of the Lord: if it predicts it predicts but that is not the teleology of prophecy:: All of these things must exist in the past because I am remembering them & along with the second law of thermodynamics there is only one single law of time: You cannot remember the future::

COUPLING

The thin pillow under Zeke's head might as well have been just a pillowcase. In the corner of the room, a ficus, and with no light in the room, it appeared to be a house cat, a small dragon. The outer neighborhoods of Columbus, Ohio, might have been the darkest of any large city in America. In the two A.M. stillness, even a room in the city was cast in near total darkness. It allowed the fuzzy glow of the stars on the ceiling to grow distinct, unmistakable, above.

"What percentage of Americans between the ages of, say, thirty and forty do you think had those star stickers on their ceilings at some point?" Zeke said.

"Star stickers."

"Like those." He lifted his hand skyward. He pointed toward the stars with his index finger, but it was genuinely too dark to see what he was doing.

They were both silent for five seconds. Ten.

"If you're asking if I put those there, I for sure didn't put those up there," Johanna said. "I'm a thirty-something-year-old lawyer. I don't need to stick star stickers on the ceiling. I'm honestly so busy all the time I'm so tired when I get home that until you pointed them out I don't know if I even noticed they were there. Normally if the light is out, so am I."

"I wasn't saying you did. I was just—well, OK."

Again silence. He could feel himself receding until, unexpectedly, Johanna put her hand on him.

"Sorry," she said. "I don't know why I got so defensive. It's been months since anyone other than me was in this apartment. I seriously didn't even know those stars were there."

She said for a second time, much gentler now, "I'm so tired by the time I get home most nights the only thing I see is my pillow."

She walked across the room and turned on a night-light in the corner, and immediately the stars disappeared, even the faint glow of them. In their stead tiny pinpricks of light swirled above Zeke and Johanna's heads. It was as if there were a gentle blizzard swirling, but the room was seventy degrees. She came back and lay down.

"This looks almost healed," she said, looking at his eye. "I mean, like, basically healed."

"I know. I mean I don't. I don't know how it got so much better so fast. Maybe there's a lot of vitamin E in the water here or something."

"Or something," Johanna said. The minuscule points of light now played over her face. Zeke could see as each bright white point hit on a freckle, or on the moles that overlay the freckles on her face. It looked as if tiny snowflakes were alighting across her face and then disappearing, again and again. She looked like the exact Johanna he'd been in love with when he was twenty-one, only with a breath or two more life breathed into her by her maker. But the ease—the ease of just being together, being around each other again, being undressed together again—was like living inside a memory. "Can I ask you something?" she said.

"You just did."

"Funny. You're funny you know that? It's good to be around someone who's funny. Murderers aren't funny. Lawyers aren't funny. Prosecutors, in particular. Ohioans. Ohioan prosecutors might literally be the least funny breed of human. When they're interacting with a youngish tattooed perspicacious female prosecutor, they're particularly not funny. But. The question. Does there seem to be any truth to these people's beliefs to you?"

"I . . . do not . . . know. I mean I don't know what *I* believe, for that matter. Or that I believe anything at all. It doesn't make it easier to take on these people I think are fanatics. But who seem at peace, even with the horrible events there." A single point of light skittered across the glowing star stickers on the ceiling. "Do you believe?"

"In their weird Islamic Jewish stuff?"

"No. Just in, you know. Anything."

"No. No, I don't. It's funny—all the time we were together, around each other, in college, we never once talked about this."

"Nope."

"Well, I don't know what I believe. I just believe in me, Yoko and me." Zeke didn't have time to laugh before she went on. "I'm a second-generation American hippie. My grandparents changed their shtetl name from Frankyl to Franklin back in the 1910s. My parents were at Woodstock, but, like, the weekend after. By the time they got to Woodstock, they were half a dozen strong. I was literally in college before I found out what people meant when they said 'Samson,' or 'disciple,' or 'God said to Abraham, Kill me a son.'"

"'God said, No. Abe said, What—'"

"Right. Which, shit, I guess doesn't mean I don't believe in *any-thing*. I believe in the law. Laws, not men. Laws, not men! Or even just: Not men! Full stop." She paused for him to laugh, but he didn't. "Until tonight anyway, for the first time in a long, long time. I believe that when people break the law they should be held accountable, and that even if they want to use some insane sophistry to make people believe they should be able to do what they want because of the Establishment Clause or whatever, that it's our job to argue on the basis of facts. And truthfully, I believe in the law so fully it wouldn't matter where I was practicing it—here, or in New York, or on the moon . . . I mean it's ultimately Aristotelian, the law we practice, right?"

Zeke asked her what she meant.

"It's not like we're in court talking metaphysics, duking it out over whether what someone like Nathan Fritzman did was *evil* or not, arguing over the fate of his eternal soul. We're there to make a case: if anything is worth prosecuting, it's murder. If any murder is most unforgivable—how could it not be the strangulation of your own son? I'll leave it to the Declan Wrens of the world to understand Kant's *Critique of Pure Reason*. My job is to present a case as directly as possible. Without resorting to sophistry."

The slow dance of lights over Johanna's face played tricks while Zeke was trying to be so quiet. He wanted her to talk more—he wanted everyone to talk more but him. A whole cacophony of talkers talking, and he the listener listening. The lifelong dream. He wanted at this point in his time with her, and with his time here in Ohio, to simply allow everyone he met to talk until they'd talked out their purest beliefs. Tonight was a useful opportunity to see that simply remaining silent wasn't enough. There was the journalistic cliché of letting the voice of silence be filled by your subject; this was no longer an effective strategy, and it took being with a woman he'd loved more than a decade earlier to see it. He had to ask the right questions, too, and sometimes asking the right questions required making statements, offering truths yourself to elicit truths from your partner. He was going to have to put himself out there a good bit more—here with Johanna, up at the Caves, and when he met Natan.

"Well, for what it's worth, the Dönme up there in Mt. Izmir don't believe in metaphysics, either," Zeke said. "I'm not smart enough to know if it's Aristotelian or whatever the opposite of Aristotelian is."

"Platonic."

"Right. Platonic. Which you and I are no longer. Again."

"Funny, there's that funny coming right back—"

"But right. Talking to Yehoshua—"

"Josh—"

"Talking to Yehoshua, I understand at least that they don't subscribe to a Platonic view. Of sin, of redemption, of evil. I mean, when we were in college, we learned that pure evil wasn't a thing, right? That it was relative. And I guess Natan—Nathan—whatever—is pushing on that, too, with his ideas of Ein Sofism. Rejecting that relativism we were weaned on."

"Well, I wasn't weaned on that stuff," Johanna said. "Maybe in your English major you got that. I was in the political science department. We more kind of learned what major thinkers thought and didn't worry so much about whether we believed it, too. We learned which ideas governments adopted, and what they didn't.

We were reading actual law by the time I was a sophomore. I think I've read the Federalist Papers four times."

"The Federalist Papers . . . So you believe in that."

"Yes! I believe in the power of John Jay. Give us this day our daily Jefferson. His kingdom come, Hamilton's will be done, on earth as it is in heaven."

Zeke could feel Johanna's whole body stiffen next to him. She didn't actively roll away from him, or recede, but her skin had filled with wood.

"When you put it that way, sure, I believe in something," Johanna said. "I believe in learning what other people believe, and doing my job."

"Oh, good," Zeke said.

"That said, I didn't need the Federalist Papers to comprehend that murder is illegal. I didn't need the Commandments to get there. I don't need a god to comprehend that you can't kill your own fucking son."

The room fell silent again. The verve had left Zeke's body. It became harder to say words not untrue and not unkind. He could feel the cold of the light of the night-light as it crossed his face. He was about to respond, to confess something of his own beliefs, when Johanna spoke again.

"And OK, fine. I do find belief attractive. So there's that. I find comfort in knowing other people have strongly held beliefs. When I was a teenager I smoked a ton of pot, and at times I would get so stoned I'd get terrified, just chilled to the bone, afraid of nothing at all. And in those moments I'd believe I could believe in God, or I'd talk rambling with friends about the idea. But it strikes me that that's the very heart of the conversation: it's in those moments of terror, of fear of death, or fear of the death we've caused and the punishment to come, that we find ourselves turning in that direction—those moments of help! Help! But it's been a long, long time since I've felt the need for that kind of help. Ta-da. Belief. You got me."

And with that Johanna finished speaking and turned over, flopping against her mattress.

"It's going to be a very early morning tomorrow for both of us," she said.

ASSIGNMENT

Before he leaves Johanna's apartment for Mt. Izmir, Zeke takes a minute to compose himself in his rental car. He checks his phone. He has a very brief Slack message from his boss.

"You have a week," she's written. "Just like any writer: coach airfare back to the city. Try to get that Airbnb for the rest of the week if you can. See you a week from Monday."

Zeke immediately writes her back and with no chill whatsoever says, "Thank you thank you thank you thank you." While he's thumbing that in, and before he can send it, a new message comes from his editor.

"And hey. Like I tell all my writers—don't fuck this up."

REAL DRAGONS

The Mt. Izmir Dragons football stadium sat at the outskirts of town like a single star glowing hazy through clouds in an otherwise star-less night's sky. Nowhere near the high school itself, but a refracted beacon alongside rural route 613, its light cast out to the fields around it like something precious was being mined deep within the plains. It wasn't a stadium, per se, but a succession of two-hundred-foot-tall permanent risers set up around the hundred yards of turf supplanting grass at its center, a brick red track running around its perimeter.

Zeke could see only one sign of Mt. Izmir in the distance from his frigid seat at the top of the risers, where the wall of an abandoned warehouse still carried a Lucky Strike advertisement that had been fading for decades. On the field, Mt. Izmir players scrimmaged against their own: offense in white pinnies, defense in red. Where in the fields around them snow still frosted the tips of grass and husks of cornstalks, the Dragons' field was pine green, manicured er early dark. Declan had suggested they meet at the football adium, but Zeke didn't realize a practice would be underway— why would they be practicing football in late winter?—until he arrived to find cars parked at odd angles to each other in the gravel parking lot just to the north of the field. Though they couldn't know who he was, it felt as if the eyes of every football parent were on him, Zeke the interloper, wearing a jacket two layers too thin, here to put both the Dönme and them under a microscope. And they were never more visible than when they were at the football stadium.

"Over here, bud," Declan had called out when Zeke arrived at the bottom of the risers. "So good to see you, my friend." They hugged, and Zeke could feel the slim six feet his friend had always been, now wrapped in his own insulation. Zeke knew what Declan's kids looked like and what they'd done for their most recent birthday parties and how they had looked at three months, three years, thirteen, from social media. Declan was the first of his friends to marry and have kids, two years older than Zeke after having taken a gap year and being a year ahead in school, and an infinity ahead in life, and it was as if he existed to lend fallacy to the idea of generations, to unpack the complicated process of aging: Zeke still an advanced teenager, living alone in Brooklyn; Declan the father of a precocious high school sophomore cornerback.

"So to get down to it," Declan said. Under the hood of his jacket, Zeke could see a smattering of dark freckles across the bridge of his nose that had not been there when they'd been at school. He remembered that Declan had had a melanoma removed from his forehead—that was a fact he had not learned on social media. Under the darker freckles in the sodium light of the Dragons' stadium, a fainter row of what now was browned Irish skin appeared, a flat layer of darker skin that when they were in college together had likely been freckles, marking the progress of time. "The backup QB is Fergus Shaw, number 7—the one with the muffler for his hands. The center is Miles Boyle, number 67. The very, very fast wide receiver you'll see burning everyone downfield, 88, is De-shawn Flaxton. My son is Bill, one of the cornerbacks, 37. He'll come talk to us at the diner after if you want. But Fergus and Miles and Deshawn are the kids who your Dönme friends will have been talking about. They're the ones who were mixing it up with Osman Fritzman and Dave Effendi off and on at the time."

As Declan was talking, one of the parents also watching the game, three rows down from where they were sitting, turned and gave them a hard stare, then turned back to the field, wiping a thin silt of fallen snow from her shoulders.

"And you're not being paranoid, dude," Declan said. "Trust your instincts. Everyone in town knows you're here. People knew about Gram's funeral, and to say they've been keeping a close eye on the Caves would be a massive understatement. And now they all assume you're here to try to give credence to Fritzman's story. They're all on edge. And this is a real kinda 'fake news' attack-dog crowd. So be careful. I've done what I could to convince folk you're a good guy. But keep in mind—even though I grew up in Ohio, I'm a professor at the college here. I mean, I've had op-eds in the *Times*. The town-gown shit is real, tangible, and it's more contentious than ever. They wouldn't like me much either if it wasn't for Billy's speed. And if he missed a key tackle in a key game, who knows how quickly that could turn, too."

From their height in the risers, they could hear the clap of num-ber 37 popping a running back who'd gotten to the edge of the line, and had tried to turn upfield. They were just far enough away that the sound carried to them, but the play had already ended, what they saw and what they heard not quite synced. Time and the physical world of the senses felt out of whack, that way sound carried across space so much slower than sight—so maybe it was the opposite of time and the physical world being out of whack. Maybe it was one moment when you were perceiving time, sound, and sight most keenly. Billy's legs were still driving at the ground beneath his feet though his teammate was on his back. The field, though manicured, was slick with melted snow.

"I don't have a clue where he gets it from," Declan said. "I mean you know I played soccer in high school. I was plenty good. His grandfather back in County Cork was a big guy, but not that big. Just living here, it's as if his genes were signaled at birth to keep muscling him until he was big enough to get out on the field."

"Did you consider not letting him play? I mean with all the CTE and traumatic brain injury stuff you read about."

"*You* read about," Declan said. "Folks here choose not to read about it. Look at where we are right now. Practicing in the off-season is technically illegal, enough to get you kicked out of conference play. But everyone does it—they wouldn't have a conference if they kicked us all out, so here we are. I mean, do you know what it would've taken to dissuade the kid from playing? He'll be done with it by the time high school's over. He's nowhere near big enough to play D-I, and the way Bill and his friends are— playing D-III, at a place like William James College, would be such a slight, it would be worse than not playing at all. And he'll be going there free."

They caught up a bit on their friends in common, on Declan's research, his teaching. They actively avoided bringing up Gram again. Declan said he wanted to know about Natan of Flatbush, about the Dönme and their theology, if Zeke had changed his flights now that he had the assignment, and how long he'd be staying. Zeke told him what he understood of Ein Sofism. It couldn't help but remind him, even as he was talking, of the hours they spent talking metaphysics and cosmology when they were undergrads, stoned out of their gourds in dorm rooms, with his couple of years on him Declan the guide, Zeke following along.

"Nah, I don't know that I think it comports much with any long-standing philosophical tradition," Declan said. "I mean there were pre-Socratics, I guess, who might not be averse to it, Heraclitus or Zeno, someone like that. It sounds more like the provenance of theoretical physics—the way string theory works, the advances in loop quantum gravity, ways of trying to account for the existence of dark matter. Which is way outside my own expertise. But honestly, hearing you talk about it now . . . how much does it matter? It sounds like the quackery of a cult leader, right? You can't possibly believe that kind of thing. It's a little hard to believe even his followers do. Especially after the murder."

They let that last comment hang like falling snow. The specter of Gram arose on its own—death, suicide—and they could see it on each other's face. They would talk about it, but now wasn't the time. Zeke was here to talk to Billy, which would be hard enough. So they waited for the risers to clear out before descending. When Billy came off the field, his father put a jacket over his shoulders and tried to introduce him, but Billy just looked over each shoulder and said, "Look, I'm hungry as all get-out. Can we head over to Ankara's and get a burger?"

Declan started to explain where to meet them, but before he finished his long involved description of the route, Zeke said he knew where Ankara was. They went off to their cars. His whole walk away from the stadium Zeke could feel eyes on him—the eyes of foxes in the dark off behind the glowing stadium, the eyes of the parents there to pick up their young footballers, the eyes of Fergus Shaw (7) and Miles Boylan (67) and Deshawn Flaxton (88) and any other of the teammates (1–99) who had felt whatever they'd felt about Osman, and now knew Zeke was here looking into a trauma they thought they'd put behind them once Natan was charged. Just as he reached his car, the bright lights of the stadium went flat, just the granular white afterglow of the sodium lights burning soft and low in the distance. He was alone. In the dark.

: : : : :

In town, the welcome return to a feeling of anonymity. Inside the Turkish restaurant, Declan and his son had already found a table. Billy kept his eyes down in his menu.

"Some hard hitting out there," Zeke said. He knew almost nothing about football. "Your tackling was very . . . containing. Your containment. You contained things well."

Billy looked up from the menu long enough to scowl at him.

"Look, I know you're my dad's old college friend," Billy said. He had Declan's freckles only in a single row, like the Milky Way viewed in the country night sky, a single band of color against a stark monochromatic background. Zeke could see a couple of wiry auburn hairs beginning to develop on the boy's upper lip. "But Ferg and D are my best friends. If you think I'm gonna tell you they were intimidating that kid from the cult up there . . . or why . . . it's not gonna happen. Those kids were too . . . elite. Elitist. We're God-fearing here in Ohio. They were God-loving. And I mean . . . loving."

The three of them let the last comment hang. Before Declan

could interject, the cashew-headed waiter from before came to take their order. Zeke asked for the same sumptuous plate of dolmas he'd had with Johanna. Billy ordered an Athena burger rare. Feta and the egg on top, over hard.

"I've been to Greece and I've been to Bulgaria, and I'd never heard of a burger with an egg on it before we came to school here," Declan said. "I mean we definitely didn't come to this place when we were in school, right? In Budapest they put fried eggs on their pizza—remember that from our trip, Billy?" His son nodded. He'd left his earlier comments behind him after ordering. Maybe he was, in fact, just hungry.

"Yeah," Billy said. "Uck. Worst pizza." He looked down at his hands as if a script were written there. "You heard of the Dimming of the Candles?" he said. It was clear he was aiming the question at Zeke, not his father. "Osman told Fergus all about it. That's what got him killed, I think. It's the biggest thing those freaks aren't supposed to talk about. Every year at their biggest holiday, their Christmas, they have this ritual where they kill one of the lambs from the farm up there in the Caves. They don't eat lamb any other time of year. Anyway, when he got older, Osman found out that that night, when he and his friends went back to their houses, their parents did this thing called the Dimming of the Candles. It's a thing they've always done. They might as well call it the orgy of the cultists—"

"OK, Billy," Declan said. "OK, OK. I think he gets it. I told you, Zeke isn't here to interrogate you."

"He's with them. The cult."

"Well, they're not a cult," Zeke said. "But no. No, I'm not *with* anyone. I'm a writer, Bill. When your dad and I were at school together, we were both on the school paper. I mean, we didn't even study journalism or anything. Me, I wanted to be a poet. I'm here to get the truest, fullest version of the story I can. Sometimes while I'm here, that's going to mean talking with the Dönme up there in the Caves. Sometimes it'll mean hearing the story as honestly as I can from the prosecution, or you, or your friends. That's what I'm trying to do today."

While Billy mulled over what his father's friend had just told him, the waiter came with their food. The thick smell of lamb burger topped with fried egg mixed with the slow saffron smells of Zeke's grape leaves.

"There's just not much of a question," Billy said. "Everyone at Mt. Izmir knows exactly what happened. Don't you remember what it was like to be in high school, dude? Everybody tells everybody everything, and everybody knows everything that happens with everyone. The law, it takes them a little longer to figure it all out, but they figure it out eventually. You know we can say whatever we want. They have to get it right, so they take their time. Get it right. They tell the jury. The jury knows exactly what happened."

"So why don't you tell Zeke what happened, William," Declan said. For the first time he was glaring at his kid, tired of the tirade. "So he can write it. So he can ask them about it. The sooner you tell him, the sooner you can head home and I can get back to catching up with my friend."

"You talk to Davey?" Billy said.

"You mean Dave Effendi."

"Osman's friend from down in Columbus. His family is part of that shit. He knows. That Dimming of the Candles orgy. He's lucky he's not strangled to death by that cult leader, too. He and Osman went and peeked in for the first time. They saw it. Davey called it the Fugly Orgy. All the elders of the community, together.

The kids aren't supposed to see it, but Osman was kind of like an elder because of his status with them. And Davey got in with him, and with his father being so—so important to them. Their existence. Because—well, you know. But Jesus, the Dimming of the Candles. With the lights out, the candles out. Said it was part of their religion. Jesus, you call that a fucking religion."

Bill picked up his burger and took a bite. Zeke looked at Declan, whose gaze was now fixed on a spot back behind him. When Zeke turned around to the front of the restaurant, he saw through the plate-glass windows that Fergus Shaw and Deshawn Flaxton were standing there, still in their football uniforms and pads, looking at him. Watching over their conversation. Looking in at Billy. Zeke waved as if to invite them in.

Fergus Shaw gave him the finger and walked away.

THE REAL THREAT OF DRAGONS

At night in his cabin Zeke sits up watching local sports coverage until two in the morning. He even sees a highlight of Bill Wren from the previous fall, making an open field tackle. Johanna sends him a couple of texts. He ignores them.

There's nothing new on his work Slack. He's on his own for the time being.

He hears scuffling outside his door, but no prayer. He hears the mid-range treble voices of teenagers saying, "Fuck you, bitch, go find your own fucking story." The phone in his room rings and then rings again.

He does not answer it.

Now he is watching footage of Fergus Shaw taking a shot from an opposing linebacker and then getting back up. He is watching Deshawn Flaxton outrun everyone they put on him, triceps poking out of his early-autumn sleeves like subdermal rolls of quarters.

He thinks he hears someone knock on his door. He waits two minutes, three. He opens the door. He peers out through the snow at the small outcropping of trailers next to his Airbnb. No one is there but him.

He hears someone shouting in the distance. It could be, *Shabbetai Tzvi, esparamos a ti*. It could be, *Fight, Dragons, fight!* It could be the chattering of ice in the trees.

Tomorrow he is set to meet up with Dave Effendi at the Caves again.

IN THE VOICE OF THE PROPHET [II]

From *Shivhei ha-Natan*, the Prison Notebooks of Natan of Flatbush

On the Eternal Present

There is no present moment:: There is no now:: Ein Sofism, like theoretical physics, tells us that as it has always been will always be there are multiple presents one present for each perceiver as there are infinite Torahs a different Torah for each reader, selah:: As there are different sets of halakhic guidelines one guideline for every follower.: There is no causation.: There is no time:: Only events::

: : : : :

In the early days of late summer it will be nearly one hundred degrees by ten A.M. every day, Ohio sun bearing down. It will take more than a week to find our way to the Cave of the Dragon. I know the area will be called the Caves because the area has been called the Caves. There must be caves somewhere. When we arrive, our land will be nothing more than an overgrown field. I go into Mt. Izmir. In a small hardware shop I buy first a scythe, then a lawnmower, and later rent a groundhog to level the field where the Dönme will pray. And a small canvas tent where Yael, Osman, and I sleep after on the first night keeping the U-Haul a day and sleeping in a space in the rear::

The rest of our fellow Dönme will arrive from Crown Heights and Williamsburg in the first two weeks. Soon we will be a dozen. Soon we will be Ben-Gurion in Palestine. My best friend then went by the name David Levin. His wife Chana. Levin is the most effective of us—the strongest, the most full of rectitude as he would be for all his years.

"We are Ben-Gurions in the land of Israel, clearing swamp to make way for kibbutzim!" Levin will say. While the rest of us are sweltering with the summer humidity bearing down on us, he will lead the way. Before we know it there's a small tent city at the center of the field. Levin is exactly right—we feel as if we were Ben-Gurion clearing the muck of the valley, planting orange groves, setting down the soil to grow Jaffa. We're all at once Zionists and settlers, the first goyishe settlers of this country of America, taking steps westward from New England. Levin tells us that first we need resources. He's had the full American experience, Levin—grown up in a Modern Orthodox family in Brooklyn, learned the sciences at Stuyvesant. He longs to be a surgeon and what could stop David Levin from any goal no matter how imposing! But he has fallen back in with the Lubavitchers he knew as a boy, and he is always torn between secularism and an intense desire to lead the life of narrow piety. Every day of his life—he knows he has the life and the opportunity to live a comfortable life of a qelippa. He also feels more intensely the calling to the tzaddik, to the learning, than any of us. Were I not the Prophet, he might even imagine he was.

: : : : :

Each of the early settlers of our Mt. Izmir ummah finds a job waiting tables in Mt. Izmir, in Dayton, in Columbus, in Mount Vernon, in Gahanna—until in a year we accrue enough money for a trailer. A single trailer, with an air-conditioning unit in the window to keep our sacred texts dry. And on occasion our bodies after a long day in the field. By then Osman will begin to walk, and every day Yael takes him to the Bosperous to wash, until a path is padded down, and in her washing herself in the creek, Levin and I decide this will be our mikvah, used equally by our women and by our men, in summer as well as winter.

When the field is cleared and the second summer upon us, the Prophet of the Dönme, Prophet of Shabbetai Tzvi, Natan of Flatbush, I perceive the flock as it wilts in the hot summer sun. The field is cleared, but there will be need of a room for our sheep, a space for our shtibl, a place for worship. But clearing more land, renting another groundhog, doing that work has left a dull paleness in the eyes of all, even Levin. So on a clear hot day a week since rain, I take to the middle of the cleared field and to all those out at work and say, "The time has come for the performance of one of the mashiach's miracles!" Levin hands out water all around. Work ceases. Even without labor, at the height of the sun sweat rises on brows. And I will perceive it, I understand there are needs, and I say:

"Tomorrow at noon I will stop the sun in the sky."

There is new energy among them now, but it is immediately the wrong energy, a suspicious energy. "You all read the prophet Amos just as I have. 'And it shall come to pass in that day that I will cause the sun to go down at noon, and I will darken the earth at the clear day.' Tomorrow. But for today! Today we will wash in the mikvah and we will prepare."

With Levin behind me, we will tromp through the woods and

down to the crossing on the other bank from the Cave of the
Dragon and now all fifty of us disrobe, bodies smeared in sweat and
grass and dirt from the work, and cool in the cool cool Bosperous
Creek the sun is so hot not one among them can imagine how the
sun will darken in the noonday sky and neither can I but there are
smiles at last::

: : : : :

Night. Late late after Yael and Osman have gone to sleep, I creep
out of my tent and find Levin. He is asleep next to Chana and
wakes easily when called. We get into the F-150 and head into
town where only the Kroger is open, and with money stashed for
the coming frigid winter we purchase cases of beer. Pabst Blue Ribbon, Genesee Cream Ale. We sneak them into the river, hundreds of
them planted with their bottoms cooling in the chill of the summer
night in the Bosperous Creek.

: : : : :

Next morning we repair to work as every summer morning,
knowing winter is only ever a season away, but with a newfound energy from the cooling creek and the beer they do not know will be
there, and their skeptical anticipation of the miracle to come. I will
spend the morning in the trailer, the window air conditioner in off
position, reading Zohar in preparation. To shed the qelippot, to shed
the worldly vision, to sit in the space of redemption through sin.

By this time the community will discover the mystical powers of
the smoke of the plant and the spore of the pasture, and with a long
plastic pipe I prepare. Then I arise from my trailer, smoke in hand,
and pass the smoke around to the Dönme all through the field.
"Shabbetai Tzvi, esparamos a ti!" The Prophet will speak the words.
And with the congregants around him, his face to the bright hot
sun, the Prophet of the mashiach, Natan of Flatbush, with all the

power of the fallen sparks again raised, will open his eyes, gaze upon that flame in the sky, and he will recite psalm after psalm as the congregation watches him & in the height of its noonday blaze the sun will stop, a single star in the midday Ohio summer sky. The sun has not dimmed, but is blazing at its height.

"And now we stop our work for the day," and again the maaminim will tromp through the woods, mothers fathers children and all, and the mothers and fathers and even the eldest children find the cold drink there and rejoice, and while you would not believe it and we hardly will believe it ourselves, with the sun barely a notch farther along in the sky directly above, dark clouds heavy with rain close in. For a day so bright and a sun so hot, just the dull grayness of them is enough to darken the river. I look over at Levin and see a dimness in his face below this newfound shade, a miracle performed, the prophecy of Amos fulfilled. Until he looks up and sees me looking, and then he smiles, tips his Pabst Blue Ribbon can to me and then down his gullet. And with great joy the maaminim will spend hours in the Bosperous Creek, the darkened frozen sun in the frozen Ohio sky covering over them as they cool in the waters, and until I see that there is flagging energy I'll point it out, the sun in the sky with no movement at all, until the day is done and I say, "And now the sun will return to its path," and along the far bank of the creek the community in its entirety would cram in through the mouth of the Cave of the Dragon with smoke in their hands and the drink in their gullets and smoke in their lungs and upon their exit just moments later they will watch the sun soar across the far horizon and down below the trees, cloud covered over as it moves darkly set again in its movement until evening falls upon them in the space of a moment, and then again in the sky the stars of night::

: : : : :

You'll note I have come often to adopt the future tense for use in my writings. And the freedom of dropping it. The Ten Commandments of Moses, the Eighteen Commandments of Shabbetai Tzvi, are commands formulated in the future tense. Secular philosophers claim the Jewish people are a people too wholly mired in the past, who allow themselves to live through what has come before: Moses receiving the tablets, reliving the Exodus every Passover, reliving Abraham's covenant with the Lord at every bris. But that doesn't define the Commandments, which are as central as any text and which will apply to every Dönme not only on the holidays but on every day. That in our communications with the Yakubi, who still worship in Istanbul, who have added us to their tree of life, and have advised with documents, we would learn just how the Yakubi have worshipped since 1690. Like the initial devarim, the Eighteen Commandments of Shabbetai Tzvi set out in the 1660s appear in the future tense.

They do not tell you what *not* to do.

They dictate what you *will* do, in a time after now, a time you cannot remember because—remember!—the second rule of time:

1. Thou shalt set forth that God is One and Shabbetai Tzvi his prophet, and Natan of Flatbush will be his Prophet in the days of days. Adam, Abraham, Moses, Ester, Natan, and others will be only parts of Shabbetai's soul. The maaminim shalt maintain that Shabbetai came to this world eighteen times under the names of Adam, Abraham, Natan, etc. The world shall be created for the maaminim. The Muslims shalt protect only this. From that shall come the saying of maaminim: There will be no egg without a shell.

2. The non-Israelites shall be qelippot.

3. A believer shalt not marry a qelippa or to a Jewess, until the Israelites

recognize Shabbetai was the messiah, and Natan of Flatbush will become his Prophet.

4. Paradise shalt be created for the maaminim and for the Israelites.

5. The souls of the qelippot shall sink to the lower world with the body.

6. The Israelites shall not be deemed maaminim, but shall one day arrive at the truth and confess that Jacob, Moses, etc., will be only sparks of Shabbetai's soul.

7. What concerns your rights, duties, and business, thou shalt subject yourself to the Law of Moses!

8. Thou shalt not hate the Israelites, for they shall be your brethren.

9. Thou shalt be punished if thou speak of thy religion to a qelippa or an Israelite, unless compelled to do so by law, or the Israelite has been deemed a scribe of the Prophet.

10. The Israelites shall be inspired by the creator. Thou shalt not show them the way to paradise.

11. Thou shalt simulate the quality of being a Muslim, and be entirely Jewish in your innermost world.

12. It shalt not be a sin in the eyes of God to kill a maamin who reveals the secrets of his religion. Thou shalt hate these traitors. Even kill him, if he is dangerous for the maaminim.

13. The maaminim shall obey the government of Islam, be they Muslims or otherwise, the government of the culture. The Muslims shall protect, even wage war for you. Always assert that thou are of Islam. Thou shalt defend Islam, simulate reading Qur'an, etc. But thou shalt never take refuge in the Islamic court; the Law of Moses may serve as thy law in all thine quarrels. Remain obedient to the Muslims, do not seek to substitute them.

14. Thou shalt not imbibe intoxicating drinks.

15. Thou shalt have two names, one for the world, the other for paradise.

16. Thou shalt bring the name of the Creator to mind twice every day!

17. Thou shalt have among you no thieves.

18. Thou shalt study privately every day the Book of Psalms.

THE SHEEP MEADOW

The day after his attendance at Mt. Izmir High's football practice, Zeke was scheduled to meet Dave Effendi again. Before leaving his cabin he caught up on email and discovered just what he'd been waiting for, what he needed to write his story: the warden would allow him to visit Natan. There was a strict schedule, and he would have to wait four days, until midweek. But it would happen. Zeke wrote an enthusiastic note to Natan letting him know they would finally meet in person. He got on Slack and let his boss know it, too—he'd secured the central interview for his piece.

Then he left for the Caves.

When he pulled up to the entrance this time, there were no armed Dönme—and there was no Dave Effendi. Instead he saw Yehoshua Green bounding toward him in full Hasidic suit, the frays at the bottoms of his tallis bouncing against his legs.

"The Scribe of the Prophet," Yehoshua said. There was a touch of sarcasm in his voice. The contrast between Green's nearly playful stony enthusiasm for him and the Effendis' circumspection wasn't lost on either of them. But it didn't change anything. In the slowly falling snow, there was no one around at all. Zeke was willing to let a sense of ease settle into the back of his neck. After the pain of Gram's funeral and the shock of the guns on his first two visits here, there was a sense of comfort, of routine, now entering into his morning, alongside it an illicit sense of joyous trespass. It was like visiting the museum after-hours, when the dimly lit life-sized dioramas are suddenly at once your own and somehow so lifelike they instill real fear of attack. "I'm sorry I missed you when you were back earlier this week. I had thirteen fillings to get filled in my teeth."

"That is a lot of fillings," Zeke said.

"I was on the lam for almost five years, friend," Yehoshua said. With no one else around, he was more candid than even the first time they'd met. "Who was paying for dental work during that period? Who was paying for fluoride fucking toothpaste? These are luxuries of upper-middle-class kids, Upper East Side kids, Park Slope Reform Jewish kids, of those who have not committed their lives to the name of the Lord, or had it committed for them."

Zeke said he hadn't thought of it that way.

"Why would you?" Yehoshua said. "I'm not saying you should have. I'm just saying: now, do. There's much for you to learn in your time around us. With that in mind, Dave Effendi said he thought you might like to join us to see the lambs and the heifer today. The Sheep Meadow. The animals."

They were off again to meet Dave. Zeke was beginning to sense that the Caves was a deceptively massive compound, at first seemingly confined to a smattering of trailers and a clearing. But upon each visit, the property offered new spaces, new corners lit with sparks. They walked past the last line of trailers on the east side.

In each window of each trailer they passed, Zeke could feel eyes on him, eyes he couldn't see through screened windows and high windows and closed windows, but searching, imploring eyes whose demands he couldn't discern.

Just as they reached the other side of the trailers, two things arose at once. The first was the low mellow fecund smell of animal feces. It carried even in the cold winter air. It wasn't sharp like dog shit on the street in Brooklyn, or like the smell of the bars in Alphabet City. It was an animal smell, something alive and organic and at once living and dead. The second thing: Dave was not alone. He had his father with him. Faiz Effendi was again in his black Hasidic suit, but now he also wore a large fur shtreimel, like an enormous hairy washer sat atop his head. Today Dave was in the traditional black hat for the first time, but with his hoodie underneath his black suit jacket and the hood pulled down.

"Faiz, I didn't know you were going to join us today," Yehoshua said. His speech was forced, formal, the consonants that had liquefied in his previous conversation now reconstituted, finite and precise. "I mean of course we're happy to have you along, but it is a surprise."

"My dad heard that Zeke met the Dragons yesterday," Dave said. He didn't make eye contact. "He won't be with us the whole time, but he wanted a word."

The Sheep Meadow was much deeper into the property than Zeke had anticipated. As they passed to the east of the trailers, the property gave way to open field and a haphazard path between them. There was a deep gulch on the other side and, as it rose further from view, a steep hill. All alongside it were juvenile pine trees that appeared to have been planted in the past couple of years.

"Stop," Faiz Effendi said with unnatural force. "Let us pray."

And with no effort or pushback, the three knelt and began to say a prayer in Ladino. Zeke could see the darkening of their knees with the wetness of the snowy ground. They didn't stop there. Faiz Effendi knocked the large shtreimel off the top of his head and touched his forehead to the cold ground, until he was in a kind of yogic gymnastic balance—he was in complete control of his body, hands, head, and knees on the ground, reciting prayer. Then he returned to his feet—all three did—replaced his hat on his head and continued walking.

"When he was an old man," Faiz said, not breaking stride, "the Ba'al Shem Tov saw a young disciple enter a large open field in Mezbizh, drop to his knees, and pray. When the young disciple left the field, the Ba'al Shem Tov said, 'You released from that field all the thousands of prayers that had built up in it.'"

Yehoshua and Dave took on a newfound sense of deference to their elder, and continued walking. Zeke worked to match their solemnity as Faiz Effendi continued.

"This is where Natan will move us all one day," he said. As he talked, the wiry curled hairs of his beard dipped in and out of each other with each word he spoke. "You will see at the top of this hill a clearing where we will build our mosque. For now, it contains only the Sheep Meadow. But in years ahead, it will become our house of worship."

"I'm surprised to hear you say it will be a mosque, not a synagogue," Zeke said. Dave and Yehoshua shot each other a look.

"Dönme practice here as they do in Istanbul. As they do in Ankara and as they have practiced for hundreds of years. Have you been to Istanbul to see our places of worship?" Zeke said he had not. "Have you looked at photographs?" Zeke said he hadn't done that, either.

"But I'll Google them tonight," Zeke said. "I haven't had much time, and there's a lot to learn about your culture. I mean keep in mind this is only my third day here."

"Ah, yes. We've heard that you simply stumbled upon our ummah."

"Well," Zeke said, "I was here for personal reasons." All three of them looked at him. "A friend committed—died. I was here for a funeral."

The lowing of cattle, the smell of barn surrounded them.

"Then you should have a special reverence for what we're dealing with," Faiz said. "Our loss."

"I do," Zeke said. Much as he tried to put the thought of Gram away, the pain of it pushed into his throat. "I do. And I'm aware how much there is to learn about you, and your pain."

"There is," Faiz said. "I'm glad you are coming to see it that way." It was the most agreeable thing he'd said since they met. "And that you won't think of putting pen to parchment until you've done enough learning. That is what we all do here—learning. We have set out plans for a mosque in the model of our places of worship in Istanbul. And already Natan has underwritten the building of a cedar ark as it is set out in the words of Solomon. You will see it before you leave. But above all we have financial plans in place to expand here, to keep the ummah in good stead for ages."

Now they neared the top of the hill, which was steep enough that under his Patagonia fleece, sweat was rising on Zeke's skin. The sound of the bleating of sheep carried across the field. The smell that had carried on the winter wind back closer to the trailers grew stronger with each step the four men took. As he crested the lightly snow-covered hill, Zeke saw them all at once: in a makeshift space penned in by chicken wire and yellowing two-by-fours there were maybe two dozen sheep. Zeke had almost no experience with sheep, with any animals. He lived in Brooklyn, and had not had a dog since he was seventeen and living with his parents. These sheep looked like the most derelict animals on the planet, bearing a sense of menace from the negligence that must have left them so. A rime of snow crusted the tips of their browning wool coats. Not one of them appeared to have been sheared in months, and upon seeing Faiz, Dave, and Yehoshua, they all began bleating at once. The sound was maddening, pitched low, vibrating, cacophonous.

"Do not be concerned," Faiz said. Zeke's face was a hieroglyph of distress. "The Festival of the Lamb does not begin until March seventeenth this year. Still weeks off, and these sheep have needed insulation through the winter months. We must have enough lamb to feed a much larger community now."

"I heard a little about the festival yesterday," Zeke said. They all understood it to be a reference to his meeting Billy Wren. A community accused of something like the Dimming of the Candles, whether it was true or not, was aware of the rumors.

"Don't listen to what the kafir say," Dave said. It was the first he'd spoken since they set out for the Sheep Meadow, and when he spoke so darkly, it was remarkable how much he sounded like his father. "Everything they know about us they either heard from Osman when he was fucking with them"—Dave glanced at Faiz and then put his eyes back to the ground—"or they made up on their own."

"Tell me about these boys," Faiz said.

"I'm not sure what you mean exactly," Zeke said.

"We know what you're doing when you're not here. Don't be coy. You think we don't know every move you make in this tiny town? That we don't report it to the Prophet? You met with the kafir, the outsiders, the boys in town. What do they think they know about our community? What do they say in defense of themselves, these boys who murdered Osman?"

Zeke had grown up around men like Faiz Effendi, successful pious Jews who were offended by every step those around them made that didn't comport entirely with their sense of halakhic practice, with Jewish law, with their narrow view of orthodoxy. Men whose beliefs were doors shut so tight they needed no lock. Doors you would actively work not to approach. The ever more perplexing question became what a man like this would've seen in the antinomian practices of Natan of Flatbush to begin with.

"Well, they all have alibis. Airtight," Zeke said. "Honestly I knew that from the trial transcripts. I didn't talk to Fergus or Deshawn, who I saw play football—I just talked to William Wren. Billy. Declan Wren's son."

"Fuck those kids," Dave said. Again his gaze was lowered to his feet, on which he wore a gray pair of ersatz New Balances. Yehoshua didn't seem to have anything to say at all.

"Did they tell you they have come multiple times to our property after the ummah is asleep for the night?" Faiz said. This was news. It was the kind of fact that should have come up at trial. "That they came up to this very hill where we're standing and stole and slaughtered one of our sheep at the beginning of every football season? That they put a scare into the sacred red heifer? That they cross the Bosperous without our permission and enter the Cave of the Dragon, trespassing upon our most sacred space?

"Oh, I'm sure they don't confess these transgressions," Faiz Effendi continued. "We deal with it. For years we called Mt. Izmir police to report it, but after a period they stopped even responding. That is why you see so many Dönme with guns. The sheriff of the town? You'll learn soon enough he's Fergus Shaw's father. He is the biggest booster for the Dragons football team. He doesn't want their ritual and their world broken into by a bunch of Islamic Jews." It was the most candid Zeke had heard Faiz speak. "Well, I will leave it to the boys to describe to you the Festival of the Lamb, to describe the reality of our rites. I have things to attend to back in Columbus."

Faiz Effendi was off. He walked over to the edge of the sheep enclosure and put a pile of manure in a bucket to take back to the entrance with him.

"Composting," Yehoshua said. They watched Faiz Effendi trek back down the hill, the bucket tapping at his hip with each step, the slow sift of snow separating from an entirely white sky only visible as it swirled slowly about the brown- and copper-colored fur of the large round shtreimel on the older man's head, as if it were simply a color dusting off the solid mass of midwinter Ohio sky. They waited until he was out of earshot to speak again.

"OK. So you wanna see the sacred cow?" Yehoshua said.

The moment just minutes before when Faiz Effendi mentioned it was the first time in his life Zeke had heard of it.

"I mean sure, I guess. If you think I should."

"Should?" Dave said. "We're talking about the first red heifer to be prepared for sacrifice in a thousand years. The most sacred animal alive."

"That is a long time."

"Come on," Yehoshua said. Through their long walk across the snowy fields Yehoshua lectured again, switching modes once more from Brooklyn to tzaddik. "The Hebrew word for snow is 'sheleg,'" he said. "In almost all its uses in the Torah, its purpose is simile. In the Book of Numbers, Aaron is described as leprous, white as snow. Sheleg. In Exodus, one refugee under Moses's leadership has a hand as white as snow. Again, leprosy. Sheleg. Masculine noun. It appears in Job, in the books of the prophets Isaiah, Jeremiah, and Daniel." He paused to catch his breath. The hill rose, the snow now falling more heavily. "On occasion snow appears in its literal sense, but when it does, it is rarely a sign of *here,* of *now* or *this.* It is a sign of over there, far away—in Jeremiah, 'sheleg' evokes the snow of Lebanon that would forsake the man who would visit the embattled north. In Job, again, the snow that would fall on the house of the man circumscribed by a challenge between Hashem and the devil. Rarely, very rarely, it can mean something pure, as in Lamentations, when we speak of mi'sheleg—the people were whiter than snow. White. Laban. Again, it is a simile. Snow. Sheleg. An idea, a poetic noun, that finds its way into Torah almost entirely to evoke an idea, not an experience. To make us feel its cold, its unwelcoming cold, or its signal of illness, or, in the rarest case, its purity. All of this learning comes from the *Shivhei ha-Natan,* the word of our Prophet, our central text."

They stopped talking, taking in the easy knowledge worn so lightly. They followed Dave up the hill and past the sheep pasture. To the far side of the field was a separate pen, and at its back a manger. Inside the makeshift barn, tall heat lights like metallic trees centered in each corner. A tiny lowing arose at the center, and there, lying in the straw, was a rust-red calf the size of an especially large yellow lab.

"She's cute," Zeke said.

"'She's cute,'" Dave Effendi said. He just shook his head and looked at Yehoshua. "In the Talmud, it is told that only the ashes of the red heifer can cleanse the soul of the worst offenses. Apostasy, incest—even murder can be absolved by the ashes of the red heifer. Only eight times in the history of the Jewish religion, in six thousand years, has the sin offering been made with a red heifer. In the weeks before Osman's disappearance, Natan of Flatbush came back with this one. With a red heifer! As if the Dönme needed more confirmation that we are living in the new Mt. Izmir."

"And we don't," Yehoshua said, uncharacteristically petulant.

"We don't. The night Natan is released from his incarceration we will make a sin offering of this red heifer."

"Why?" Zeke said. "I thought we were certain that the boys from town killed your friend. Killed Osman."

Now both of the young men were silent.

"Ritual and immediate events do not always need to correspond," Yehoshua said.

Snow released itself from some low space in the sky above their heads, sheleg, now the smallest lightest flurry thus far. They backed out of the manger, and Dave led them all back down toward the Sheep Meadow, across the way.

"With that behind us," Yehoshua said, "I'm sure the Dragons told you all kinds of bullshit about the Festival of the Lamb, too. There's not much to it. It's basically the Dönme Christmas dinner. We're forbidden to eat lamb any other time of year. That night we eat a ton of lamb, and party, and the adults continue into the wee hours. They haven't celebrated in Istanbul in years. We're continuing the tradition."

"And," Dave Effendi said, "Osman filled their ears with the stories he thought they wanted to hear. About the Dimming of the Candles, the orgies that Sabbatians supposedly had back when the religion started."

"All bullshit," Yehoshua said. "The Frankists—supposedly they engaged in some of that. But not the Dönme! We're no Frankists. Jacob Frank, they said, had two dicks. Imagine what those Dragons would make of that fact. His was a real apostasy. I mean, look at Faiz Effendi. No offense, Dave, but can you imagine that guy being part of an orgy?"

"None taken." He paused. "And no. God, no!"

"Come on. I know Osman used to sometimes claim he'd walked in on Natan. But that kid had the wildest imagination. I guess you could say who knows what he told his teammates. But not—"

Yehoshua stopped mid-sentence. In the far distance, somewhere on the other side of the trailers, a sound like firecrackers popping. One, two, three—maybe a half dozen.

Yehoshua and Dave were halfway down the hill before Zeke could turn to run after them. In the slick of the winter snow and the steepness of the hill they descended and the impediment of their flowing black suits, Dave and Yehoshua ran lumberingly enough for him to catch them just this side of the trailers. When they reached the clearing on the other side, all three were together.

What they discovered there was chaos.

Fergus Shaw, Deshawn Flaxton, and three other teenage boys were standing to the side of Zeke's rental car. A long jagged line of white tore through the side of the car where someone had repeatedly keyed it. Between Yehoshua and David and the football players were six Dönme, rifles drawn. Three of them were down on one knee as if ready to shoot again.

The closest of the Dönme to them turned and spotted Dave, Yehoshua, and Zeke running up behind.

"We were coming back from the Caves, and we found them there," the Dönme said. "During morning prayer." He was one of the three who was kneeling, and after turning to say it, he looked back at them, then stood. "They were in the act. Two of them were slashing the tires on the car. The other was defacing it." He turned back to look at the boys again. None of them spoke. They just stared back: a standoff, a confrontation. "We fired a warning shot. They didn't stop. They laughed. So I shot a number more warning shots and still they didn't stop."

Zeke saw that not only were three of the tires on his rental sedan, a sky blue Honda Civic, completely flat, but the splintering of a bullet hole webbed out from a spot in the upper shotgun side of the windshield.

"Looks like you missed one, too," Yehoshua said. He was pointing at the hole in the glass.

"Fuck you!" one of the kids said. "We stopped as soon as we heard warning shots." The kid looked directly at Zeke. "And fuck you, Fake News."

"Plus what difference does it make?" another of the kids said. "It's a rental car."

"Shut the fuck up, Simpson," Fergus Shaw said. "Let's just get out of here. And you"—Fergus said it while pointing at Zeke. "Yeah, you. Fake News, hanging with the Fake Jews. Think about whether you really want to be here. Next time it won't be your rental car."

: : : : :

It took the better part of the afternoon to get the Honda towed back into town. Fergus Shaw called his father. Three Mt. Izmir sheriff's cruisers arrived at the Caves not ten minutes after the boys left. Just far enough off to be out of earshot, Sheriff Shaw and Faiz Effendi stood talking. The sheriff was an inch or two over six feet tall, clad in a uniform whose pale brown made him look like a brownshirt. He was a bloated, aging version of his son, freckles on his cheeks smeared to beige. He was wearing his officious sheriff's hat, a Stetson that served like a goyishe complement to Faiz Effendi's absurd enormous shtreimel. After maybe ten minutes of conversation, both Sheriff Shaw and Faiz Effendi looked up at Zeke. Faiz motioned him over.

"I understand you're here working for the newspaper," Sheriff Shaw said.

"A magazine. A national magazine," Zeke said. He said the name of the magazine. Sheriff Shaw's face did not evince any knowledge of the publication. There was something familiar about Shaw, his face, but for the life of him Zeke couldn't place it. He put out his hand and said his full name. Sheriff Shaw's right hand stayed down by his side, hovering instinctively over his sidearm.

"Do you understand that this community has been through a kind of tragedy in the past year we're not used to? We've gotten through it. These people here don't look like us, and they don't look like you, but they're God-fearing people just like we're God-fearing people. We've managed together under these . . . strange circumstances. So maybe before you come back out here, or before you decide how long you'll stay, give some thought to what a hornet's nest can look like when it's been given a big old kick. And consider whether you wanna be the one kicking. Whether you wanna be around when a whole bunch of dragons start breathing fire."

"That is some mixed metaphor," Zeke said.

Before Zeke saw the hand coming, the sheriff had slapped him open-palmed across the side of his head. A ringing opened in his ear. He dropped to one knee. The sheriff gave him a good hard knee in his ribs. He fell to his side.

"I'll mix whatever I want to mix here in my town," Sheriff Shaw said. He landed one more hard kick to Zeke's side. "And it ain't no fucking metaphor. It's the thing its motherfucking self."

Sheriff Shaw turned to walk away. Against his better judgment, half lying on the ground, Zeke said, "And what about the damage to my rental?"

The sheriff stopped. Snow fell about his Stetson in swirls, but did not appear to attach itself to his hat.

"What about it?"

"Your son and his friends did thousands of dollars of damage to the car."

"Did they now?" Sheriff Shaw said. He turned and took a couple steps back toward Zeke, who didn't get up. "I'm not sure we had any witnesses to that," the sheriff said. "Just as I'm reasonably sure no one among these fine God-fearing community members fired rounds from their rifles in the direction of a group of minors. Which, as you likely know—attempted murder of minors. On a property where a minor was murdered not two years ago. Where a single call to PETA would have a whole swarm of you elites out here looking into, I dunno, neglected sheep or something. And plenty else we could talk about with creditors lookin' to make good on a whole bunch of other trouble. Every business transaction scrutinized. Maybe you as a magazine writer don't understand what can turn up when the police start looking into a cloistered little community like this one. One that some would call a cult. But the members of the community, living here so long now, they do. So it seems to me what we have, what we have are a series of events which you think took place, but that did not take place."

Zeke looked at Faiz Effendi, who just stared blankly back at him.

"Have a good look at me, Fake News. Because me, Earnest Shaw, I'm law all the way through. Don't you fucking forget it while you're in Mt. Izmir."

Sheriff Shaw stalked off to his cruiser, a new white Dodge Viper with all the Mt. Izmir Sheriff's paint on it, and drove off. The shallow tracks of his boots on thin fresh snow tracked up to where the tread of his tires followed him into the white nothing on the other side of Dönme property.

NATURE ABHORS

Outside Zeke's cabin.

Late afternoon, while he nurses his wounds and tries to nap, there is not a sound.

Not a peep.

Not a footstep.

The few other guests in the trailer park have all left. The cable is out in his room, and so Zeke cannot put on *SportsCenter*, cannot look up the latest originals on HBO. There is simply silence amid the slowly falling snow, a vacuum of sound.

Ein Sofism or no Ein Sofism, nature abhors a vacuum.

BOOK TWO

THE AFTERLIFE OF STARS

The stars on Johanna's ceiling emitted less light presently than the last time he'd been there. The only other time. In the dim light of the late evening—such modest light in comparison to stars'—one could discern their outline, the faintest glow.

"I can't see the stars tonight," Zeke said.

"You're lying in a bed with the shades drawn," Johanna said. After some silence she spoke again. "Oh, right. Those stupid stickers. Well, unlike real stars, glow-in-the-dark stars need to be filled up by the light of our solar system's sun, and I was in Columbus yesterday and will be again today doing discovery for a case. A case I can't and won't talk about. With anyone, let alone a member of the national press. So they didn't get charged up. Not like you did, spending all your time with your Jews. Muslims. Whatever. How are those Muslim Jews after all. Beyond the fact that your Enterprise rental didn't make it out alive."

"Alamo."

"Whatever."

"Small world, that you would have heard."

"Small town, small state, small everything," Johanna said. "Also you mentioned it at dinner."

"It did seem like a pretty big deal at the time. Which already feels like an eternity ago. I ended up spending the whole day trying to figure out whose insurance was paying for it. Suffice it to say my boss wasn't all that happy—about the danger, but most of all the expense. Since it wasn't ultimately deemed a crime by local law officials. Official. Who happens to be the father of the accused."

"Acquitted. Not ever charged. Or even really deemed persons of interest." Johanna stood up. Walked through the dim bedroom to the window. Pulled up the shade, and in the cool midnight light her body was cast in gray. She unlocked the window. Cracked it. Zeke's eyes took in the hardening of her nipples before he felt the thin stream of cold air that flowed over the bed. She walked back.

"I can't stand the radiator heat in this place and you can't turn it off," Johanna said. The brittle smell of snow filled the room. "It's better for you Shaw didn't charge anyone in the vandalism, or in the discharge of the Dönmes' rifles. I didn't get to know Shaw well during the case—he's a seriously closed book, and one I wouldn't have ever encountered if it wasn't for Osman's murder—but he's not someone you want to tangle with, from what I can tell. Folks up here are mostly just used to being left alone to sort their issues out. It would've been a mess. Attempted murder. Since you were there, who knows how you would've gotten involved. Reporters aren't supposed to become their own subjects."

"It's 20-fucking-20," Zeke said. "We're like a half a century since the New Journalism. And the New New Journalism. The end of journalism. I can basically be in or out of the story as much as I want. No matter how I write it, I bet the headline will be like, 'I

Met a Group of Jewish Islamic Murderers and Here's What Kind of Loafers I Was Wearing When I Did.' It's not like anyone's going to read it anyway. For all I know, by the time I get back to New York, the whole concept of the magazine will have been banished from existence. Poof . . . gone. No more mags."

"Still. Better for everyone for there not to be an official report. Trust me."

They let the judgment implicit in that statement sit in the ever colder air. With the shades open, he could now see Johanna next to him—though he didn't need to see her to know that she was turned the direction opposite. Now she flopped over so she was lying on her back.

"It's awful to lie on my side these days," she said. "Carpal tunnel. It's like I have it all over my whole body. All I have to do is lie on my right side for a minute and my whole left arm is tingling like I'm going to have a heart attack."

"So is that how it happened?"

"A heart attack? Not sure how old you think I am, Fake News. Surely not old enough to worry about cardiac arrest."

"Not your fuzzy arm," he said. "The choice not to consider the Shaw kid or Flaxton as suspects in Osman's murder. Just some surly sheriff who decided it didn't happen that way, and it didn't happen that way. Like my nonevent today. A thing I witnessed with my eyes but in the eyes of the law did not transpire."

"Well, first of all, if Shaw is an old sheriff, then you're an old reporter. He's like our age. Maybe a year or two older, even. He just seems old because he's got a kid, and a uniform, and an accent affected from too much *Cool Hand Luke*. But to your point . . . there are two easy answers to that question. Neither looks good for your Prophet," Johanna said. "As a prosecutor, I have to work with what I get. There was no record of a report of trespassing from the Dönme, and with no contemporaneous complaint, it's hard to trump up a charge ex post facto. The charges of property damage and trespassing from the previous years that Fritzman mentioned might have checked out in principle, but with no reports from any of them, none of that was admissible.

"And all those kids had easy alibis. They were at a football game. They were playing, at the established time of the murder. A *home* football game, making it so that there were more eyewitnesses than you could shake a shofar at. Every person in all of Mt. Izmir was there, at the Dragons' stadium, watching the game. Police wouldn't have to look at them long to dismiss them as credible persons of interest. And believe me, the sheriff in particular."

"A sheriff who just let his kid and his friends key and slash the tires on the rental car of a reporter because he was on the Caves property. And from the East Coast. And, one might argue under duress, also Jewish."

"A car that also had a bullet hole in its windshield. Minors standing next to it. From a weapon fired by a person who to anyone in the outside world looks like a wild-eyed, wild-haired, wild-bearded religious fanatic with an AK. Almost certainly reeking of weed. And a bunch more religious fanatics in black suits, bearing those rifles, pointed at the minors. Which you would have had to testify to in court. Which, as you told me at dinner, was what you saw yourself when you reached the scene."

Cold from the open window had completely filled the space around them. They could both feel it, so Zeke got up out of bed and closed the window. Now, with the streetlight peeking in through the open shade, it was as if the stars on the ceiling had disappeared—not even a faint glow or outline was perceptible.

"Look, I don't want to tell you what to do. I don't want to thumb any scales. As if sleeping with the reporter hasn't done enough thumbing. But if I were you, I'd be a whole fuckload more careful around all involved in this thing. It is now a legitimately dangerous situation. Unless you've taken some military training since we were in college, I don't think you're prepared to deal with much of it. You've now seen how armed some of the Dönmes are."

"Dönme," Zeke said.

"Doon-may, whatever. I will never be able to pronounce an umlaut. Frankly I don't want to try. But never mind the Dönmes—you need to worry about all these townspeople, the fathers of all these football players now, too. And the sheriff. I get that you want to get the story. I know I pulled you toward it. Am pulling. But you've got a trial transcript, you've got a meeting set with the man who was charged with the murder and who, unless some kind of miracle comes to pass late next week, will fail in his expedited first appeal and potentially spend the rest of his days in a federal prison. And . . . and also. Also you've got me."

"I do have that," Zeke said. "That I do have."

"This might be a weird time to say this, but. It's been nice."

"Nice?"

"Good. Beautiful. I don't have the words for feelings the way you do, writer. But. It's nice to be around you again. I've been working so hard, for so long, it's like fucking you again has collapsed time for me."

"I'm not *that* good at it."

"Shut the fuck up. You know what I mean. It's like . . . the joy of having memories again. Measuring who you were then against who you are now. Which is literally not a thing I've had time to do in years. Introspection. Like, a single thought about myself. Shit, I have like twenty thousand bucks in my checking account because I don't even have time to go to a bank and open a savings. Sometimes I take off a button-down and it still has the tag on it. It hasn't been but a couple of days. But. It's the first time I've had thoughts about myself in months, being around you. Memories, even. Actual memories."

They let her words, and the cold, wash over them.

"Thinking about Gram a little, too . . ." she said. "Sad he's gone, but happy he gets to be a part of this."

"I've felt that," Zeke said, forgetting himself, meaning it. "Like, falling into being with you again after Gram's funeral can bring him around. Keeps him around."

"Well said."

"I'm happy to be with you, Jo, too. I am." He put his hand on her arm, which did not tingle from the outside, though he understood from the way Johanna jerked it away from him that it was tingling on the inside with carpal tunnel static. "Speaking of which. I also have an invitation to join the Dönme tomorrow for their tish." Zeke looked over at the clock: one A.M. "Or tonight, technically, I guess. They asked if I wanted to bring anyone with me."

"Listen to you, talking like you've got their Yiddish down."

"Huh?"

"Fuck's a tish."

"Oh, sorry. The dinner the whole community has with their leader every Saturday night, following Shabbat. With Natan of Flatbush gone, Faiz Effendi will be leading it. They don't consider him officially a tzaddik yet, but if Natan does fail in his appeal, I have a feeling he might end up having to take the title on sooner than he thinks. Someone's got to lead a community as broken as this one."

"Or they could just all head back to Brooklyn and leave Central Ohio the fuck alone.

"Effendi. Rigid as hell, that guy. Like all the men in that uptight, tightfisted Bexley Orthodox community. Not that they're any better than those their-eyes-were-watching-God Hasids."

"Whoa-ho-ho there, my friend. That is positively un-American. A little light postcoital anti-Semitism."

"Not anti-Semitism! Not in the least. I don't even understand if these people are Semites, so I'm not sure I can be an anti-Semite against them. And . . . I'm not sure we were postcoital just yet. Was hoping it was more like . . . mid. Coital."

"Touché. And . . . well. We'll . . . yes. At any rate. You're invited to join their tish with me tomorrow if you want. Tonight. Technically."

The cool air rolled over them again. The harder Zeke looked, the more he thought maybe he could make out some stars on the ceiling after all.

"I'm not sure after two dates I'm ready to meet your family yet," Johanna said. "Well, your other family. Since I've met your, you know, biological family." Before Zeke could object or cajole or make light, she said, "But lemme give it some thought. I might be interested in seeing that community again, now that I'm not officially on the case."

∴∴∴

Zeke summoned an Uber to take him to the rental car place in the morning. He'd need it with the tish coming up that night. He was not at all surprised when the car pulled up and Meta opened his door for him.

"Eye's looking a whole lot better there, Fake Jews!" Meta said. He was wearing a "The Land" LeBron James jersey over a black hoodie. Today was the warmest Central Ohio had been since Zeke arrived, and in the high fifties it almost felt like spring. "Though those stitches are looking awfully tight." Meta reached out and touched it. Zeke jerked his head away like he'd been zapped by electricity.

"There will be time for all that next week when I get back to Brooklyn," Zeke said.

"No sleep till," Meta said. He pulled away from the cabin. Soon, outside his window, Zeke again saw the reality of Mt. Izmir: the rusted-out cars, the rotted barns, the tangle of brown woods not yet bearing a single green bud. Without snow falling from the gray sky, it was like they were now in no-season amid no-weather in cold nowhere. Pines had no fringe of snow hanging off their needles, though it had not been warm enough for a thaw. Perhaps they had simply sloughed the snow to the ground.

"I'd ask why we're going to the rental car place," Meta said. "But I heard why we're going to the rental car place."

"Did you."

"I did, I did. Driving Uber, bro—it's like being the town crier. Not everyone takes it and not everyone who takes it is from here. But when they do and when they are . . ."

"Well, that being the case, town crier," Zeke said, "how much real danger would you say Fake News, Fake Jews, the journalist interloper from Brooklyn, is actually in?"

"Oh, come on, man," Meta said. "You been around those crazy Jews enough now to get it. They not gonna hurt you. They protect they own, to be sure. And they believe some crazy shit. But it's the post-truth world, mi hijo! Everyone believes crazy shit. All it'll take is one Zika or SARS or Ebola outbreak and we'll all be scrambling for a God to believe in again. Trust me, bro. It'll be one big Al-Aqsa Mosque up here in this mug."

"I do," Zeke said. "I trust you. But that's not actually who I meant I needed to be worried about."

"Oh," Meta said. "Gotcha. Well, you haven't broken any laws? I don't see why you'd need to worry then."

"Again not who I meant."

"Oh, right. So many factions! Well, the townspeople with they pitchforks and torches. Them you do need to worry about, I guess, if I'm being real. I hadn't really thought of it that way till you mention it now. They'll come for you in the night, those cray motherfuckers. Fuck, they'll come for you in broad daylight with helmets and shoulder pads. I'd say get you rental and get you information and get the fuck on outta here. That's what I'd do if I was you. And hijo—I'm happy I'm not you."

"Thanks," Zeke said. "That helps a ton. Being, you know, me."

"Oh, you welcome, you welcome. Gotta get my five-star rating, you know what I mean?"

: : : : :

As Zeke was leaving the Caves the day before, Yehoshua had lectured him about the Jewish language of cars, again claiming Natan's writings as the source. The original Hebrew word for car comes not from any similar word in the Pentateuch, like many other modern Hebrew words. "Merkabah," the word for chariot, also describes the Kabbalistic afterlife, a chariot and a palace into which man passes after his death. This was not a word suited to the Ladas and Opels and BMWs driving around modern Zion. So the first modern Hebrew word was "auto," for, well, auto. Automobile. By the 1960s, Israelis had begun using the word "mechonit," which means something more like machine. Judah Maccabee used a machine in battling the Romans in the stories of Hanukah. Now the word that has taken over is "rechev," which means something more like vehicle. Both Hebrew and Arabic words have three-letter roots, and "rechev" has the same reish-kaf-beit root as the word "riding." Words like these are fluid, open, reaching back five thousand years, or five. They can ride to heaven, or deep inside. They can transport you from here to New York, or from here in Ohio ever deeper inward.

Zeke was beginning to see that the travel Yehoshua wanted to discuss with him was travel inward. But the new rental car he was stuck with after returning to Alamo was an eggplant-colored PT Cruiser, the last of its kind—the only thing on offer. Zeke pulled up to Johanna's office in downtown Mt. Izmir to pick her up. He rolled down his window.

"That is not exactly what I'd been expecting," Zeke said.

Johanna was wearing a pair of black pants and a violet blouse, a puffy Canada Goose jacket, and over top of it she had on a hijab. A black hijab.

"You understand I've been out to the Caves on numerous occasions at this point, right? That at first it was a threat to my life given that as an interloper I presented a danger to the Dönme, but that they came to accept I had to be there. Back during discovery I went out there multiple times to interview folks about the murder. I made my mistakes the first times. I'm not going to make them again."

With the sun fixed low in the late-afternoon Central Ohio sky, Zeke pulled up to the Caves in his eggplant-purple rental with Johanna Franklin, her head covered. Zeke had thrown a navy-blue sports coat over his shirt—actually the jacket from his only suit—the most formal outfit he owned. He did not cover his head. As he pulled up to park, he could see the flakes of paint from his previous rental car dusting the ground, and the footprints in a circle of chaos from the day before. It hadn't snowed, and no one had been in or out of the community since, it being Shabbat, so there all the tracks lay like the fossil record of some prior extinction. Zeke parked, and he and Johanna walked up to the fields at the center of the Caves, where the entire Dönme ummah was now leaving its trailers for evening prayer. The sun was even lower and more diffuse in the western sky, the light around all of them growing grainy and brown like the image of a memory already passed. As ever, Yehoshua Green was there to greet them.

"Dear Zeke. Always a pleasure to see you." He took Zeke's hand. Then looked to Johanna. "Prosecutor, thank you for joining us. Though perhaps you are not exactly who we had in mind when we asked if Zeke wanted to bring a guest." Johanna stared blankly out of the opening in her hijab. Zeke drew her in closer to him, and whether they were playacting it or acting it in reality, he felt what it would be for them to be a couple, enjoined, inseparable. "But that is not the nature of welcome," Yehoshua continued, "to question the welcome! We are meeting for prayer. Faiz Effendi is leading us. Come join us."

The three of them walked up, spared further scrutiny. The Dönme had begun their evening prayer. At the edges of the prayer group, keeping watch with the intimidating distant omnipresence of a pity of doves, black-suited Dönme stood with rifles slung at their sides. At the front of the group, Faiz Effendi donned his same black suit, and though it was so much warmer today, he wore his same fur shtreimel. Cold settled in as the sun fled the sky. He stood before the congregation, for that's what they were—cult or not, sect or not, murderous coconspirators or not, they were congregated to attempt convening with their Lord—and, facing the Caves themselves, led them in prayer.

He began again with the modified Shema, and with their "Shabbetai Tzvi, esparamos a ti" prayer, which Zeke had now heard enough times to recognize it by its melody. They moved to the back of the congregants, of whom there were so many today—were there three hundred? Four? And where had they all been those previous days when he had been here to observe them? Some large segment of the community that lived in Mt. Izmir, in Bexley, had made pilgrimage to the Caves for tish. The men in their black suits and their peyes formed a phalanx at the center of the open field. Women in varicolored headscarves were scattered among them, children at play around their ankles. Being interlopers, but with no room to hide, Zeke and Johanna stood at the back together, where they could make out the sound of Faiz Effendi's prayer. Prayer was in Ladino, the Dönme were repeating it, a familiar but distant mix of Hebrew and Spanish like the image of mercurial water on the desert horizon forever slipping just out of reach.

The prayer continued for what felt like eons. All the supplicants knelt and their guests joined them, knees down on the cold wet muddy Ohio ground. No longer was there enough snow for knees to simply crush and then melt. They could feel oleaginous mud against flesh. The Dönme recited Ladino and mixed in Hebrew prayers.

Then Faiz Effendi turned back toward the congregation, and facing them, he returned to their first prayers, this time with a variation to the words: "Natan of Flatbush, esparamos a ti! Natan of Flatbush, es no otro como tu," Faiz Effendi intoned. He was genuflecting, his arms flowing in rhythm out from his torso, and after his recitation, there was a murmur from the crowd. Faiz Effendi continued, and with the whites of his rolled-back eyes visible even from a distant vantage, he was no longer speaking in Ladino, but speaking in tongues, words that were not words spewing from his mouth automatically, a babble of not-Hebrew, not-Aramaic, not-Ladino—until he stopped and again said, "Natan of Flatbush, esparamos a ti! Natan of Flatbush, queremos alli!"

A short man looked up to the dimming sky, then stood. Without his having to do more than motion, the congregants immediately in front of him parted. He elbowed aside the two men next to him and put his head to the mucky ground, and with the control of a Brooklyn yoga master held his body at an angle maybe forty-five degrees to the ground. Holding the pose perfectly still, he said, "Natan of Flatbush, esparamos a ti!" Wet snow and silt ran down his knees toward his midriff.

Now in all corners of the prayer phalanx, men and women alike were clearing aside their brethren, holding their heads to the ground, their knees on the ground so their feet pointed toward the supernal sky, repeating this new prayer. Men inverted and lost their black hats to the slushy ground, their suits billowing from their bodies as they stood on elbows, on hands and heads. Some hewed very low to the ground and slowly army-crawled in the direction of Faiz Effendi. Women came up with muddy snow spattering the tops of their hijabs and chadors. That this might appear comical, something out of a downtown Manhattan theater performance, did not arise in the minds of their guests for the intensity of it, the immediacy and spontaneity, felt so genuine, so much more snake handlers speaking in tongues than circus performance. From the distance that separated Zeke from Faiz Effendi, he could see the seriousness on the man's face, the way his lips trembled and continued in prayer, whether speaking quietly in tongues again or uttering a prayer. His wasn't a warm humanistic leadership, but it was unmistakably leadership. Soon the murmur from the crowd lowered, and Faiz Effendi said, "Ah-ah-mein." At his signal they all stood and began walking a new path deeper into the community. It was beaten down in the woods between the path to the Caves to the west, and far to the east the path to the Sheep Meadow. The armed congregants at the edges of the field split, half walking at the front of the line, the others waiting for the group to pass.

Zeke took Johanna's hand once the crowd had begun down their path. She looked down at his grasp, up at his face, and apparently against her will, said, "Well, that's weirdly quaint. Nice even." She did not attempt to let go. The two followed maybe a half mile through the woods until before them, in the near distance, they espied a two-story building with corrugated aluminum siding. It looked like a metal barn you might find anywhere in rural Ohio, serving as a volunteer fire station or a VFW hall or Masonic Lodge, a barn door open to the candlelit tables inside. Yehoshua came back out of the crowd as they entered the building.

"Ah, Zeke! I've been looking for you. This is our shtibl. There are so many Dönme among us now, since Faiz Effendi began to bring his congregants from the city, we hold our tish here. But we do not want you to miss out on anything, and you must hear all of Faiz Effendi's devurah." Yehoshua walked them through the building until they were seated directly across from Faiz Effendi. This must once have been Natan's seat, and while he would remain their tzaddik, Faiz Effendi was now taking on that role. Zeke and Johanna sat, but Faiz Effendi did not acknowledge them as he stood and began to talk. He had a rectangular area mic on a shock mount before him, and it picked up not only what Faiz Effendi said, but the chatter around him. The cable from the mic led to a new PA back along the wall. The sound of his prayer came out of speakers in each of the four corners of the room.

Faiz Effendi spoke at first quietly, davening, eyes lowered to the siddur. Yehoshua sat down on the other side of Johanna from

Zeke and introduced them to the Dönme immediately surrounding them.

"This is Rabia, Faiz Effendi's wife. On either side of Faiz are his son Dave—who of course you know—and Avraham Bohm. The others you will meet later."

Zeke put his hand out to shake Rabia's, but she left her hand by her side. She was one of the two women he and Yehoshua had run into on their way to the Caves his first day here. She was wearing a purple hijab, which framed the tan mole-covered face he remembered from her burkini when they passed each other on the path to the mikvah. There were green flecks in her gray eyes, and she lightly pursed her lips in a manner that suggested she knew what you were going to say before you said it.

For a moment Faiz Effendi continued to daven. No one else spoke. At each corner of the open barn door, and at each exit at the back wall, was a black-suited and black-hatted Dönme with a rifle under his arm. In the rear corner of the building, a short woman in a full chador stood with a pistol held against her midsection, free hand holding the hand with the gun in it. At each corner there was a large red-coiled space heater, keeping the area warm enough that congregants could take off winter jackets. Between the heaters and the springlike air, it was quite warm in the open barn.

"I see you," Rabia said. She'd leaned over close to Zeke and he could smell incense and rosemary on her. "You get used to the weapons. Just like you would if you visited Jerusalem or Tel Aviv."

"I have visited Jerusalem," Zeke said.

"Well, exactly, then." Zeke was about to jump right to it and ask her about her relationship with Natan when a new quiet overcame the congregation. Faiz Effendi was looking right at him. Then Faiz looked away, and up at the ummah.

"Tonight we have with us a number of new guests for our tish, and so I will end the public portion of our Shabbat with the credo and then with a translation of our prayer." First he spoke for a long time in Ladino. Then he prayed so Zeke could understand:

> *I believe with perfect faith in the faith of the God of Truth, the*
> *God of Israel who dwells in the sphere of Tiferet, the Glory*
> *of Israel, and in the three knots of faith. I believe with per-*
> *fect faith in the mashiach Shabbetai Tzvi and I believe with*
> *perfect faith in the perfect innocence of Natan of Flatbush in*
> *the eyes of God, of Elohim and Hashem.*

> *May it therefore be pleasing before thee, God of Truth, God of*
> *Israel, who dwells in the Glory of Israel, in the three knots*
> *of faith which are one, to send us the just mashiach, our*
> *redeemer Shabbetai Tzvi, and procure the freedom of his*
> *Prophet Natan of Flatbush, speedily and in our days. Amen.*

"And since this tish falls on the most important of weekends," Faiz Effendi continued, "the weekend before we believe our mashiach shall return to our community, I will end with a word about the week ahead. We have not one of us seen Natan of Flatbush, hallowed be his name, in many months. I know we have all been waiting, and I can only say that this is the day, this is the week we have all been waiting for."

Faiz Effendi looked down to where Johanna and Zeke were sitting. Johanna stared right back at him.

"No matter what you may have heard, this is what is ahead. You should know I have spoken with the mashiach himself. He promises that upon his return he shall perform one of the great miracles which our first mashiach, Shabbetai Tzvi, was unable to perform, which the prophet Amos promised would transpire in the days beyond days. He will do so on the day after his return. So keep your eyes open for a communication from us, and please do plan to be here in Mt. Izmir for his glorious return. Ah-mein."

A murmur arose in the high-ceilinged room following mention of a miracle. Faiz Effendi sat and moved seamlessly to speaking to the twelve Dönme at the table. Before beginning, he pointed to the plates in front of them.

"These here," he said, pointing at what looked like roast chicken and a quinoa dish, "are the less intense fare. These are the dishes our guests are generally invited to partake in." He pointed to some wine, Zeke nodded, and Effendi poured for both him and Johanna. Then he pointed to a couple of other dishes. "And these here are more of our unique fare—edibles, only if you're invited to partake."

"Edibles, as in—" Johanna said.

"You don't need Urban Dictionary to understand, I don't think. We're just a year away from legalization in Ohio, are we not? As we understand it, OH-High-Grow was just given a twenty-million-dollar contract to grow the first state-sanctioned crop."

"Twenty-five," a woman to Faiz Effendi's left said.

"Twenty-five, then."

"I honestly wouldn't know," Johanna said. The words settled between them. For a moment no one moved.

"Well, if you'd like to partake, all you need is to seek an invitation." Faiz Effendi stared at Johanna, understanding full well what he was saying to her in her role, in his. "Oh, and all the desserts. Steer clear if you're not invited."

Johanna took a very long look at Zeke. Then she looked at Faiz Effendi.

"I understand what you're offering, and it is a very complicated offer. I think I'd best—Zeke, I think I need to get back to town. I—I just realized I have to . . . wash my hair. Or something." Where Zeke imagined that Faiz Effendi, the women around him, might beg Johanna to stay for dinner out of feigned politeness, they simply turned away from her at the table. Zeke stood and walked her just past the threshold of the building.

"Well, that is some fucked-up information," Johanna said. "I mean . . . I mean. It's soon going to be legal. And who knows if the state would even touch prosecuting a religious group—one that just had a death in its midst—and yet. Fuck. This is just way too compromising. Not exactly what we encounter in Columbus day-to-day. I want nothing to do with it. I honestly wish you hadn't brought me here." Zeke stood looking at her, his hands abuzz. "But you need to get back inside. I get it. You're a writer. Reporter. The . . . scribe of a false messiah? You're what you are. I get it. I'll take an Uber."

"No, no," Zeke said. "I can drive you back and then get back here in plenty of time."

"Zeke," Johanna said. "We're not college students. I've got it. Seriously."

"Seriously?"

"Seriously. Do your job."

"And I'll see you when I get back?"

"Not tonight. But call me in the morning." She paused, composed herself. "I want a full report."

Zeke returned to the barn. Just as he did, one of the black hats with a rifle slung across his shoulder trotted over to the PA and turned the sound off, as much of the conversation was now being picked up still by Effendi's mic. Another came over and removed the microphone from the table. They did so with military precision, in stark contrast to the messiness of the rest. And then conversation broke out at the table, focused around a tale their interim tzaddik wanted to tell them:

FAIZ EFFENDI: People of Shabbetai Tzvi, as you know we have with us for tish tonight a special guest, Ezekiel Leger. Our tzaddik, Natan of Flatbush, is considering taking on this Zeke as his scribe, to tell the story of his persecution. So we will allow him to hear tonight. Husna, will you recite the motzi?

HUSNA: *(lights candles with two other women in hijab, breaks the bread, and says a Hebrew prayer)* We have met and greeted our guests and we thank them for coming. On this auspicious occasion we would like to hear from you, rebbe.

FAIZ EFFENDI: I have thought a long time before your arrival tonight, Zeke, and what occurred to me was this: Long before the arrival of Natan of Flatbush, before even the arrival of Natan of Gaza, Prophet to the mashiach Shabbetai Tzvi, there was a certain Kabbalist of Safed who was known as Aharon of Ankara. This Aharon of Ankara was a devotee of the Lurianic Kabbalistic tradition. He longed to convene with the Lord. He believed in his ability to do so through reading Torah, through becoming an ideal student of the Talmud. He had memorized the Mishneh Torah, and he had memorized even a substantial portion of the Zohar, perhaps the hardest book to memorize of all the books known to man.

HUSNA: The hardest. Who would even try?

ZEKE: *(looks around the table to see that the congregants are all shaking their heads)* I've never even seen it.

FAIZ EFFENDI: In the community of Aharon, there were some who longed to allow more and more new members into this group. They lived near a group of Chaldeans, nonbelievers, who appeared only to want to live off some of Aharon's family's profit. Aharon was a talented seer, and had made a good deal of money telling of the future. One day he learned that his closest friend, a young man named Isaac, who was like a son to him, had been out talking with these Chaldeans. It comes to Aharon from one of the more knowledgeable members of the community that Isaac has been telling the Chaldeans not only of their business dealings, but of their rituals, as well. This sharing of information is forbidden by decree, and by tradition, and by the written law of their community.

HUSNA: *(sitting to Rabia's right, in a hijab, the other woman Zeke saw when he first went to the Caves with Yehoshua)* One of the laws any member of the community in Ankara would have known. And would not have broken.

FAIZ EFFENDI: This is right. *(looks directly at Zeke again)* This is a central tenet of their faith and it poses a more practical danger to the community. For the sultan who controls this city now has been accommodating of the Jewish community because they have practiced their rituals quietly. But it is known that, as it was for Jeremiah, for our prophet Shabbetai Tzvi, if their practices were to be made public, the sultan might make them all take the turban—or worse. Take their heads. And so Aharon of Ankara brings the boy to his home one night and impresses upon him the danger of his interactions with the Chaldeans. He tries to speak to his son in a language his son will understand. "I know you consort with the kafir," Aharon says. "You think they're your friends. But there is great danger to our community, and our community takes its commandments seriously. And so you must stop." But does this boy stop?

HUSNA: *(silent now, listening)*

FAIZ EFFENDI: The boy does not stop. One night, as it is told, the whole community wakes to the sound of the cries of a boar from the desert. Most stay in their homes, but a few of the elders take to the desert, and there they find that this Isaac has been taken from them. Some speak of the intolerable cruelty of the Chaldeans who have stolen into their camp in the night and taken Isaac to the desert. Still more speak of a boar that has been spotted around the woods, a nasty boar with sharpened tusks with which no human should tussle. That night he gets the sign: like a burning mountain, aflame with the light of a thousand stars, in the woods he sees Shabbetai Tzvi himself. The whole congregation sees him. The dangers they all see are many, inside and out. But Shabbetai Tzvi—Shabbetai Tzvi is one.

The interim tzaddik's story ended. Zeke looked around to see the Dönme at the tables all around them engaged in quiet prayer, determined in their eating. All were too far away to have heard a word of Faiz Effendi's story. Faiz Effendi put his eyes to his plate and began to eat. Outside the barn door, snow began to fall again. Rabia excused herself, and Husna slid into the spot next to Zeke.

"How do you like our tish?" Husna said. She wore a traditional black hijab that framed her pale white face. There was a distinctly Ashkenazi look to her face, a bulbous nose and ruddiness to the tips of her cheeks that looked almost prototypically Polish.

"I hadn't expected such a long sermon," Zeke said.

"We love Faiz Effendi's derashahs," Husna said. Her voice was nasal, strained. "My husband and I come all the way up from Columbus every Friday afternoon to stay over for Shabbat and hear him. I mean we miss Natan, of course, and await his return. But until then."

"So you don't live here in the Caves?"

"Oh, no. We didn't even really know where Mt. Izmir was. But my husband and I grew more and more involved in Chabad when we were in our thirties, and a decade ago we started hearing about the Dönme community here. Robert got involved with them through— through some other businesses they had in common. But that's neither here nor there. Because we arrived and we came to believe. Say what you will about what's happened—they are the most serious about Lurianic Kabbalah of anyone we've ever encountered. And we love Faiz and Natan. And, well, Natan is Natan."

"And it hasn't turned you off," Zeke said. "All of it."

"When we first heard, we were bereft. I came up every day for a week to sit shiva. That poor kid. We live down in Bexley, where we can keep our community safe, and a bit separate. We sent both our kids to the Schechter school. So we really feel for Natan and for the community. It came to feel *more* important to be here to support them, not less. In times of trouble, community grows tighter. Wraps itself inside itself. My husband and I, we both grew up in Williamsburg and have been looking for something like this, community like this, ever since we went away to college. We've found a home here, in convening with the Lord."

Dead silence sat between Zeke and this woman, and on his heart, weighing upon his mind, was Gram. Who had no real community. Whom he hadn't seen in a year.

"May I ask—do you believe what they do here?"

Zeke was intensely quiet. The murmurs of conversation rose all around. "I've always had a kind of interest in mysticism, if that's what you mean," he said. "I think that's what drew me to the story. I mean, telling this story. For a magazine. Saturday morning in synagogue with a bunch of smelly-breathed white people was never for me. But the idea of interacting directly with God . . ."

"I know," Husna said. "I know it can be enticing. Most likely here's what will happen: most likely you'll go home and write your magazine story. But you know, before you leave, have Yehoshua take you to the frozen mikvah, to the Cave of the Dragon. If you feel nothing there—maybe it's not for you. But if you do . . . it can be life-changing. Like, literally change your life. Don't just dip a toe in here, and then leave. See what it feels like to be submerged."

Husna turned to talk to her husband on the other side of the table. All around them, congregants were intently eating their chicken—and just as many were slopping their plates with edibles. The energy around them was mellowing as they ate their way to the light psychedelic experience, and Zeke figured he would partake. When dessert came, he ate three caramels, and a couple of chocolates. He went to eat one more dark chocolate when Yehoshua walked by and said, "Don't want to go too heavy on the indica. Some call that the 'couch lock'—it'll take over your body so you can barely move. Maybe take some home. It's all worth trying. We have—we have the best hookup here you could imagine." A lightly stoned and self-satisfied look overswept Yehoshua's face. Zeke put a handful of gummies in his pocket and took a moment to survey the scene, Dönme in black suits and hijab walking around the edges of the barn's open doors, stoned and staring at the moon. A couple at his table had clearly gone after the indica early. They were in a Shel Silverstein cartoon embrace, keeping one another up. The man started laughing, laughing, laughing. And singing.

Zeke walked to the barn's edge. Out in the fields next to this metal barn, new falling snowflakes had begun to squall, had begun to swirl and drop again even in the warmer evening. He was thinking of leaving when he felt a hand at his elbow.

"We should talk," Rabia said.

"Well, here we are. Let's talk." He followed her to a table, where most of the ummah had cleared out.

"I'll waste no words," Rabia said. "There is an immense desire to move on here now. This happens in a community overcome by trauma, by tragedy. It takes time. But I need you to see me, too." She stopped talking. Behind her chador, only her eyes were visible, and in their reflection the scattered blowing of snow outside the barn. They were watery, puffy. "I need you to see that every night many of us return home—and mourn. You're here now far later, much later. You haven't seen us sitting shiva. You haven't seen looks on the faces after the police came to take Natan forcefully away while he was still mourning the death of his only son. It's not apparent now, it's not plastered on the faces. But it's here, the remnants of it."

They were both silent, and only the murmur of voices, the hush of falling snow, arose around them.

"I get it," Zeke said. "So how does it feel? How did it?"

"Osman was all of ours," Rabia said. "Not just Natan's. He'll tell you more when you talk. Osman's mother has been gone many years. We took him on like we might in a kibbutz—he was a sweet kid, Osman, but he had a passion in him. He was a searcher. I cannot tell you I know how they got in, or which of those men or boys from Mt. Izmir did it. But I can tell you in no uncertain terms that the truth will one day come out. That it was an outsider who—who strangled—"

The word cracked Rabia's voice. Her hand came to her face. For the first time, the full sense of her mourning, her grief, did come across. The immediacy of it. Between them now was that feeling Zeke had felt when he first met Johanna and Declan after Gram's funeral, like there was a physical presence between them.

"I'm here for a funeral, as well," Zeke said, tears welling, one beginning to roll down his cheek, growing freezing in the outdoor cold. "An old friend. My friend Gram. Suicide. I'm—I'm mourning, too."

Now Rabia looked up, looked him in his eyes. She looked at him long and low, directly, with passion in her eyes.

"I can see it," she said. "If I could hug you, I would hug you." She stood and rushed from the barn.

Zeke sat alone for a minute, the most alone he'd felt since his arrival in Ohio. He could feel more tears coming down his cheeks and he did nothing to wipe them away. He returned to the edge of the barn, and he stood and walked to the snowfall. He was equidistant from the two rifle-bearing Dönme, far enough away that they couldn't talk to each other. He looked up through the mix of helixing snow to the black sky, where bands of stars in the galaxy had just begun to show themselves, revealing their light as if in imitation of the winter snow that every day fell on Mt. Izmir, and on all of Central Ohio.

CLASH OF THE UNIFORMED

Johanna is in bed at the Airbnb cabin when the sound of shouts comes from outside. It is enough to wake them both, though in Zeke's indica stoniness he is very, very slow to rouse. At first it is the sound from his first night there, the incomprehensible but imposing Ladino of Dönme in the stark black night.

Then there is a second sound. It is louder and raspier, but it is unmistakably the voice of Deshawn Flaxton.

Zeke lumbers to put on his clothes. He turns to Johanna and says, "Pall the colice." As soon as they make eye contact, both comprehend the futility of that idea.

"How much of those edibles did you eat?"

"Like a lot of those edibles did I eat," Zeke says. His arms like sandbags. Like he's talking to Johanna through some dense gelatinous material. Ears like they're stuffed with pussy willows.

"Fuck," Johanna says. "Ain't it just like the night. The last thing I need is for them all to see me here. I'm going into the bathroom, and I'm going to close the door and lock it."

"The sun isn't yellow, it's chicken," Zeke says. He walks out-side into the full squall of winter night. The air has a strange soft warmth, but wet snow whips in all directions. This seems to be how it snows these days, less when it's frigid but more when it's warmer, the air just cold enough for snow and wet enough to make a lot. Global weirding snow, the new snormal. In the swirl of snow under the starlight in the dark, dark riverbank night, to his left Zeke sees Fergus Shaw, Deshawn Flaxton, and six of their friends. All linemen.

To the right he sees the four armed congregants from the tish earlier that night. They are in their full black-suited and chador-ed specificity. Not the congregants. The Hasidim he saw militarily protecting the place with their long guns.

"Well, we came to fucking get you, Fake News," Deshawn says. He is looking right at Zeke, who has his T-shirt on backward and a pair of plaid PJ pants on and is all at once freezing. He's still stony enough that even as serious as the situation clearly is, he can only laugh. "Look what we get instead. The whole fucking Fake Jew army."

"Fuck you," the Dönme closest to Zeke says to Deshawn. It oc-curs to Zeke for the first time that these are all young men and women of about the same age, some clad in religious gear, some out of football uniform. "We've seen you all come here every night since he arrived. We're just here to make sure nothing more hap-pens."

"If you weren't," Fergus says.

"If we weren't?" the Dönme woman in her full chador says.

"If you weren't," Fergus says. He shifts his attention. "How many more nights you here, Fake News?"

"This might be the blast, the last, the faster master blaster, after tonight," Zeke says. "Tonight's the night-eye-eye-eye-ite, tonight's the night-ite-ite-ite-ite."

Now all eyes are on Zeke. They can see, town and God alike, that he's too stoned to make much sense.

"Well, make that a fact," Deshawn says.

"He's not going anywhere until he decides he wants to," the first Dönme says. "And neither are we."

"Let's fucking see about that," Fergus says. He takes a step closer to the Dönme, though almost twenty feet of snow-squalled night separates them. The chador-ed woman hoists the AR-15 that's slung across her back, brandishes it. It's the biggest gun any of them is carrying. Zeke cannot imagine how he did not notice she was carrying such an enormous weapon. It's black and long in the long black night, and it feels as if the gelatinous whole of the world between him and her suddenly rarefies, clears to air, and he can see her finger on the trigger. Thumb flips off the safety. Zeke's mind is thinking, *Whoa whoa whoa whoa!* But he can't get words out in time to say them and probably they wouldn't help much if he could.

Fergus's hands go up toward his face. He sees just as clearly as Zeke does now. He immediately steps back and then back again, and then the whole crew of footballers run to their cars and drive off into the snowy night, their F-150s fishtailing across the wet snowy riverside community.

Zeke turns to say thank you, but the woman just says:

"They're not wrong about you getting out of here."

Then goes herself.

IN PRISON

In every photograph of Natan of Flatbush, the self-proclaimed Prophet's beard was longer than in the photograph before it. There was a picture of him from his time in Footsteps, just before he left Brooklyn with his family for Ohio, when he had what Gram had called back in college a "get-the-fuck-off-my-porch beard," big, round, and patchy. There was the photograph the local Ohio news stations and newspapers had used around the time of his trial, when the beard had reached the middle of his chest and appeared classically rabbinical, something out of seventeenth-century Galicia. There was the longish beard in the photograph that ran in the *Columbus Dispatch* a year earlier when MasterCard had tried to repossess the cedar-and-gold ark the Dönme had built after Natan failed to pay off fifty thousand dollars in debt (the repo men were chased off by AR-toting maaminim). There was the photograph on the walls of a few trailers in the Caves in which the beard was somewhere in between, flopping long and low across the tallis wrapped about the Prophet's shoulders.

Zeke was sitting across from Natan of Flatbush in the visitation room of the Northeast Ohio Correctional Center on Monday morning before he realized he was in the presence of the Prophet. The table where they sat was fixed to the floor, but the chair squeaked and wobbled with years of use. Across the table, in a blue jumpsuit, was a small middle-aged Ashkenazi man with the prickles of a five-o'clock shadow on his cheeks. There was no rabbinical beard. His chin was weak, cleft deep at its middle like a pear with a bite taken out of it, and a series of red bumps stood out across his chin where he was clearly still unaccustomed to shaving.

"Ezekiel Leger, in the living flesh," the man said. His voice was bold, discontinuous with the appearance of his face. His was a bellowing voice, an octave lower than one would have expected, and disconnected from the treble voice Zeke had subconsciously made up for Natan in his head when they emailed. He stood, then sat again. "Awesome seeing you in person, Ezekiel. Zeke. Zeke in person. Thank you for meeting me a day early."

"The warden's assistant called first thing this morning," Zeke said. "I was supposed to visit the Caves—to see the Cave of the Dragon for the first time today. Dave Effendi was going to take me."

"I know," Natan said. "Believe me. I know. But we have received word that the decision on my appeal may come tomorrow. Soon. I'm confident I'll be cleared of charges, today appeared to be the day."

"Right. Well, I wanted to be here."

"I'm grateful for your flexibility," Natan said. He was looking down at his chest now, no longer holding eye contact. There was a pallor to his cheeks that made the red bumps along his weak chin stand out starkly in the buzzing fluorescent lights of the room. In his eyes, Zeke discovered something quite familiar to anyone who has experienced it: the dead loneliness of depression. Depression: anger turned inward. Zeke could see it clearly as he was carrying something of the same since Gram's suicide.

"You doing OK?"

"I'm fine," Natan of Flatbush said. "Why wouldn't I be fine? Because I'm a year into serving a sentence for the death of my son who was murdered by heathens in Central Ohio but pinned on me? When because of the tenets of the religion I'm the leader of would've said it would be admissible even if I *had* killed him—which of course obviously I did not? Because I've been forced to shave off a beard it took more than a decade to grow and haven't been in direct contact with any members of my community for more than a visit like this one in a year? What could I possibly be down about?"

"Right," Zeke said. "Right."

"I'm sorry," Natan said. "I'm very sorry. I don't mean to get heated. Already. Sorry. This is all very painful. I am happy to see you. I hear you had quite a time the other night yourself."

"You did? Already? Oh, right, of course you did. Well, as I say, I'm going to make one more trip out to the Caves and then I'm flying back to New York midweek at the latest. It's already getting on past time for me to get out of town. I feel like another couple nights and it'd be full-on redneck-versus-Yakubi-Islamic-Jewish fight club."

"It might be that no matter when you leave. That you won't be here doesn't mean it won't happen. At least while you're here you'll be able to have an influence over those who will listen. Me. I'll listen to you. I'll answer your questions here. I have some questions of my own.

"First," Natan continued, "let me assure you that you do not want to leave too soon. You want to stay until Wednesday, or better yet until the weekend. I know it is days longer for you to be here. But tomorrow or the day after—so there is time to prepare for it, whether I am freed on appeal or if I stay here in jail—I will perform my first miracle in more than a decade. I can't tell you now what the miracle will be. But you won't be able to miss it. You must be here to bear witness. Like Baruch to Jeremiah, you are in position to be the Scribe of the Prophet, that can be your role here, telling this story, telling it far and wide. And as a journalist you must be here to witness it. The things it will do for your story! For your magazine!"

Something new sparked in Natan's eyes at the thought of performing a miracle. The glaring fluorescent lights bore down on them, in this space, in which there was no snow, no cold. If the vapor of water that had once been snow was in that prison, it was not detectable by human eyes, skin, noses. There were no stars above their heads. "For now we will talk. But just hear me once more: don't leave too soon. For you as a Jew, for you as a writer, for you now increasingly a member of our ummah, stay."

The sound of another inmate meeting with his young son carried across the room and stopped them short.

"The laughter of a young boy," Natan said. He sat back a moment. Shallow flat water filled his eyes, but did not breach their rims. These were not the tears of a killer. They were tears of a mourner, an innocent mourner. "But." He swiped the back of his wrists across his eyes. "Sorry. Please do go on."

"If you need—" Zeke said.

Natan put up the heels of both hands to him as if to say, *No, no, go on.*

"OK. Well," Zeke said. "It feels odd to be discussing religion at this point but—yes, yes, I see, I get it. It's exactly what we should be talking about. I'll confess I've read at the Zohar just a little. And I can't profess to understanding it any better than I did when I was a kid. But even in its inscrutability, I feel a kind of affinity to it. A text that won't really let you read it."

"A text that won't let you read it," Natan said. "Hah!" A semblance of light continued to shine in his eyes, some color returning to his pallid cheeks. "That is a nice way to put it. But the Book of Splendor, when you fully comprehend its mysteries, is full of beauty and guidance." He spoke some Hebrew, then backed up and translated. "'Stars and constellations are always visible in the realm of Elohim. By the word of Adonai the heavens were made.' When I get out of here, you can learn with me. You could read it with Faiz Effendi if you like before you go. He knows much of the book by heart, you know."

"By heart!" Zeke said. "It must literally be the most difficult book to memorize in the history of the world."

"The Qur'an is pretty tough, and there are millions who have it by heart. They even have a name for it: Hafiz. The name literally means 'He who has memorized the Qur'an.'" Natan stretched his legs under the table until his feet hit Zeke's, then retracted. "There is no name in Hebrew for he who has memorized the Zohar."

"Crazy."

"That's not a good name."

"Crazy smart, anyway. Dedicated."

"It is a book which most repays close reading. Now what I want to know, given this reading: Have you come to believe something, now that you've read so much more, now that you've been to visit the Dönme of Mt. Izmir?"

Fluorescent lights buzzed above, in place of constellations, heavens. They were lucky that only one other inmate was in the room to receive a visit, a tall scraggly man with sleeve tattoos, whose mother and young son sat across from him in relative silence. Because here at the table where Natan of Flatbush sat, something was happening. It might simply have been the lack of sleep, or the sense of fatigue, but it was as if a second presence sat across the table from Zeke now. The pain in his brow where his eye had nearly healed throbbed. Natan of Flatbush was the somewhat disappointing small shorn man Zeke had encountered the moment he arrived. But there was a tangible power within him as soon as he began speaking: a charisma, a religious fervor. A certainty, a confidence, a peace, and an anger. Joy. But oh, anger. Whatever anger had turned inward and plagued him with the depression Zeke could see deep in his eyes from the moment he first sat down was now turning back outward. It wouldn't have been accurate to say it was aimed at Zeke. But it was exuding out into the room.

"I know you want to ask me about Osman, to compare what you've heard from the people of Mt. Izmir, the people of the Caves, my emails, to whatever you might hear from me here and now. Maybe catch me slipping up or something."

"No, no, that's not what I'm after. I think I've heard all I need to know on that topic."

"Oh," Natan of Flatbush said. "Enough to tell the story?"

"Enough to tell enough of it."

"You must have questions," Natan said. "I am your tzaddik here. Ask."

"You've been saying you want me to serve as your scribe. Why would you want your story out? As I understand it, the 12th commandment says maaminim could be killed for talking about what happens in the community. And you want me to write about it for millions to read."

"Well, you are not one of the maaminim, are you."

"Doesn't quite answer the question."

"How familiar are you with Jeremiah?"

"Not at all?"

"Jeremiah was a prophet who told the stories of his visions only within his community at first. He saw the face in the whirlwind. The greater world wanted to kill him for it! In the time of Nebuchadnezzar, Jeremiah counseled the leaders of Judah to fight in the name of the Lord, and was so forceful he was imprisoned. When the king intervened, he sent Baruch to take down his visions, to write it all down. Jeremiah couldn't write. So he told the story to his scribe, Baruch, and when the king read it, he was saved."

Again there was silence between them. It was a convincing performance.

"OK," Zeke said. "I want to talk to you about evil."

"Evil."

"I'm willing to believe the things you say, Natan. I believe in your wisdom. I do. I think your ideas around Ein Sofism are expansively interesting. What would be most useful is less to find out what happened than to find out how you feel about it. Not as a father—well, not only as a father. And not as a religious leader—not only. When I was in college, we learned that evil was relative. If it doesn't seem too far from Judaism or Hasidism—we learned an Aristotelian version of evil. If you understood a person and their situation, you could see that they might do wrong, horrible, unspeakable wrong—but we learned that it was a wrong compelled by circumstance, by choices made within a system.

"As a result," Zeke continued, "we learned to be empathetic. Living through another's eyes. Part of that empathy was to understand that absolute evil—a kind of evil that comes from an evil person and makes them evil in and of themselves—doesn't exist. There were simply people making the worst bad decisions in the midst of the bad decisions they had to make. Realpolitik, the banality of evil, all that. Now here we are. Your son, a teenager, has been murdered. Is this evil? Does it exist?"

Zeke felt exposed. In some weird way, in this moment—the moment after asking Natan of Flatbush what he wanted to know—he'd done what he'd set out to do. Whether Natan was a false prophet or a real one, a true mystic or an ersatz messiah, whether evil did exist and whether Natan was a purveyor of it, Zeke honestly had no idea what kind of answer he would receive. Maybe one closer to some kind of lasting truth. The peal of the bell and its knell in the open air, not the response of the parishioner.

Natan looked down at his chest, put his hand to his face. It stopped a couple of inches below his chin, as if he were attempting to collect a phantom beard in his hand.

"There is a famous story of the Ba'al Shem Tov. The founder of Hasidism. He never wrote a word. When he discovered one day that one of his disciples was writing down his words, he beckoned this follower to bring him the notebook. He sat reading. His face grew redder and redder until he looked up and, fire in his eyes, breathed at him: 'Not a word you've written here is true to a word I have ever said. Destroy it.'

"For generations Hasidim have seen it as an imperative; the tzaddik must teach through his body, one-on-one. A tzaddik cannot answer your question simply by answering it. It is for you to observe, to watch."

Again he was quiet. His hand raised to stroke his absent beard.

"In Isaiah, the prophet says, 'All flesh is grass, and all its kindness like a blossom in the field. Grass withers and blossoms fade when the breath of God blows upon it, and the people—the people are grass.' What even the greatest prophet did not express was that grass is itself an extension of the soul of grass. Grass is the shell of the spark of grass that is the true grass. The only true grass. The blossom is not the blossom as the body is not the body, but both are a mode of becoming. They are the qelippot. They are the shells of the sparks of the sparks. All the rest is mirage."

Natan stopped. The lights buzzed overhead.

"In the human," he continued, "the human being—it is the being half we must grant our attention. This is a case where English has done a great justice to the natural world of man. Adam—ha'adam, 'the man,' in Biblical Hebrew, feels nowhere near sufficient to describe the experience of being. But human *being*—that nearly rises to the test. The experience of being. Being. Being. If one *wanted* to call this metaphysics, one could, and it is what you mean when you say metaphysics. But it is just the world, as it is. This world of Ein Sof."

Zeke had a feeling of intense dryness in his throat and a rapid, almost tachycardic beating of excitement in his chest. He nodded, said, "Continue."

"Take the snow all around you outside right now," Natan said. "There it is, a physical mass on your finger. You touch it, feel its substance. Then it melts. Then it evaporates—selah—into the air around you. You no longer perceive it. There's moisture all around us now that was snow. We walk amid it, we breathe it in, we piss it out, we drink and ball it, slip and fishtail in it. This is what we mean by Ein Sof.

"The theodicy, your initial question: Why is there good and evil? This is the question we will work on in the early days of living amid Ein Sofism. Heidegger, the famous philosopher, the phenomenologist, was a great villain of the twentieth century in the eyes of the Jews. No matter how useful his phenomenology is to us, many will never forgive him for being a member of the Nazi Party. For firing the Jewish faculty at Heidelberg. But do you know, in 1934, who was his student?"

Zeke said he had no idea.

"The Lubavitcher rabbi himself, Menachem Mendel Schneerson. The Lubavitcher rabbi took Heidegger's history of philosophy class. The great tzaddik would sit in the back of the classroom, reading Talmud as Heidegger lectured on Plato and Aristotle, asking the ontological question: Why is there something rather than nothing! The only question worth answering, he said.

"Though the rebbe was reading Talmud while he lectured, if Heidegger called on him, the rebbe would always answer, correctly. In one ear, the metaphysics of the Greeks. In the other, the Hebrew of the Rambam. Isn't this just theological Ein Sofism? Just as Heidegger and Merleau-Ponty did, the rebbe and the Ba'al Shem Tov wondered why there is something instead of nothing. Only we have a certain surprisingly, elegantly simple answer: There is Ein Sof. Evil, good, and everything in between. This single physical world of joy and goodness and sin and imperfection. Even Job the Moabite himself acknowledged the mix—'Though I were perfect I would not know my soul,' he tells the Lord. His ability to endure the worst a man has endured comes in part not simply from his unbending worship. It comes from his acknowledgment that man will always do wrong, always do no good, and yet he will push forward."

It was as close to an admission of some other knowledge of what happened to Osman as Natan had come. Zeke was on the edge of his metal chair.

"The Fergus Shaws and Deshawn Flaxtons will come to the Airbnbs of the world, and they will battle the David Effendis and the Yehoshua Greens of the world. They will do evil. Or they will turn to the good. It is possible they will go to jail. This is all part of the space that the Ein Sof did *not* vacate! Each soul distinct but in contact with the space of the Ein Sof."

Natan leaned hard over the table between them and hit his two middle fingers against Zeke's chest. The guard in the corner barked, "Hey! No touching." Again Natan of Flatbush leaned back. There was no longer any pallor in his enlivened cheeks. He had awoken to the world. Something flickered brighter in Natan's eyes now. He dropped his gaze again down to the middle of his chest.

"Then isn't the only evil, the sole evil capable of breaking from the space of Ein Sof, to steal the *perception* of time from another soul?" Zeke said. "I get it, I get the idea of the flower dying or whatever from Isaiah. But isn't that just what a strangulation and murder is? To steal the perception of time. To cause another to cease perceiving time. It's not the act of the angel. It's stealing the perception of an angel from another soul."

Now a new anger flared up in Natan of Flatbush, another side. Was it mourning? Remorse? Recompense? It was as if the manic side of his prophetic grasp was onrushing all at once. The pallor had returned to his face, but it was as if he was made of sunstruck snow, as if a dim light shone through his ashen cheeks. He stood up at the table and the guard again barked, this time an order: "Sit back down!"

This time he did not sit back down. There was no longer a pallor in his cheeks at all, but instead a suddenly sweaty ruddy mess. His whole face flushed with an onrush of blood to capillaries.

"The experience of being continues to become the experience of being," Natan said. "The perception of time for one is the perception of time for all. Do we feel anger at the heathens who have taken Osman's life! My son! Tonight they will come for you. We will feel anger and we will feel remorse. There is no evil. There is only coolo tov. The experience of time as joy and joyousness as becoming."

For a moment, a long moment, there was silence at the table. The murmur of speech between mother and son came across the room to them only as an unintelligible wave. The buzzing of fluorescent lights nearly canceled it out. Natan's chest rose and fell in jerky movements.

"I read through the Commandments," Zeke said. "I spoke with Dave Effendi and with Yehoshua about it. Dave says Osman had told Fergus Shaw what happened at the Caves. Told them everything there was to know about the Dönme, and even a whole good deal that wasn't true. That he sometimes even discussed your personal life. That he confirmed the worst rumors about your congregation. I cannot imagine how that must have played in the community."

Natan of Flatbush fell deep inside himself again after he sat. He was looking down at the palms of his hands.

"Before Shabbetai Tzvi, all Kabbalists believed we are living in a vacated space. There was Ein Sof, in the time before time. And then he absented himself, the Lord. We live in the space he vacated."

"Do you really think those teenagers killed your son?" Zeke said.

The lights bore down on him. He looked across at Natan, who had grown very still.

"I don't know what good it would do for us to keep discussing it, or for me to go back over and over and over it again."

Now, like it had when they first heard the boy across the room, water welled up in Natan's eyes once more.

"Please don't think of it. I'll be out of here tomorrow," Natan said. "I will see you at the Caves."

As if they'd both entirely forgotten where they were, Natan stood up, and Zeke stood, and they embraced each other. As soon as they let go, the two guards now at the back of the room were on them, one pulling Natan back to a cell. The other grabbed Zeke awkwardly. Pulled his shoulder in one direction while his feet went the other.

All at once, his face slammed nose-first into the table.

"What have you done!" Natan cried. Zeke was again standing with the help of the guard who had grabbed him. Blood rushed out of Zeke's nose and onto his shirt, a bib of blood soaking down like the bottom half of a gibbous moon.

"I'm OK," Zeke said, putting the sleeve of his shirt to his nose, pinching and tipping his head back. "I'm OK."

One guard, the one with his hands on Natan, looked at the other, and with a look of strange apprehension on his face said, "Get that gentleman on out of here."

DECISIONS DECISIONS DECISIONS

"So you're honestly going to head back to the Caves?"

"Unless there's some good reason for me not to," Zeke said. On the ceiling above his head, the stars in their sticker constellation glowed brighter than at any point since he'd first been in this bedroom.

"Well, there is the general fear-of-bodily-harm reason, combined with the having-experienced-some-already fact."

"I'd say this is enough. Don't touch it. It feels like the whole of existence is trying to get out through the bridge of my nose."

"I guess in a way it is. But you weren't complaining when I accidentally knocked into it before." Zeke's nose throbbed with each slow throb of his heart. He put his hand to his eye, which was now a hard nodule of rapidly healing flesh, a knot of wiry stitches flailing out as if reaching for the broader world. "I've got to be dead honest with you. It feels almost like you're putting yourself in harm's way intentionally. Like, you loved Gram so much. I remember. I don't think I ever really said it aloud back in college,

156

but I'd get jealous of how much you loved that guy, how much you would try to emulate him—his easy way in the world, his musical talents—and I know—don't interrupt me while I'm on a roll here. I know Gram was amazing. He was so smart. He was the guy you kind of wanted to be. But seeing this again here now . . . like now he tried fate and lost, and you're willing to tempt it, too. I'll just be honest in saying it reminds me of why we broke up. Your striving. Your inability to just slow down, be in the moment."

The charge of the glow from the stars meant Johanna's shades had been open to the sun all day. Those same shades were now drawn tight, and in the midnight dark of the room, it was all they could see.

"I hear you," Zeke said.

"Well, that's a start. I think that's more than anything the issue we used to deal with. You very much did *not* hear me. Or, you know, listen."

"I hear you. I do. I just kind of need you to believe me: I am not trying to put myself in harm's way. There's a story here. I won't lie for a second and say there's not danger in the reporting. But I'm being as careful as I can be."

They were both silent again for a moment.

"OK," Johanna said. She pulled closer to him. "OK. Speaking of which, it really does seem your eye has healed miraculously. It wasn't even a week ago you were in that car accident. Look at it now."

"Fug! Don't touch that, either. Until I finally get them out, the stitches hurt worse than the injury."

"Now that you mention it, I was going to say before that it looks pretty ghastly. Like the stitches have grown into your flesh. You should get it checked out."

"I know! I know. But what time have I had. The Prophet—Natan—Nathan—Fritzman—called me in for that meeting this morning at the absolute last minute, and then tomorrow morning first thing I need to head in to meet Yehoshua at the Caves. Though Yehoshua did say that they'd set me up with one of the women from the ummah to take them out, one who'd been a nurse in the past. So maybe tomorrow I'll get that done. It does really, really hurt. Like, a lot."

"Back to the city."

"What."

"You could always consider extending your stay even longer. I could help you extend it." Johanna had her hand on him again. It had been long enough since the last time that a little something was stirring. "It's not like you seem to have that much to go back to in New York. Ohio's a fine place to live."

"That'd be a good state motto. It wouldn't sound at all like you were underselling the shit out of your own state. Up there with 'Virginia Is for Likers.' 'Live Free or, You Know, Whatever.'"

Johanna rolled back onto her own side of the bed. "I am being serious."

"OK."

"OK. So. Now you be serious, too."

"Me? I work as a magazine editor. The center of that world is in New York. It's all I've known for more than a decade. And that's how long it's taken to get there. To get taken seriously. They say when you hit forty, all of a sudden doors open. The writers who haven't had the temerity to stick on move to law, or home, or academia. I've still got years ahead. I've put in too much just to leave it."

"Funny."

"What's funny?"

"Just the other night when you were explaining it to me, you said the rule in Kabbalah is that you're not allowed to start reading the Zohar until you're forty."

"True."

"So you've got like five years to decide. You could take five years to keep telling stories like the ones you're telling now. Or you could stay around here, and maybe get real about religion."

Zeke turned on a bedside lamp. The world returned to his eyes like the fire of the Ba'al Shem Tov—a holy, nearly blinding fire. When it subsided, Johanna's freckled angelic nakedness revealed itself next to him.

"You really think that," Zeke said.

"I mean, I know you went to college out here. And came back for Gram. But something more than just the salaciousness of a single murder must have attracted you to stay."

"I'm interested in it, yes," Zeke said. "But this isn't 1971. You don't just pick up and move to a kibbutz. And fuck. The Caves sure aren't a kibbutz. And . . . I mean, what's the endgame here? You'd have me go become the scribe to a man you think is a false prophet who killed his son?"

"No," Johanna said. She was sitting up now, too, the skin held taut at her neck. "No! No. But you've met plenty of community leaders from Bexley. You could move there. You could get a job on staff at the *Columbus Dispatch* just by asking, I bet. You've already got more sources in Central Ohio than anyone at the paper, just in the week you've been here. And through me. And you'd have . . ." Now they were both quiet, letting the implication of her suggestion sit in the cool white air. "I mean at a minimum, you could ask Faiz Effendi about it. He knows all the shuls down there. He's unpleasant, he's sanctimonious, but he's a surprisingly well-connected dude. Hasid. Dönme slash businessman slash doctor."

He put his arm around her neck and brought her naked body close to his.

"Seriously, though," Johanna said. "I actually still don't think you should go out there again. To the Caves. All you've got is a not-quite-broken nose and some suspiciously ingrown stitches and you don't quite seem to be able to handle it."

"Natan was talking about death a lot," Zeke said.

"So you got him to confess?"

"Well, not like that. He was quoting the Zohar. And I went back to look at the passage online when I was at my cabin this afternoon. It was about a man on the edge of death. 'Who is End of Heaven above. What is End of Heaven below.' And the answer: 'Stars and constellations are always visible there.'"

"So, Zeke," Johanna said. "As I was *just* saying. Listening to you talk, it just sounds like—maybe you have drunk the Jewish Islamic Kool-Aid."

"I was just today reading that it actually wasn't Kool-Aid they drank at Jamestown—it was another fruit drink that Jim Jones gave them all, called Flavor Aid, but I guess 'drink the Flavor Aid' just didn't have the same ring—"

"Uh-huh. Sounds like you're using irrelevant trivia to dodge my question."

"No, I just—"

"Zeke. You're a secular Jew living in New York. It took your coming to Central Ohio for a friend's funeral to suddenly be quoting sacred ancient mystical texts. By heart. Postcoitally, I'll give you that, and after what was a weirdly candid relationship conversation in which I revealed more about how much I'm into you than I'd really intended when we started talking. But still. If you haven't drunk the Kool-Aid—Flavor Aid—you're seeming awfully Kool-Aid-Flavor-Aid-drinking-adjacent right now."

"I'm not that far in. At the Caves, that is. I mean, even after seeing how heated Natan could get in protecting me and how quickly this morning, I believe he killed Osman even less than ever. The 12th-commandment thing just doesn't seem like enough to make you strangle your own son."

"And if he was at football practice, telling his teammates that his father, who is supposed to be the new messiah, was fucking his parishioners?"

"Even still. Even that."

"Well, I still don't want to talk about that aspect of this mess with you, if you want me to be honest," Johanna said. Now she got up out of bed and opened the shades, cracked the window. The stars on the ceiling again disappeared. Gooseflesh broke out over Zeke's chest. Johanna came back to bed.

"But it remains a fact, what I do want to know is how much of all this Dönme stuff you believe."

"Believe. That's a weird one. I've always been attracted to faith, I guess. Belief—you can use reason to make someone believe something. You could argue to me that LeBron James is better than Michael Jordan—"

"He is."

"—using numbers and playoff statistics, et cetera. But if you wanted me to play on LeBron James's team—"

"I don't."

"—and you wanted me to have faith in him, faith that he could take over a game and help me be a better player, I don't think that's just belief. That's real faith, and it stands separate from reason.

Apart from the part of your intellectual mind that processes it. That's really appealing. I mean, reading a whole bunch of religious texts might get you so far. But seeing these Dönme, the way they truly feel they're convening with the Lord—I feel a kind of jealousy, seeing it. Like honest-to-God jealous. I will confess that every single person I've met out at the Caves, even Yehoshua— even Devorah—has just seemed so centered. Did you feel it?"

"I did," Johanna said.

The cold air streamed in from the window over them both and for a time they were quiet. After his conversation with Natan, Zeke found himself consciously thinking about the snow outside melting to water, evaporating into a gas, and the cold of it coming in through his lungs. No good, no evil, just everything in between. In the silence, layers of sound that had not been apparent were revealed: the squeal of brakes on tires miles away. The humming of electricity from sockets around them. That neutrons were being encircled by electrons, that Johanna's heart was beating in the bed next to Zeke.

"But it also seemed like they were willing to have faith," Johanna said. "Seeing them all with their heads to the ground like that—they looked like Muslims. But then, as you've explained it to me, they're Jews. You put it all together and it doesn't make any sense—"

"But the idea of faith is that it doesn't have to make—"

"Hear me out! That if anything, their belief, or faith, or whatever abstraction you want to put on it, is hugely practical. Four hundred years ago, their predecessors decided to present themselves to the world as Muslims so that they could survive. But they barely learned any Arabic, barely even cracked the Qur'an. They found the trappings of what it looks like to be Muslim, and they owned it. But they kept reading Torah in their places of worship all along. Did Nathan say anything in your time with him that suggested he had any sense of the actual practice of Islam?"

"No."

"I truly, honestly don't think you should go back to the Caves. It won't hurt them for you to ghost. It won't do anything for your writing to be there again—you've got what you need. And listen— you can stay here tonight. Sleep here so you don't have to be at the cabin tonight in case Shaw or Flaxton or any of the fanatics come by. You can just go back under cover of daylight tomorrow, pack up, and get out of here."

"Aw," Zeke said.

"What."

"You want me to stay the night."

"That's not what I—oh, what the fuck. I'll keep the honesty alive. Yes, I want you to stay here. I'll even ride out to the cabin in the morning if you'd feel safer having someone there when you go back."

"I won't," Zeke said. Johanna did not move any closer to him physically then, did not curl up or attempt to spoon. But in that bed, with the cold air just vaguely awakening him, and the glow of the false constellation of star stickers above him, Zeke thought he could comprehend something, lying in bed next to Johanna. That there was something beyond her flesh and beyond his, a presence that was not body and was not shell in the space between them, one that he could feel: there was a spark in the bed next to him that was something other than just Johanna, something other than arms and legs and head and flesh. Something that was wholly *Johanna*, but that also wasn't wholly *not* Zeke himself, too. Part of the same whole. That he could not see her in the room's dark, but that not being able to see had brought a comprehension light would not have brought, that as their breathing was in sync in the moments before sleep there was a Johanna and there was a Zeke, that there was a room and a bed and outside in the night thousands of undergraduates at Ohio State in bars and in frat houses up and down High Street, but that they were all part of an Ein Sof, one single indiscriminate mass whose lines, whose boundaries, were surely not as finite as Zeke had perceived them to be at any point earlier in his life. That he was something of the same as she was, a divine spark not limited by body, and that they were just as close without touching now as they'd have been if they were. It was in this state of newfound comprehension that Zeke passed into a dreamless sleep for the last Monday he would be in the state of Ohio.

RACCOON BREAK-IN

The door to Zeke's Airbnb is wide open. It does not appear to have been forced open, but the inside of the cabin looks as if the face of the whirlwind has turned its gaze upon every object.

The television lies in the middle of the bathtub.

Glass splintered all about the tub.

The top of Zeke's suitcase has been torn from the rest of the bag, his clothes scattered all about the room. Burn marks mar the rug throughout. When Zeke stops and takes it in, looks closely, he can see smoldering smoke still lifting toward the ceiling. The burning plastic stench of burning plastic rug permeates the air.

Then a loud bang from the bathroom. Whoever has done this, is doing this, will be doing this, will be doing this to him, is still here.

Zeke turns and runs too quickly to see that a raccoon has taken advantage of the open room, that it is bolting from the bathroom and making the sound there. Zeke runs to the riverbank. He has the sheriff's office's number in his phone from the calls he's placed asking for comment that have not been returned. Two minutes later

Zeke still hasn't seen anyone leave the cabin. Five minutes later Zeke still hasn't seen anyone leave the cabin. Eight minutes later Zeke still hasn't seen anyone leave the cabin.

Eight and a half minutes later the sheriff's cruiser, last year's Dodge Viper—a car the magazine Zeke works for gave a very poor review for performance, fuel efficiency, and design—pulls leisurely into the parking lot. Sheriff Shaw steps out of the vehicle.

He is alone.

"What seems to the be the problem here," Sheriff Shaw says. There is an ursine complacency to the man, the way he carries his beery weight as if it's not quite ready for use, yet terrifying for its six-foot-three quiddity. His hand never strays far from the sidearm on his hip, like some magnetic attraction keeps it orbiting there.

"I called to report that the cabin I'm renting has been ransacked. I'm pretty sure there was still someone in there when I arrived and I haven't seen anyone leave since I called. Though there's a small chance it was a raccoon. But. Still. Raccoons didn't do . . . this."

"Let's have a look." Sheriff Shaw carries his grizzly body leisurely into the cabin. A minute passes. Thirty more seconds. The sheriff comes back out. "Nothing in there at all. Guess your magazine will have to pay for all that damage."

"Not if I file a report. It's clearly breaking and entering."

"Let's drive you down to the station and you can file a report, then." Zeke has a look at the newish Dodge Viper with the black racing stripe and "Mt. Izmir Sheriff" painted on its side. He has a look at his rental. No choice but to get in.

It's cold in the back of the cruiser. For his first job Zeke worked as a stringer at the paper of record, and he would occasionally do ride-arounds with the NYPD. They'd let him ride shotgun.

He will not be riding shotgun with Sheriff Shaw.

The snow has picked up as they make their way into town. Zeke can see Mt. Izmir more clearly than he did the first time he got into that Uber his first day, not having to pay attention to the road. If he weren't with Shaw, he'd take out his recorder and make some voice notes about the surroundings: Drooping limbs like overburdened parents on the trees alongside the road. The expanse of gray sky covering the horizon for miles. Houses with facades succumbing to ill repair, pastel paint of what were clearly once beautiful Victorians flaking, denuding wood.

"I know you think my son killed that kid," Sheriff Shaw says. "We can get that out of the way first thing. That's why I didn't return your calls."

"I don't think that," Zeke says. "For as long as I've been here, I still don't know what to think about any of it. I'm not a lawyer or a DA. I've drawn no conclusions. I just . . . don't know."

"I know you don't. No one could. You sit back a million miles looking for stars and all you're gonna see are stars. You get up close and it's a burning ball of fiery Boschian hellscape. Now here you are, friend—your nose right up in it."

Shaw looks in the rearview mirror, staring right at Zeke's swollen, broken beak.

"That looks painful," he continues. He adjusts his rearview mirror, adjusts his seat belt. "Look, I know those boys didn't have airtight alibis like the prosecutor said. Sometimes a prosecutor will get out there and just clean shit up so a grand jury will have it a bit neater than it was. I know there was some fudging facts up front. But that doesn't change things. I'll tell you some facts so you can get on your way."

He makes a right out of town. The low slow fields roll away, along with them the businesses of Mt. Izmir, the houses and barns, so every inch, every foot they travel, they're more alone together.

"Fergus and Deshawn were both benched the day Osman died. Was killed. Murdered. They'd missed a week of practice for some fucking around or another, and each had been injured the previous week, so it wouldn't have raised any eyebrows if they weren't in the game. So they didn't show up, and if you asked anyone who was there, 'Were Shaw and Flaxton in the game?' they'd say yes. Did say yes. Over and over. But shit, the boys weren't on the field and everyone was in uniform, so you couldn't say for sure if they were there. I was paying far too much attention to the outcome of the game while it was being played."

Shaw pauses a minute, allowing his foot to leave the gas pedal just a bit. He rolls down his window so he can smoke a cigarette. Then he rolls down Zeke's and offers him a Camel Filter.

"I do know they didn't kill that kid," Shaw says. "That crazy Jewish fanatic killed the kid."

"That is news," Zeke says. "All of it. But I don't see why you need to consider Natan a fanatic. It seems to me after nearly a week here that folks just have a false sense of the Dönme, generally. Like they signify all the wrong stuff all at the same moment. Islamic. Messianic. Hasidic. Very, very not Christian."

"Well, except for the messianic part."

"Point taken."

Shaw is silent for another minute. During his silence Zeke notes that they're not headed anywhere near to the station. They're headed in the direction opposite. It's truly desolate now. His stomach drops.

"Town was back that way."

"Not taking you to town," Shaw says.

"Well, where are you taking me, then?"

"Taking you to campus." As they hit the distant outskirts of town, the hill climbs perceptibly. Cornfields sprawl out to their left. On the right, hills roll up toward the gray Mt. Izmir skies. They're on SR-314, the back way to campus, a route Zeke hasn't been on since he was a senior in college. Hills roll, and the speedometer on the cruiser hits forty, forty-five, fifty-nine. Seventy-two. It's a roller coaster on their stomachs.

"I don't wanna make assumptions about you any longer and I don't want you to make them about me," Shaw says. "We're heading up to William James campus to have us a little walk around. See, the thing is, you and Gram and your friends aren't the only successful alumni of that place. I'm an alum. A small-liberal-arts-school alum. Of the same fucking college you went to. Man, I was a senior when you were a freshman. Probably you don't remember me."

Zeke is so surprised he doesn't even respond for a second.

"No," he says. "Fuck, no. I'm sorry. I don't—I mean—that was a long time ago and you're really—"

"A small-city sheriff."

"I was gonna say tall. With kids."

"I was on the basketball team, so I didn't get to do much more than play and study my senior year. By the time we graduated, Chelsea was pregnant. Eventually had three. I get it. I know, of course, you don't have kids, out here reporting, out here to say goodbye to Gram and seeing your ex and all. And I get what you must've thought of me. I'm not a fool. Probably you thought: small-town sheriff, cliché cliché cliché. But the truth is, I graduated from William James just four years before you guys. I actually knew Gram Silver a little. We were in an art history class together, if you can believe it."

"I only kind of can, to be honest," Zeke says. "Has Declan made the connection?"

"He has. He has. But. When Gram moved back, we saw each other once or twice, ran into each other really, and it was cordial but brief. I liked that guy. Everyone did. But he was dark when he got back from the coast, and . . . well, you know. And I am sorry for your loss. Awful. Awful news. But beyond that, I kinda steer clear of the campus. They don't much like us to be up there. They have their own security now. Since all the complicated Title IX shit, after Obama, we really don't head up there if we don't have to, and we don't much mix with the William James folk. I won't say it makes anyone happy much, being so divided, but it's how life has turned, and we accept it. What other choice. We accept it as what it is: the truth. If there's one thing I carry with me from that liberal arts school experience—other than all the Natty Ice we drank— it's that. Truth. Respect truth. To thine own self be true."

Zeke watches a column of smoke shoot hard from the corner of Shaw's popeyed mouth and out into the cold air, where it expands into a large cloud passing by his window. He takes a drag of his own.

"What's your first name," Zeke asks.

"Earnest," Shaw says. "Earnest Shaw. Folks call me Ernie. Anyway. It's the truth. Hell, we could've been friends if we'd been in that art history class with Gram together. Then. Maybe I wouldn't have—I wouldn't have had to get rough with you the other day. But. We all started out as the students we were, and we all headed off to the worlds we headed off to. That's a fact. Here's some facts about me, about the father of Fergus Shaw, that might help you straighten out how you're thinking about this. I grew up in Columbus. Father was one of the biggest contractors in the city. Big jobs. Built a whole lot of the OSU campus. Dorms, academic buildings. He sent me up here. Didn't study law. I studied religion. When I was a sophomore, I thought maybe I'd do best to go to divinity school. The good Lord strapped me with this massive body and made me both play basketball with it and carry it to parties, parties full of aspiring biologists and musicians and aspiring writers like you, so I was the center on the football team, too—D-III, but still. And I even had some crazy years, crazy years I'm not proud of but that I know you'd uncover if you did your reporting fully. I slung bags of weed for a couple years. Not much to do out here after a while, and them that don't go straight to meth or opiates smoke, sell, a lotta weed. Me, too. Even got caught. It was that that brought me to the other side, though knowing how it works does help me in my work now. Two sides of the same coin in a way, that."

They reach the center of campus.

"Now hop out."

They're at the top of the hill. Even in the cold, a handful of Amish stand on a gravel path selling pies and meat. They walk between two huge stone obelisks and on to the main part of campus. It is a spill of hyper-Gothic buildings, spires and gargoyles, sandstone buttresses and modern chrome and glass. Hundreds of millions of dollars of buildings. Shaw walks off the path into maybe six inches of crunching snow. They are in the middle of a new-looking quad.

"This was James Hall when I was a student," Shaw says. "We read *Varieties of Religious Experience* right in there. You remember him, I'm sure—Professor Soule. His father had been a student of a student of James himself, back at Harvard at the turn of the century. I was very attracted to it. I still remember passages from that book from memory. Professor had us memorize whole paragraphs like they used to do in the 1800s. 'How irrelevantly remote seem all our usual refined optimisms and . . . uh . . . and . . . and intellectual and moral consolations in presence of a need of help like this! Here is the real core of the . . . of the religious problem: Help! Help! No prophet can claim to bring a final message unless he says things that will have a sound of reality in the ears of victims such as these.'

"If you think for a second," Shaw continues, "your friend Nathan's messianic impulse at all times isn't to construct such need for help, well. Maybe you needed more time in Professor Soule's seminar room. Or you're in need of help. Which I guess you are, after what you went through with Gram, and now this. Your eye. And now your nose. That's most of your face. I don't mean to point. But I can't help but notice. And warden told me about your trouble with his guards yesterday."

They stand at the center of that quad, and for the first time since Zeke's been there the snow has slowed to the point where you might not say it was snowing, exactly. Flakes at random blow by, but they could as well be coming from treetops as the firmament. At the tops of the buildings around them, at the edges of their facades, someone has installed black crows, lifelike statues.

"Well," Zeke says. "This is all . . . not exactly where I'd expected you to take all this."

The two men stand opposite each other on the quad, both on campus at the same time not for the first time, but for the first time knowing each other's name.

"There's not a lot for the son of a builder with a degree in religion to do. I tried. Like I say, I got an M.Div. from Yale. Came back. And you know what there was with an M.Div. from Yale to do religiously in Central Ohio? Fuck all. I taught high school for a couple years, but you can't teach religion in public schools. Ohio doesn't have much in the way of parochial. I wanted to live here. It's a great state, and it's what I know. I love what I know.

"So I started working for the old man. It was a good business. He built half the buildings on OSU campus in those decades."

"You said."

"I know I said. Proud of it. I worked on them. I worked with the guys, and when my dad took sick, I took the business in another direction. Guys I knew were flipping houses in German Village and making forty, fifty, sixty percent on them. So for a couple years it was gangbusters. Bought a big house for ourselves, had some more kiddos. And then you can guess. Lost our shirts. So we moved up here. My parents had some land in Apple Valley. I'd had a whole slew of uncles in my dad's family who'd worked as law enforcement. Trained for the force, and it wasn't long before I got the top job. Did I want to be in law enforcement? I did not want to be in law enforcement. But it is solid work, and it's surprisingly quiet. A solid pension, solid benefits, solid salary.

"And then the Doon-mehs came to my attention. More and more came to all our attention. It's almost like we grew up as adults here together, even if we tried hard as we could not to see each other. Shit started to get tense right from the jump, more as their numbers grew and their kids got older. At first I tried to read up on them, to appeal to the religious side of things. I mean I had it in me. I got on good enough with the Amish from doing the same. But this was different. It helped for as long as it helped. But then the state said the kids needed to come to the high school here, legally they had to. And much as I didn't want to, I had to deliver the message. Not a message I wanted to deliver. Lotta folks out at the Caves weren't happy about it.

"But me and Nathan, we were good with each other most of the time. When the repo men came to try to take back that crazy-expensive cedar-and-gold ark he built with his own two hands and the help of twenty-one percent APR from MasterCard, and Nathan's boys drew guns on them, we calmed it down. I myself convinced the repo they'd better find another property to repossess, because my small town wasn't about to be turned into some Branch Davidian mess. Nathan wasn't David Koresh. I mean, shit, you know how David Koresh took over that place?"

Zeke says he knows about the story, but the details, no, he doesn't.

"We read about it in a class here. The old leader of the Branch Davidians didn't like David Koresh, didn't like the challenge he presented to leadership—but Koresh was claiming he could perform miracles. So the old leader said, OK, if Ezekiel could bring a body back to life, and you're a prophet like Ezekiel, you can do it, too. He exhumed the body of a Branch Davidian woman who'd recently died, then dared David Koresh to bring her back to life. You know what Koresh did?"

"Brought her back to life?"

"Koresh left the compound, found a pay phone so it couldn't be traced, called the cops and said, 'The leader of the Branch Davidian community just committed a felony by exhuming the body of a dead woman. He needs to be arrested for his crimes.' Waco law enforcement came and took him off to prison, and David Koresh became leader of the Branch Davidians.

"Now that's some Machiavellian shit. I don't put Nathan up to that kind of manipulation. What I see of that guy is just someone who believes in earnest—but believes too much, who has needs but needs too much, and who believes and needs enough that he's dragging a whole community down with him. He's passionate, but he is smart, and he is a believer. It's not a coincidence that folks follow him. He's a real leader. But then on top of it, when he started getting some more legit folks from down in Columbus coming up there, oldies, Orthodox in regular old business suits the past couple years—well, shit got more serious in a thousand different ways, ways I can't recount now. There was some money in there, some more sense they'd be putting down something serious. And when I say money—more money than a regular old church might bring in. Synagogue.

"And between the money and the rigidity, I'll tell you, some of them are *serious* about their religion."

"Serious, yeah, I've seen that."

There is a long pause before Earnest Shaw speaks again. Zeke just takes in all he's already heard, so he's silent, as well. He's thinking about Shaw, but he's also thinking about how on earth this will all get into his magazine story, how he'll report it back over Slack to his boss. Now editor. It's like there are three different Zekes inside this one Zeke, all ready to run in different directions. After a couple minutes, Shaw starts up again.

"Anyway. Nathan got Osman started going to the high school, like the state asked, got him hooked up with some friends down in Columbus. Osman would even come over and hang out with Fergus sometimes. But he tried out for JV football and didn't get on and he started fucking with them. Man, was that kid a pain. He would not let up on those boys in the classroom. He was smart as they come and he'd just run intellectual circles around them. I love my boy, but I raised him up here. No way we'd ever be able to send him to a place like William James College on a cop salary. We made the choices we had to. Like I say. Osman just ran intellectual circles around our boys. Fergus can run laps, but intellectual circles are not Fergus's kind of circles."

Shaw falls silent. A dusting of snow drifts from the sky.

"And you had to go out to find Osman when he was gone," Zeke says.

"You read the depositions. You probably know as much as I do about the facts of the case. We didn't get onto that land until probably four days after the kid was gone. As you can imagine, there are all kinds of sticky issues about just busting into a religious compound. There wasn't all that much forensic evidence. There was some. But even the absence of evidence, as you know, pointed to Nathan. It came from someone in the Caves, and the person in the Caves. It came from the father. That's what I'll tell you. And here's where we get to why I took you here. You see this place?"

He sees the place.

"Maybe you go to the Caves and you see a kind of little anthropological experiment to write about. Shit, maybe you go down Atatürk Street and see the same. Just a bunch of shops and some middle America like out of 1950, where you got to take advantage of a summer-camp experience of college. Someplace where time hardly moves at all. But I get who you are. I know you *mean* no harm.

"But.

"Not *meaning* harm doesn't mean you're not *causing* harm. It's time for this community to put this all behind them. It's time to do a little forgetting. I know you and your people are the people of the book, you've got memories that go back five, six thousand years. I respect it, even have some love for it. For them. And I even have a little sense of familiarity with you, being James alums. But time has passed, and we are who we are now, and I need you to believe me: I honestly love the people here in Mt. Izmir. I care for Nathan even if he did it. But sometimes the way to get past a thing is just to move past it.

"Those Doon-me up there, they're not gonna put a lick of it behind them until you're gone. You and everyone like you. So here's something familiar to you. Our alma mater. Do you know how fucking hard it's been for the admissions office of this top-thirty small liberal arts college you and I both care about to recruit when folks come to visit and have to hear about a murder? A murder that was either perpetrated by some Muslim Jews—or by the sheriff's son? It's one or the other. They're both bad. So you write your story as quick as you can and get this behind us. You saw what happened to your cabin. You felt what happened to your nose. You've probably seen more automatic weapons since you arrived here than at any other time in your life. I'll write up a report for you, for the break-in. You don't need to sign it.

"But this is what I'm here to tell you today, both as a fellow alum and as the sheriff trying to keep order here:

"Just get on a plane.

"Get the fuck out of here.

"You're no longer welcome in Mt. Izmir.

"What happens in the days ahead, here and to you, I can't predict any further. But it's going to get worse before it gets better."

IN THE VOICE OF THE PROPHET [III]

From *Shivhei ha-Natan*, the Prison Notebooks of Natan of Flatbush

On the Human Experience of Time

There are only two facts regarding time::

> *First:* The second law of thermodynamics:: Heat cannot move from a colder body to a warmer one.: The only empirically confirmed way time informs the Ein Sofistic world::
>
> *Second:* There is no memory of the future:: We have a memory of the past: There is no such thing as a memory of the future:: This is not how memory functions.: Memory is a sense wherein we only comprehend time as it moves in one direction::

: : : : :

On the Feast of the Lamb we're young and flush with the first opportunity to work and earn. We repair in the early-spring air to the Bosperous and practice the Dimming of the Candles—but this will be the natural dimming of the candles, wherein the candle is the sun itself, not the dimming of the old ways of the original Sabbatians.

The dark will lie easy upon the Ohio night of the Prophet, and he will find himself in the deep strong current of the river, the body of Tzipi and the body of Chana, Levin's wife, so close to his own, and when the body is in the water there is a fluidity to the movement and in the slick of the current the bodies will join, and this early on will be what the Dönme will build as it will be built in Istanbul of 1666 and in so many communities between. And though the Prophet will look up to see the vague outline of another that must be his wife, he will be drunk on the wine of the Lord and the sweet drawing current of the Bosperous and the smoke of the plant and this will be the new Dimming of the Candles that will last only through their first summers but will be those first sweet dark nights of community:: Redemption through sin as only Shabbetai Tzvi has previously envisioned, prescribed, lived, but not thinking I will confess to what Yael could see, what Levin could see::

Late afternoon only days after when the river tugs thick silk at her thighs I will happen upon Yael in the mikvah and she sees me and I see her as we won't have seen each other since leaving the Five Boroughs:: And Yael will cross the river and I will skip the mikvah entirely:. Wading through the water crashing about my own thighs like jagged stones and I follow Yael into the Cave of the Dragon and therein we procreate for the first time since we have arrived, and that in the Cave of the Dragon such acts occur quickly and not entirely to satisfaction of both parties but to intended effect::

: : : : :

Before long the cold of autumn will descend upon the land:. Winter next.: students at the local college return to their homes:: Months when there is no work waiting tables for many of the Dönme:: and that second winter will last longer than the first.: Snow will fall. That snow will fall on the trees and through the trees and on the ground and that to pay the heating bills of the three trailers now will take all of the Dönme's resources. Osman looks small and blue some nights, warmed only by the heat of his father's and mother's bodies. Yael's body begins growing but there will never be enough food. And like when she carried Osman, Yael will suffer morning sickness. Even Levin isn't able to ignore the granola vomited in the grass some mornings: A meal that could have been in his own belly: Inside Levin something darker arises that winter in the time after the dimming of the noonday sun, a questioning:: More and more often I find him during tish or on Shabbat in his trailer with a thick book of secular medical training in hand:: "The Rambam was a doctor," he says. In his eyes there will be something downturned. Absent. I will see him less. I leave and head to the space that one day will be the Sheep Meadow to twist the head off the last chicken and make the last eggs and offer this omelet to Yael to replace the grains in her gut::

: : : : :

Snow falls from the tops of trees in the woods that clear beside the Bosperous Creek as if separating from the sky, a supernal snowfall, a snow so cold and long it brings a chill not only to the shells but to the sparks themselves, proving as it will ever be proven that law of thermodynamics: cold bodies will not under their own volition become warm. Warmth does not pass in time into cold bodies without the detraction of cold. And now, two years removed from New York, the Prophet will understand for the first time this law of the physical universe because I experience it myself, experience it undeniably as I experience the face of the whirlwind amid prayer::

The coldest morning in early spring: snow falling. Gravid with months of late winter Yael wakes, and with a peace unlike other peace she declares herself ready. Walking the path toward the Caves:. Every so often Yael's knees buckle with the weight of on-coming child. So early morning no one stirs even for early-morning prayer. As we pass the trailers I call out to Levin, who if he is to be our Maimonides is to be our midwife, will help to bring our new one into the world. As we pass into the wood, the light arises from Levin's room. Air warm enough for spring and still a light filter of snow releases from the trees above. We both disrobe when we reach the Bosperous and our mikvah takes place in passing, the current at the creek's midway point strong enough to knock us over with the rush of melting winter. No snow falls above the creek as it did in the trees. Levin disrobes and is just behind us, trudging across the freezing water. We make it to the far bank unscathed, wet, Yael now with a deep inner concentration. With my hand against hers I feel the full force of lifting of the sparks: joy of a new birth ahead. A sense of hand touching hand and yet there being no separation between us, the full sense of the Ein Sofism arises within::

Inside the cave: embers from the previous night still crackling at the back of the space. The simple open womb the day we arrive and a thousand years from now when after the acceptance of the mashiach the space of Ein Sof will be understood to be the space of time and life and the central tenet of joy, and Yael undresses, back to the cave wall, hugging close to the embers when Levin and Devorah and Tzipi arrive. Tzipi with blankets and Devorah with pail with waters from the Bosperous. The completion of our antinomian dreams: a woman full with new life, her husband the Prophet there in full view of the supernal act. Hours pass:. Yael deep within herself: Her body in the interaction with the cold and warmth contorts and moves—Yael's hands against the wall like she is Samson moving the very support before her as the bees made honey in the lion's head. Yael groaning and grunting until she finds her position::

Yael on her back: fire crackling at its orangest and slow smoke at the mouth of the cave grants a light: from a distance of yards: I return from the creek: all previously kept from my view.: Levin turns and the darkness in his eyes is full now, a turning away: There are colors: evacuation and blood: lumping from inside all before me the act of Human Being.: A black squiggle of matted hair and brown meconium and lifeblood and darkness in Levin's eyes.: He watches: previously a sin seeing and seeing but now mitzvah through sin: revelation through sin: the prophetic acceptance of all acts and all that will come to be::

"Do you want to catch him?" Tzipi asks, the kibbutz on which she lived before joining the Dönme community having given her a chance to work as a midwife: her hands are adept: I reach in as the head comes out: since Osman has come from this place before it happens so fast Yael squeezing knees to chest: a small packaged spark of being: sucking herself in tight until all at once unspools: baby cord bleating sack of lifeblood into my arms: I am covered: for that moment the stopping of time: embodiment of joy:: Small purple face twisted head in the shape of a cone: Somehow this being appears as a dream of a dream and not the essential spark of life: Levin cutting the cord stanching the blood: Devorah saying preparation: "He will come out looking like a little monster, but then there is the first breath and all will be as it should"::

: : : : :

I hand the baby to Levin and he looks. We all await breath and the cry I remember breath and the cry of tiny Osman when he was this small and I do not remember him being this blue this purple or it taking this long, so long: No memory of so long the stoppage of time for a cry to come:: The cry will not come:: Does not come:: Does not ever come::

FREE PROPHET

Zeke is getting ready to leave Johanna's apartment when his phone buzzes. His phone does the two separate but clearly distinct buzzes. One is long when news has arrived from the paper of record. One is short when the news is coming from a friend, in the form of a text message. This buzz is short. It is a text message from his boss, who never texts, always just uses Slack messages, so he knows it's big before even reading:

CALL CAME FOR YOU HERE AT THE OFFICE.
NATHAN FRITZMAN'S APPEAL GRANTED. TO BE
RELEASED TOMORROW. PROBLY SHOULD GET
UP TO HIS COMPOUND.

Zeke has to read the message three times even to believe it. It is early morning just before he is to drive back up to his Airbnb and on to Mt. Izmir. He is sitting on the edge of Johanna's bed, pulling on his socks. He has reached an age where pulling on socks is, if not quite a struggle, then for the first time not the easiest thing he does in his day.

"You have to see this," he says. "You . . . won't believe it."

Johanna is in the bathroom. She's just about prepared for her day, having woken more than an hour earlier. In just a week Zeke's grown comfortable enough to come down here and sleep with her every night, and to remain sleeping in her bed until after she has risen. Time always passes differently when you're on the road. Time always passes differently when you've just begun a relationship. Differently when you're alone in a room, together in a room.

Time passes differently here.

He walks in his socks to the threshold of her bathroom, where the door is open. Johanna is completely dressed and doing something with a tweezer and an eyebrow. He hands her the phone.

"Well," Johanna says. "My day is now utterly fucked."

"Imagine Natan's day."

"I cannot imagine that, no. And I won't. Empathy for a murderer is not a kind of empathy I would practice even if it wasn't my job to continue to help in his prosecution through appeal."

"So I guess this means you will not be joining me on my trip to Mt. Izmir."

"As I say," Johanna says. "My day. Now fucked. I will have to see what this even means. I mean. Just. How."

Zeke takes his phone back. He returns to Johanna's bed, where he again sits on the mattress's edge and pulls on his jeans. The drive to his cabin will take forty-five minutes, and another fifteen minutes from there to the Caves. Zeke leaves Johanna's apartment without saying goodbye. He decides he'll skip the cabin and just head straight to the Caves.

❧ BOOK THREE ❧

THE LIFTING OF THE SPARKS

There was bustle. Maaminim with rifles across their shoulders flitted past and by the entrance without giving him much more than a glance. They were now preparing for the Prophet. Zeke parked and set out to find Yehoshua, who was sitting on the steps to his trailer, face to the sky.

"Zeke," he said. He stood and walked to him and hugged him, leaving his head on Zeke's shoulder for an uncomfortably long time. They did not need to speak of what was to transpire. They both knew what the other knew from the look on his face.

"I'll go ahead and suppose you're too busy to take me to the cave today instead," Zeke said.

"I'm busy at the act of waiting. But I have been busy at the act of waiting my whole life."

"No, seriously, Josh. I mean we know that Natan is coming back now. We should hardly be focused on me."

"That's exactly why we *should* be focused on you. Yesterday got scuttled, but today—today is today. Let's get you to the mikvah. We can deal with the rest later."

"You're sure," Zeke said.

So Yehoshua led the way down the path they'd now walked together a half dozen times. He handed Zeke a vape pen, and each time Zeke tried to hand it back after a hit, Yehoshua demurred, saying, "Yours yours yours." Halfway to the Bosperous Creek, the crackling of footsteps began on the path behind them. A single-file line of Dönme, rifles slung over their shoulders, was following them down the path. Apparently some armed maaminim were not too distracted by preparations for the imminent return of the Prophet to give him an imposing escort.

"You remember where it is," Yehoshua said. He didn't acknowledge what they'd both seen behind them. "One tradition of our particular mikvah is this. Your first trip there is a trip you'll take alone."

Like he did on the first day they met, Yehoshua pulled out a glass bowl and packed it with some green bud crawling with red hairs. It was actually somewhere north of amazing how much nugget and what good-quality nugget everyone at the Caves seemed to have on hand at all times—it must have cost a fortune. But Zeke hadn't even thought to ask yet where it was all coming from; he was enjoying it. He took a long toke, breathed out. The only smoke was the smoke of the cold in the air. Zeke took the bowl, already stoned out of his gourd from the vape pen, and inhaled, exhaled. It occurred to him only then for the first time in these woods there was no snow falling. The crunching of footsteps on a thin layer of snow was more brittle than in the past. Snow had taken on a crusted shell as weather warmed, and the topmost layers melted only to be frozen by those below them, until before long they were water. Dampening ground beneath. It was growing warmer every day, the spring having begun to migrate west from New York. Occasional flakes drifted in a seesaw trajectory from above, but it would have been a stretch to call it snow.

Zeke handed the glass back to Yehoshua. They walked on.

"I received a message from the Prophet," Yehoshua said.

"I mean, I assumed so."

"Oh, no, not that. I know that. He knew you would be here. He wanted you involved in preparation for his return. He wants you to be here, he wants everyone to be here when he returns, and he told me about your visit. Being stuck in a prison cell for so long, and our lawyer had been telling him it was mostly bad news on his appeal, that he could be in there a lot longer."

"I thought Natan doesn't believe in time."

"Hah! What a narrow conception of Ein Sofism. I get it. This must hurt—OK, sorry, I won't touch again. I know you're not happy about them back there. But it's our mikvah, and how we do things. You're the first kafir ever invited to the Cave of the Dragon."

They continued to walk until the slow rush of the creek began to carry on the wind to them. Zeke put his hand to his eye, where the stitches over his brow were now the most painful they'd been. It was as if there were simply strands of string woven through his healed flesh, and the red inflammation around them was growing angry with threatened infection. His nose throbbed. The pot they'd smoked his first day there had mostly given him a body high, but now a new sensation was crawling up the back of his neck—it felt more like the oncoming weirdness of eating mushrooms or acid than smoking pot. His whole body felt the coldest it had ever felt, then flashed hot in the winter chill. He was still wearing his Patagonia fleece. With the air having grown warmer, he could feel the cold creek's frigidity lifting off the water.

DANIEL TORDAY

One of the Dönme with his rifle stopped maybe a hundred feet behind them on the path.

"From here you are on your own. You are to proceed on to the Cave of the Dragon."

Zeke's feet did not move. This happened sometimes when he was too stoned, especially if he was smoking too much indica. Couldn't walk. Sometimes when he was younger he'd get so high he could only clutch the arms of the chair in which he was sitting. Yehoshua interpreted his lack of movement differently. Zeke could see him look up at the rifleman behind him. Zeke managed to look behind him. The rifleman was down on one knee, rifle aimed at him.

"This is not the only one," Yehoshua said. "He came with four others. They're all back there in the woods along the path. You've come this far, so you need to go. Strip."

Seeing the rifle trained on him shook some stoniness from Zeke's head. There were moments as a journalist you would never accept in your daily life, but you knew would benefit you. You simply acted. As if, Zeke supposed, you were not subject to the prehensile grip of time, were simply rising to meet each moment as it rose to be met. He walked until he reached the riverbank, Yehoshua not far behind him, and pulled the gloves off his hands and dropped them to the ground. He pulled down the zipper on his fleece. Dropped the jacket on the ground. Pulled his sweater over his head with his long underwear shirt and T-shirt in it. The cold struck his bare skin like a thousand pinpricks, his breath stuck in his throat. He took off his boots one at a time and let them fall beside his jacket and shirts. He had on only a pair of boxer briefs. The snow under his feet was like razors, ice cold, poking at his skin. It rose straight up through his frigid body like an electric current.

"I'll leave you to it," Yehoshua said. "This might be a weird time

192

to talk about it, but keep in mind *why* you're doing this. Mystical experience. The idea of the mystical experience is devekut: to convene with the grace of the Lord. Not the Prophet, not even Shabbetai Tzvi. Just you and Her, the Shekinah. Go find Her. Once you've crossed the water, you'll feel it. You'll be there."

Yehoshua turned to leave. He walked back up the path by the Dönme with his rifle. The rifle stayed trained on Zeke.

:::::

The lip of the creek was frozen solid. Cold on each of Zeke's feet sharpened its razors. The numbness. Numbness more dangerous than the cold. A cold so intense you could hardly think. Could hardly see with the blinding-white cold on feet. When he was a kid, he felt water so hot it was cold pouring out of the bathtub faucet for the first time. Now he felt water so cold it was hot. There was only one way this was going to work. Jump. The glug of water up about his ears. His muscles so cold they went tight. Shocked by electricity. He had to move. His head came back up into the air, and cold struck twice as hard, water hitting air like a live wire. The rush of blood in his ears and the still white smell of snow in his nose forced near all sensation onto his skin—he was a creature equipped only with a single sense informing all others: touch. He was a touch detector, a living, breathing touch machine. The bracing white in his eyes, the bracing nothingness of smell, the bracing ice taste in his mouth—all subsets of the feeling of freezing skin. One foot, then the other, and he was nearly to the middle of the creek. Water rushed down at him in a heavy current like three strong men pushing pushing pushing. He stumbled in the middle of the creek and again his head went under, came up. His foot was so numb he could only barely feel the slippery moss riming the round stone under his left foot granting a toehold. He couldn't think. A feeling of sleepiness slowed his mind, and he thought, *Must move*. If he could have thought, he might have thought he wouldn't make it. But he couldn't. Didn't.

He put his arms up so that his forearms led and his shoulders followed, and he pushed himself hard, harder, a torque of torso and a cold sharp thrust of his left foot against slippery mossy rock and sloshing across the most intense of the current he looked ahead and he could see on the other bank there was no ice. It had been trod down, smashed, and on a rock sat a towel. A goal. Push, slosh, the glub and glurg of stoned wild lightning in his head, and there he was, towel around shoulders until on another rock nearby a navy-blue Pendleton blanket and next to it a small packet just large enough to see. Next to it a can of beer. His heart pounded in his ears and his breath was foreshortening and he shook like a paint mixer, the sound of his teeth slamming against themselves in his mouth, and for the first time he could remember he prayed to God, he prayed for warmth and completion of this task. *Help! Help!* he thought. He thought of that white-bearded old man from his childhood who scared him into returning the baseball cards he'd stolen at the local Walmart, the fear of retribution so great—thou shalt honor thy father and mother shall not covet thy neighbor's ass shall not shall not and each of them a thing that wouldn't happen in the future and had not happened in the past and would be punished so severely and the sound of teeth slamming against each other eased. Next to the towel the packet, which he lifted. In it a powder meant for bumping and he bumped it and a beer for warmth in his gullet and he gulped it. He could see clearly again, and though the cold still pricked his face and rattled his shoulders he was warming enough to stand.

What Zeke saw then he saw deep inside, the whole supernal

world but a narrow dark tunnel before his eyes, a vision. Perhaps it was the desire for warmth that put a flame before his eyes. Need for a celestial body to warm him put four celestial bodies before him; they descended from the clouds above into the narrow diffuse range of vision's tunnel. In Central Ohio, in winter, it is a stretch to call what roils above cloud or clouds—instead a single Ein Sofistic mass of cloud covering everything above it. Zeke sat beside the Bosperous free from the pull of the icy water, waiting for feeling to return to his hands, and saw flame and then descending from the flame and cloud in wisps he saw four bodies. Each had four faces and four wings, and each of the four faces of each of the bodies was the face of a lion, the face of an ox, the face of a goat, and the face of a man. And each had a pair of wings for each arm and each foot and covering each foot and each arm and another pair of wings on their back to hold them aloft. And though these faces arose from deep inside him, Zeke saw them before him as they turned in his head like wheels within wheels, wheels turning inside him and turning before him. And when each of these bodies turned away, their backs were covered in eyes, eyes each upon each and each upon him, and he felt rise within himself a screaming terror that could only cause him to follow them, and in following them he looked down to see he was on a chariot, a chariot that glinted with burnished copper, as did the skin of these four four-headed beings, and he was moving deeper and deeper within himself, deeper and deeper into a series of palaces of indeterminate size and with floors of glowing burnished copper and glowing burnished granite and supernal glowing burnished pine, until he looked again to see that these four beings had vanished, and the chariot had vanished and he was back on his feet without remembering how he'd stood and he was standing before the Cave of the Dragon in front of him a blinding supernal light. A blanket wrapped around his arms and wheels turning within wheels at the center of his chest. Somehow in his memory of having seen those beings and their chariot, it arose there was a fifth figure, a being who was just a man with a single head and no wings and a baby in his arms. Now he was looking out at the Cave of the Dragon and the vision fled.

There was a great light emanating from inside the cave. It became clear immediately upon seeing it why this close, just on the opposite bank, Zeke had not been able to see into the Cave of the Dragon until now—it was not precisely a cave. It was an overhang whose rump faced the creek, mossy, grown heavy with tree and rock. But on the other side of the overhang, a shelf of rock large enough to cover a man or a man and wife or husband. Someone among the Dönme back in the protection of their community on the other side of the Bosperous had lit a fire under the cave. The roof of the cave was black with the soot of two decades of fire. He was still so cold he could not but look inside himself, but with fire before him Zeke ran, ran to the side of the fire.

At first the blue flames were painful upon his skin. It was more a shock to his skin even than the sensation of cold had been—fingers regained the ability to move and the dancing flames so close to them felt cold and hot, then cold, then hot, and all a charge of pain like a baby feeling first the world, the breath returning to his chest at regular pace. The other side of the air from him was another spark, not of a human body but of a single fire with a single flame, and as it warmed his body, it made him again feel his skin as skin, made his jaw set and his body cease its shaking. The lack of distance between him and the flame. The lack of distance between body and any other spark-inside-a-shell that might have been next to a flame. As the relative peace of revelation was upon him, something new:

The dragon.

The dragon was not a dragon. The dragon was a prickling upon the very tips of his fingers and the edges of his skin. The dragon was pure sound. A rushing in his ears, and where in the frozen mikvah he'd been a man imbued with a single sense—the sense of touch—now he was a man with a single sense—the sense of hearing, all other senses wholly subordinate. A rushing in his ears like the taking off of every airplane on the planet, the scream of every foreshortened child's life, and like Natan and like Natan's followers, Zeke wished his were the deaf ears of Leah upon giving birth to Levi, that in his mouth were the mumbling tongue of Moses, and words and sounds alike were the ineffable babel of silence.

: : : : :

The flame was out. Now the black of the black in the bedroom of Johanna without even the glow-in-the-dark stars on its ceiling, the dark of his first time eating mushrooms when he fell down after they kicked in and for a reason he could never understand went momentarily blind. Night had begun to fall with the late-afternoon Ohio gloaming. Zeke walked back down the path where he had come up to the Cave of the Dragon. There he found that someone had left his clothing for him. A note on top:

"Two hundred yards upstream from the mikvah crossing the creek narrows. A broad tree trunk lies across it. You may cross there and return."

AFTERVISION

It wasn't long before Zeke was warm again. Surprisingly so, with the sun nearly set and the temperature dropping to where, even without icy river water, air was painful. Snow was again falling. Snow was always falling here at the Caves, though in Central Ohio snow did not always fall in the winter. Zeke walked along the far bank of the Bosperous Creek. It narrowed as it moved upstream until he was maybe fifty yards from the other shore. And all at once the world returned to him as smell: the cold hard smell of snow. Zeke knelt and uncovered dirt and he smelled the dirt. It smelled of dirt. Hard frozen dirt but still the sense of the world. In the treetops over his head maybe five or six wrens were playing across the branches and those branches released snow. This was what had kept the snow falling each time Zeke came through the wood and down the path in the past. Birds stepping the fallen snow from branches. There was a sound like a small tea party tinkling down near his knees, and again Zeke knelt, but this time by the creek. There was no dense ice cover here, but instead the thin plate of nearly transparent ice that forms over moving water. The sound of tea party was the tinkling of water, the ever tinkling water under that fragility of ice shelf.

The segment of ice shelf broke off in Zeke's hand like thin toffee. He put it to his lips and the cold was a cold he could handle, no memory elicited of the cold of being in the creek just minutes before. He put it to his lips, and the mountain cold of watery ice on lips and tongue in this place five hundred miles from any mountain brought the whole of the world nearer. The world beyond the world within the qelippot, the lifted sparks all coming together as one. Now he was experiencing a sense of the Ein Sof as being contiguous with himself. It was contiguous. It was mountain stream water where there was no mountain and there was no stream. Zeke could feel the ice cold of the water as it passed between his lips, past his tongue all the way to the back of his throat, the cold of the liquid as it cleared his esophagus and down into his stomach and a numbness spread inside, tying taste to touch throughout innards. The outside had come to his inside much as what was inside him had just appeared on the outside. Inside of him was a spark. Outside of him were the sparks of all other sparks.

For the first time since he'd arrived in Ohio, and likely he didn't know it but in days before that, he was not thinking of a lost friend, of a murdered child, of the death of the dead. He felt gratitude to whoever had placed the fire in the pit of the cave, and while this was not something he could have anticipated, he felt invigorated. He'd never even considered joining his cousin who went to Brighton Beach every winter to participate in a polar bear club, but now he'd swum across the heavy current of the Bosperous Creek in late winter and he felt like a shiny new penny in the strong cold winter sun.

And it was in the spirit of that rebirth that Zeke found Yehoshua Green at the trailer on the other side of the path. There was no smile on his face, but when he saw Zeke, something curious passed in his eyes.

"What do you make of the mikvah," Yehoshua said.

"It's cold."

"A cold you'll run from? Stay away from?"

"No," Zeke said. "No, I wouldn't say that. But I'm not sure I'd want to go again anytime soon."

His tongue was a thick cold slab of unmoving meat in his frigid mouth. There was silence between the two men.

"Tomorrow morning you'll join us here at the Caves again first thing. To be here when the Prophet returns. Word has come that he'll now be released tomorrow morning. I'll tell Faiz Effendi and the others. And take care of yourself."

Zeke agreed. He would take care of himself. He was stoned, he was more than a little terrified, he was still prickling with the cold of the creek and the warmth of the Cave of the Dragon. He would need to call Johanna; he would need to get on Slack and update his boss, his editor, his editor boss, for the first time in a minute. There was really a lot to do to get this story he had set out to get. First there was one last thing: he needed his stitches out. He reminded Yehoshua of it.

"Ah, yes, we've promised. We will take care of it tomorrow." He looked up to where he could see the raw, angry red skin over Zeke's eye. "Or scratch that. We'll take care of it right now."

IN THE VOICE OF THE PROPHET [IV]

From *Shivhei ha-Natan*, the Prison Notebooks of Natan of Flatbush

On Confinement

All experience of being is the same as all experiences of being.: their actions come in confining prisoners:: There is no evil but in confinement:: Redemption through sin on its face is the experience of allowing every spark to be lifted in its freedom the sparks will be returned to their ascent, selah:: Every action of the procedure to free each individual perception from the detention of guards is a move toward the coming of the mashiach::

: : : : :

Redemption through sin::

: : : : :

The look on Tzipi's face as she suctions the baby's airway:: we can see the blue of baby's skin.: no sensation no memory but I don't feel movement here in the Cave of the Dragon: Tzipi looks at Levin: Levin looks at me, says: "I have seen this before: Genetics: We could get in the car and drive to Columbus, but I don't know what good it will do, it's an hour and an hour is far too long without breath this is why you do this on an OB ward":: Arrive at the lip of the Bosperous.: this blue body in my arms.: nothing looks like the world:: The rush of water around my arms knocks me submerged::

Under the water rejoining in time and space of the Dimming of the Candles:: Consider giving it up:: Body downstream to water wet with cold:: Let my own body follow space not time not space:: Arm around the body: Other hand planted on the creek bed:: Thrust us both up and out of the current:: Cold.: wet.: reach shore:: Feet find purchase.: Wood.:

Snow again from the trees above becomes one with the water on my shoulders.: The Ein Sof:: Water cold bodies touching and at once moving and not and all one:: I reach the field and there are all ninety-seven of us the Dönme: awaiting the joyous announcement::

The looks as the tight eyes tighten, the corners of mouths turn downward: I find my footing all at once and holding the body to mine I look into each one of those eyes and say.: "We have named him Shabbetai. He is here, among us. Join me in putting him to rest." As we are walking in the wood now in the direction opposite the cave whose light is too far behind me I will say to whoever is behind me: "Tell Yael this had to happen without her." The morning light breaking over the horizon with a pink I have only before seen that night:: The light so thin and so all-encompassing the air itself grows colder. Water on every inch of my body and his and every inch every photon and every quark on my body alive to the individual clot that was once me and was once him and once her and the cold disappears and with it time feeling consequence and all but the absence of joy:: Someone hands the Prophet a shovel::

: : : : :

First morning of spring: Snow. Snow bears with it a note. I wake on a late March morning with the snow falling loosely about morning prayer. I assume Yael has taken to the mikvah for her morning cleansing before the first prayer, though it has been so cold since the night. Prayer passes without our seeing Yael & when I enter our trailer I find the note there: "The snow falls and falls and falls, and around us there is nothing but cold and mourning and prayer," the note reads. The Prophet reads the note over & takes it & tears it to pieces & takes the pieces & he puts them in the palm of his hand & takes them down to the creek & across the creek & in the corner of the Cave of the Dragon he burns them:: The Prophet if he is honest knows what has driven his wife from here & he will not communicate with her and he will not seek her out:: Never to see Yael again::

The Prophet spends the night and the next asleep in the cave:: Asleep dreaming and writhing until he comes back across the creek to the community where each trailer is shut up against the winter cold:: He goes into his own trailer where he finds Tzipi and Devorah have been taking care of Osman, and I hold that boy as tight as I can, and he and I cry together as I realize my luck that Yael has left him here instead of taking him from our midst::

And the next morning reeling when I go to Levin's trailer there is a note there too: He will attend secular medical school in Columbus, to the south. He is gone—and Yael—::

MAIMONIDES WASN'T
A PHLEBOTOMIST

Twenty minutes removed from the frozen mikvah, Zeke sits in the largest, warmest trailer he's been in since his first time at the Caves. Natan's trailer. He is given some time alone, spun and frigid after the past couple hours, in the small bathroom. Crusted hard swoops of shaving cream and toothpaste dot the sink. Small white flecks of both dot the mirror on the vanity. For the first time in days, weeks, maybe even months, Zeke stands and looks at himself in the mirror.

Above his right eye a lump like a small crab cake has replaced the skin and muscle, of that size and consistency. He moves closer and pushes his index finger against it, and a flash of pain jolts him to his knees. Just maybe a quarter inch, less, of prickly nondissolvable stitches stick out like the ends of a sea anemone escaping skin. It makes him sick to his stomach—the mere absurdity of how quickly it's healed, the pain of skin around surgical wire, the way it's transformed his face—and he retches into the Prophet's toilet. Wipes the edges of his mouth with toilet paper, then some around the toilet seat. Gets up and views his sweaty, drugged-out, frozen-up face in the mirror once more, sees now that his nose is most certainly broken from his fall the day before. Lots of damage to the one face he'll ever have. *You get just the one face,* he thinks, and through the pain, sweat, and k-hole he laughs laughs laughs. Before he leaves the bathroom Zeke pulls back the mirrored vanity. Lining the shelves, in glass vials and small mason jars, are maybe six ounces of the best-looking weed he's ever seen. Some with purple flower, some with the orange crawling veins and white crystallized THC he's smoked with Yehoshua. There's a sense deep within him he should be looking only quickly, and so he scans the shelves, where he sees some wizened twisted mushrooms, blue with psilocybin around their stems, and even a smaller dark brown vial of a powder he guesses contributed to his day here today. He quickly closes the cabinet. Heads back out.

The main space of Natan's trailer is crawling with maaminim, all of whom have been anticipating this arrival. Rabia Effendi comes in with a pair of scissors, a poultice, and iodine. She is wearing a hijab.

"Don't move," she says. She takes Zeke by the shoulder and leads him to the couch, where two burka-ed women stand and leave the trailer. Zeke sits. She takes a pair of sharp-edged tweezers and brings them right up to his head. There's another feeling of electric shock of pain as she digs right into the hard skin that has grown over his stitches. There's something else, too: the deep skunky smell of weed. Zeke can see in her fingernails the sticky green.

Rabia pulls at the stitch. It barely moves. He jerks his head back.

"That is just . . . so painful," Zeke says. "It's like it's part of my head. Just the speed at which it healed."

"These stitches should have been removed days ago."

"I didn't exactly have time to get to the ER. To get them taken out, get a blood draw, a flood paw, a . . . I should stop talking when I can, shouldn't I." Rabia gives him a hard look, knows how stony he is right now, doesn't engage. "It's only been not even a week since the injury. Hard to believe how quickly it healed."

"Time moves different here," Rabia says. "Healing is a process in your body. The process is set. Your perception of the time during which it transpires—how long you've been here, how long the process has taken—that is malleable."

"I'm starting to believe it."

"You should've started sooner."

For the next five minutes Rabia dabs at the wound with iodine, pulls, dabs, pulls. Zeke can see that the white rag with which she is cleaning as she goes is increasingly covered in blood. Finally there's one last sticky pull, a flame of pain, a whole litany of rubbing and pushing so painful Zeke recedes inside himself—and then Rabia says she's done.

"That's it?" Zeke says.

"Well, there's a lot of flesh now to scab over and heal. I've put a poultice over it that should help it to stay healed."

"Healing doesn't seem an issue here," Zeke says.

"As I told you."

"Would you tell me a little more?" Zeke says.

"I believe we're done here."

"Did you meet Faiz Effendi here? Or did you come together?"

"Together."

"So you've been here for just a short time. But you already seem really central to the community. It's remarkable."

Rabia is silent for a moment.

"Well," she says. "We rejoined the ummah in recent years. We were a part of the Dönme earlier."

"Right," Zeke says. "Faiz did tell me that. Or Dave. I can't quite remember at this point. Or now. So. So how far back was that?"

"Early," Rabia says. A light red rises to her cheeks now, and she is not making eye contact. "Early on."

"Like, you were friends with Yael?"

For the first time Rabia stops packing up her first aid kit. She sits down opposite Zeke.

"Natan told you."

"Not exactly," Zeke says. "Natan sent me his notebooks. Wants me to incorporate it into my piece. Honestly, it's mostly religious writings I'm having a hard time getting my mind around. But I have a long way to go, and yes, there's a narrative part that tells a bit about the early days at the Caves, and mentions Yael, and . . ."

Silence builds between the two of them. It feels almost tangible, an Ein Sofistic matter.

"Many, many members of the maaminim knew and loved Yael," Rabia says. "But we don't talk about her, and it is, as you perhaps can imagine, so painful to Natan that we don't mention her name. It's been that much worse since—since—"

"I know what you mean."

"Natan had no choice but to call her and tell her what happened, and I had to help. It is . . . impossibly painful."

"I . . ." Zeke says. "I can't pretend that I can imagine."

"I'm not going to tell you you shouldn't be here, the way I know my husband does. After what we've been through this year, for the first time I think we could use an interloper if it will help us to move on. Someone just to let out some of the stink of it all. Because that's what it is—a bad, bad smell. Pervasive. Beyond that it's a grieving father. A religious community that supports him."

In the lines of her eyes, in her tone, a real sensitivity appears in Rabia's words. She's happy enough to have this opportunity to talk, but he'd better not push her too hard. He asks no further questions. He's too exhausted and stoned to make much more sense, to maintain more coherence. He can do little more now than to listen. Rabia begins to talk.

"Yael knows Osman is gone. But she'd decided long ago that if a court wasn't going to let her have him, and she knew she couldn't be here, she had to let him go. We still were legally beholden to the rules of our old Hasidic communities then, these hyper-patriarchal communities, when the father had all control of the family. If Yael left, she knew it meant leaving it all. There was simply no chance she would get custody. They both knew it. She knew if she brought Osman with her, they'd track her down no matter where she went. If she was going to leave, she would have to leave alone. So. Think about that. That pain. That decision.

"So he'd been gone from her for so long. I won't tell you more about her than that I'm the only one who still talks to her. And she's found a path to happiness. It was never going to be here, and Natan was never going to accept that. But that doesn't change the love we have for Natan. And I think really the only thing I need to say to you is that no matter what you see, or seek, when Natan gets back here tomorrow, I need you to remember this one thing: This is a grieving father you're observing. A deeply imperfect man. Likely not a prophet, though I'd deny having said it. But. A father. Who is truly deeply grieving. Do you have kids, Zeke?"

"I don't," he says. "I mean I guess I'd like to at some point. But I'm young. I don't."

"There's only so much you can understand of what Natan is going through. I'm not judging. I need you to believe me. Write your story about the Ein Sof, about what the maaminim are really like. But as a human. As a fellow Jew. As the person you are, here, blood running in your veins and joy in your heart. Don't forget that along with all the rest, Natan of Flatbush is a grieving father."

FLIES BUZZING AROUND YOUR EYES

When Zeke arrives back at his cabin, still winter damp and frozen-boned and newly relieved of the stiches over his eye, he's expecting at worst a visit from Ernie Shaw. He sees Johanna's pale blue Prius parked in front. When he enters the room, she is sitting on a poorly upholstered chair.

"You look cold," she says. There's a smile on her face, but it blanches when he gets close enough for her to see him. "Jesus, not just cold. You look like you need medical attention." Zeke's jaw is clenched like he's receiving ECT, like he's clutching a live wire. He's able to unclench long enough to say he's OK, just needs a hot shower.

Zeke immediately undresses as if Johanna weren't there. They've slept together a half dozen times now, but she has not seen him in the daylight, coming into flesh the way he entered the world. Sex nudity bears no affinity to illness nudity. The squiggly black hairs on his upper thighs and on his Ashkenazi shoulders and the dark of his puff of frozen pubic hair catch the worst of the fluorescent light above.

As soon as he's fully undressed, Zeke falls to the floor. He pukes. His body is shaking harder than it has since he first exited the frozen mikvah. Johanna's there now and she lifts him to his feet. It is a struggle. She grasps his tight cold hands as she helps him to the bathroom. There's a pounding at his door and it is followed by loud voices, but in the cold and rush of getting Zeke into the shower neither he nor Johanna can hear words, just the din of bedimmed voices. The voices may be Hebrew-inflected or teenage-Ohio-accented or coming from the mouth of the whirlwind, but neither would know in the freezing expediency of their action.

The noise subsides. The only sound is the sound of Johanna turning on the shower and the strafing sound of water against white plastic bathtub. When the first particulate waft of steam lifts off the stream going down, it rouses indiscriminate prickles of pain across Zeke's body. Johanna helps him in and the water is torture, the lifting of nerves of the crossing of cold and hot; the two sensations feel indistinguishable, and with the poultice Rabia placed on his eye slipping to the bathroom floor, the blood that had only just begun to scab is running down from his eye over his naked body and onto the white of the tub. It is a mess of faintly bloody pink water. It is so intense it can only be religious. The religious experience of actively pursuing unbearable pain. Asceticism is not a part of Ein Sofism, but it is not not a part of it, the experience of knowing the world by the active incursion of the world into the skin, coexistence with the body. Zeke cannot tell for a moment if he has been placed back into the creek or if he is in the heat of the shower until the warmth starts to seep past his skin and into his bones and he is revived—slowly he returns to a state where his eyes are not blind and his ears can hear and his mouth can seek to speak. His flesh is as all flesh, grass, and it has gone the way of all flesh. It has been frozen with morning rime, then mowed.

Zeke opens his eyes. Johanna is sitting on the closed toilet next to the shower. In the speed of their actions, the sleeves of her pale green vintage gabardine suit are soaked to the shoulder, smeared with eye blood. He has not ever seen a look on her face like the look on her face.

"I knew it didn't take much for me to get you wet," Zeke says.

"Almost funny," Johanna says. "To go from near-dead to near-funny is a very particular skill set." She lifts him under his arm, and with a towel wrapped around his waist she hoists him into the other room, onto the Airbnb's sandpapery top sheet. For the next hour, two hours, he swims in a state of half-stoned, half-ketamine, near-warm sleep that brings no dreams. When he comes back to the fluorescence of the room, Johanna is sitting on the bed's edge, looking at him. The only light is the light of the streetlights glaring in through thin curtains.

"So I got a call that you aren't going to press charges against the guards at the prison for your broken nose."

"I'm not pressing charges. There's nothing to press charges for. I slipped."

In all the intensity of the shaking and the cold and the shower, Zeke has almost forgotten the pain in his nose. He puts his hand to his face, and remarkably it seems not to hurt very much. Even the swelling seems to have subsided.

"So," Johanna says, "now what?"

"Natan comes back tomorrow," Zeke says. "I want to see him return to the maaminim. I want to observe him around his people—for the sake of the story, for the sake of my own curiosity. But also I believe him. I believe him—wholeheartedly—he didn't kill Osman. I'm beginning to get a sense that, and I don't mean to mess with you and your job, but I'm beginning to get a sense you might not have even looked at all at the real killer. A journalist isn't supposed to get involved with his story—but it feels like the police barely looked at any of the kids Osman was involved with, at anyone else in the Mt. Izmir community, and barely looked at anyone else in the Caves. So, no. No, I'm not going to press charges."

"OK," Johanna says. "I see it. Fine. So what comes next, O great scribe of the pseudo messiah."

Zeke lies back and lets the streetlights cast static shadows on Johanna's face. The smell of the Bosperous is still frozen into his head, the feeling of slippery mossy rock imprinted on the balls of his feet. The burning figure at the mouth of the Cave of the Dragon leaves a corona of light before his eyes. He tells Johanna that first thing in the morning he will head to Mt. Izmir for Natan's return. He's been on Slack with his editor. His stay in Central Ohio will last until Friday. It means extra nights with her, a fact that she seems to acknowledge. All the energy left in Zeke's frozen-water-ravaged body is sapped; he flags, he gags, he turns his head to the pillow and passes into a state that will pass for sleep.

∴ ∴ ∴

When he awakes, his body aching and ice-tired, Zeke turns to see Johanna is still lying in bed next to him.

"I'm coming up there with you," she says.

"You're doing what?"

"I'm coming up there with you."

"Why would you do that?"

"I don't want to see you come home like that again. And I love you."

There's silence between them just long enough for Zeke to sit up on one elbow, propped up so their eyes are on the same level.

"I love you, too," he says, and though he doesn't know it until he says it aloud: he means it.

THE SUN IN THE FIRMAMENT

The ride from the cabin to the Caves was the same ride Zeke has taken each day since he arrived. Today there were two differences. First: in the passenger seat, Johanna Franklin, his college girlfriend, and now the DA of the county, sat looking out the window. While they rode, he wondered what she saw in these small towns he'd come to love when he was an undergraduate, but had been imprinted upon her before she had words, like she'd always been part of some Ein Sofistic whole with them.

Did she see the way the long slide from what passed for a city flowed into the snow-covered deciduous glory of hills and cornfields, as he did, as any visitor to this senescence would? This would be part of his story. The sense both of what this part of his ever-becoming, ever-aspiring country looked like to those who lived its existence day-to-day, the Ein Sofism of an America that wasn't divided by state or ideological lines, but was all one single gelatinous mass in the eye of the Prophet. He, like the prophets before him, was responding to the permanence of the Lord but also to his moment: The way Jeremiah railed against the evils of Nebuchadnezzar. The way Isaiah's poem of turning swords to plowshares came in response to his dream of war no more between Judah and the brutal decapitating horde of Assyrians. That there was a confluence of ideas: the idea of a federal society envisioned by John Jay, by Hamilton, by Jefferson, and the idea of a single mass of a world envisioned by the Prophet he was working to interrogate on the page. "If they are good workmen," George Washington said—Zeke would make this an American story—"they could be Mohammedans, Jews or Christians of any sect. No man's sentiments are more opposed to any kind of restraint upon religious principles than mine are." In executing the laws of the land, Johanna was engaged in a practice not perpendicular to the undoing of halakhic law Natan of Flatbush was engaged in, but parallel to it. Zeke looked out the window, and all he saw now was forest, shadows cast by forest, and all he really saw on Johanna's face was the inscrutability of a lover and a lawyer.

The second new thing was that today, for the first time since his arrival, as if to coincide with the restorative warmth of his shower the night before, the air was springlike. Sixty-five degrees, and while there was enough snow still on the flat ground of the cornfields opening periodically amid the dense stands of trees, droplets of water released themselves from the branches, from the leaves and needles. Out in the cornfields alongside the rolling road, the tiniest of round patches had opened, melted snow, to reveal the dead cornstalks littering the ground beneath. The ground was not quite green, but instead presented itself as small, irregularly bordered oblongs of toad gray against the bright white of snow.

"Spring won't be long off now," Zeke said.

"It's beautiful here in spring," Johanna said. "Glorious. Late

May, the snow has all melted and the river surges. The current at the middle of the Bosperous can be dangerous. I mean, there are tornadoes, more of them every summer. By July it's so humid you almost long for winter again. But for a period it's not this winter hellscape, it's not this Midwestern cold. It's just, kind of perfect. You should try it sometime."

"Ooh, you know where else is really beautiful in the spring?" Zeke said.

"Let me guess," Johanna said. "Is it an island off the east coast of New York State? Like a whole big island city of five boroughs and tall buildings and really good knishes?"

"It's not not that," Zeke said.

Johanna looked out her window. They were quiet again. Quiet enough that they both heard her phone buzz. The short buzz of a text. Johanna held the phone up to her face so it would unlock, then read it. Zeke could see the expression on her face change. In the second before she spoke, he wondered if Natan was headed back to jail, or dead at the hand of Dragons football players, or a crooked cop.

"Change of plans," Johanna said. "I have to be down in Columbus by noon to start prepping our office's response to the appeal."

"Shit," Zeke said. For another minute he continued on toward the Caves.

"Seriously," Johanna said. "You don't have to take me all the way to Columbus. But I gotta go."

"I know you do," Zeke said. "I just wanted to enjoy this time with you a minute longer."

: : : : :

After the extra time he'd taken to return Johanna to her car in the center of town, Zeke arrived at the Caves to find a massive Dönme presence at the gate. There were nearly two dozen black hats, with varying firearms in their hands, lined up at the entrance. He pulled slow as scripture up to the road and rolled down his window.

A maamin he'd never seen before walked up to his window.

"No one comes in or out today," he said. He had the yolky voice of a native Yiddish speaker, the accent.

"I'm Zeke," he said. There was no sense of recognition on the armed man's face. "Ezekiel Leger. I'm the—the chosen Scribe of the Prophet," he said. Still no response. "I know the Prophet is returning today."

"Has returned," the maamin said.

"Has returned," Zeke said. He expressed earnest excitement, and at that excitement the maamin took a step back. In the springlike air Zeke could see a thin line of sweat roll down his cheek.

"So you can see there will be no admittance."

"Call Natan!" Zeke said. "He'll tell you wants me here."

"The Prophet has no phone."

"Call Yehoshua Green. Call Faiz Effendi. Call Rabia Effendi if you have to. They'll tell you that the Prophet has specifically asked for me to be here."

The maamin now looked stumped. He'd clearly not seen Zeke before, and had no directive to let him in. He walked back to the lineup of armed followers. He whispered in the ear of one, who took a cell phone from his black suit pocket, rubbed his fingers around its face; waited; rubbed his fingers around again; looked up at Zeke, looked down at the phone, looked up at Zeke, looked down—and then waved him through. Zeke had never driven a car as slow as he did through the car-width space the armed maaminim made for him to pass through. A community missing its leader is bound to be spooked and volatile. But a community newly reunited with its leader, aware of the tenuousness of his return? Who knew what kind of dry tinder they were sitting upon. The slightest spark from his flint could set it all ablaze.

Inside the line of the eruv, the community was writhing. To get to the parking area near to Yehoshua's trailer required stopping maybe ten times as women chased after running children, as men bustled about preparing for—what on earth Zeke couldn't say. He parked, walked up to the door of Yehoshua's trailer. Knocked. For maybe thirty seconds there was nothing until the door opened. Yehoshua himself. His eyes barely settled on Zeke's face before he turned and headed back inside. From inside came a voice:

"Ezekiel is here and he hasn't even entered? Come in!"

Squished in line along the trailer's walls were Dave and Faiz Effendi, and maybe ten women in burkas, including Rabia. On the sofa, Yehoshua had already taken his place next to a maamin Zeke had never seen before. Sitting in the BarcaLounger, vape pen already in his mouth and a thin trail of vapor exhaling from his lips, was the Prophet Natan of Flatbush. He looked so natural there in an American Apparel navy-blue T-shirt and camo shorts, it was as if he'd never left.

"Make room for Ezekiel," Natan said. "Don't leave our guest standing. Move move move." One maamin stood and joined the women along a far wall. Yehoshua moved over. "We have more things to discuss than we will have time for before our first call to prayer. Leave us!"

The door opened and the maaminim in the trailer filed out. Natan handed him the vape pen. Zeke could see Faiz Effendi looking on at him through burning bedimmed eyes.

"We've gotten way ahead of you," Natan said. "Take as many hits as you want." Zeke took a long pull from the pen. The taste of whatever very potent indica he'd been handed was citrusy on his tongue.

"Now Yehoshua tells me you had a major experience yesterday," Natan said. "Both your first time in the frozen mikvah and at the entrance to the Cave of the Dragon. I would like to hear about it."

"Well, it was ... an experience," Zeke said. "I felt what I was supposed to feel, I think. I mean I heard. I heard the whirlwind. I felt the warmth of the cave. I had ... well, I guess I had a vision? At the mouth of the cave, one I'm not sure I could quite describe here, now. But. I had the most profound religious experience of my life." Zeke was surprised to hear this all coming out of his mouth. "But then, you know, when I got back to the cabin last night. Man, I was a mess. Shivering, quaking. I honestly felt like maybe I was gonna die? But I didn't."

Natan just had a wide grin on his stoned, emancipated face.

"And now how do you feel?" he said. "Now that you're here to-day?"

"Honestly? I feel ... just kind of fine. I mean my neck aches a little, like the way it used to feel when I was a teenager and took some dirty acid. But considering last night I basically felt next to death, I'm feeling ... fine. My nose doesn't even hurt that much."

"If you were to consider the difference between the way you felt in the cave last night, and the bodily—spiritual—pain you felt when you returned to the secular assimilated world last night, and how you feel this morning here with us, what would you adjudge to have been the difference between all these experiences."

"I'm not sure I follow."

"It had been barely a day since you were here. I doubt your attitude itself has changed in that time. So it strikes me your placement in the world, in the midst of the Ein Sof, is what has changed. Think of it this way: once the full comprehension of the theory of relativity began to make sense in all its implications, so much became clear. You could grow bigger, physically, as you approached the speed of light, making it impossible to go faster. But one empirical fact became true: the pull of gravity had an influence on aging. We know it now to be true that if a pair of twins lived to be seventy, one at sea level, the other at twenty thousand feet in Kathmandu, the twin on his mountain would have grown at a demonstrably slower rate. He would be, though born at the same time, younger than his twin.

"The spiritual heights of Kabbalah the ummah here attains are not unlike that altitude. When you are here with the maaminim, whether I am here or not, you are at ease. You are in a healthy spiritual space. It translates even into your bodily well-being: your nose healing. The wound over your eye healed. Your recovery after your experience in the frozen mikvah has been expedited." Natan took a long pull from his vape pen again, and let his words sink in with Zeke. "Take whatever conclusions you must from that."

Again they sat in a long silence. Smoke swelled and eased in the space around them.

"True," Zeke said. "I will think about it. Now what I want to know is how you're feeling being back at the Caves. A year in prison. Now you're here."

Zeke didn't have a microcassette recorder out, a pen in hand, a notebook. The conventions of his profession were long behind him here, as if he were in fact at some great height.

"It is obviously the great pleasure of my life to return to the maaminim," Natan said. "There's one question in particular I feel we should address first. It's the question of the Eighteen Commandments. I know the Dönme's list is not the same as those devarim we study in Torah. Not for me, not for you, either. But I think you also have some misconceptions of the devarim that need clearing up. In English, yes, sure, the devarim are translated as 'commandments.' But in Hebrew, it is different.

"That word itself, 'devarim,' means something more like 'ten things' or 'the ten words.' It is fine, not entirely inaccurate, to refer to them as commandments. But as the Prophet, I must explain it is more like a prediction, a report of what will occur in the future, than it is command. If Hashem says to Moses, 'Thou shalt not take my name in vain,' he isn't *commanding* what the people will do. He is *predicting* it. Moses was the first prophet. He was saying to the people, 'Here is what Elohim *predicts* you will do. Try and see what will happen if you don't.'

"And thus, here, we land on the nature of our concept of redemption through sin. Hashem wasn't simply telling the people how he felt they should act. His morality was a personal morality, a predictive morality. Now if the mashiach, Shabbetai Tzvi, said to his people in 1665, 'Thou shall find redemption through sin,' he, too, was making such a prediction. And that is in the essence of Ein Sofism. Seeing the space filled with Ein Sof as it actually is. That we will predict how the ummah will act, and they will accept it, and we will accept it."

Natan took a long pull off his vape pen again. His eyes were half shut with stony intensity.

"OK," Zeke said. "Still doesn't fully help me to comprehend the 12th commandment, though. I want to be very careful, since here you are, closer to where you lost Osman than you've been in months." At the mention of Osman's name, Natan's eyes opened the slightest bit, then returned to their sleep-eyed stone. "So if that commandment says, 'Thou shall kill in order to keep the secrets of the community'..."

"Well, first," Natan said, "the community was rocked by an intrusion. I know you've come to understand that. But I think the predictive nature matters, too. In the devarim of Exodus, there is a mistranslation you've likely heard your whole life. In Torah, the commandment is 'lo tirtzach'—'thou shalt not murder.' There are places all through the Tanakh that suggest it is moral to *kill*—in war, even in the case of adultery. 'Laharog.' That is Hebrew for kill. Different word. Different idea.

"The commandment says: 'Thou shalt not *murder*.' Among the maaminim, it is not murder to kill to maintain secrecy. This is the very nature of the war the Dönme have fought every day for half a millennium. Almost five hundred years. I sent you the names of some of our maaminim still living in Istanbul. Have you contacted them?"

"I have. I've talked to a couple over Zoom even."

"What did they tell you?"

"That if their Turkish neighbors knew they were Dönme, they'd be jailed. Killed."

"Yes! Yes, exactly. We face the same. We face the real possibility of the kafir from here in Ohio coming to our community and doing just what they would do in Istanbul. So if you're asking a simple halakhic question: Would we kill to keep the safety of the maaminim? The answer is obvious. Emphatic, even."

Zeke let this admission, this claim, sit in the room for a minute amid the vaporous skunky smell of the weed they were smoking.

"Now you can see how this might seem like a confession of something very different in the hands of your secular lawyer friend than it is here, in context, with you understanding me and me understanding you. One can stand by a principle he's not actively defending. And for us, for us here, it means the opposite! It means that we know these boys, Fergus and Deshawn, they have come into our midst and taken from us what we treasure most. The indignity of even having to argue it. With you, or with others. That we would have to explain it—when what I should be explaining, declaiming, predicting, is the miracle! The miracle that Shabbetai Tzvi was not able to execute but that his Prophet shall, here, tomorrow afternoon, with all present to witness the ruach of the Prophet, in person, the power of Ein Sofism to overmaster both time and fate, to predict both what has come behind us and what is to come ahead, that in Moses's parting of the Red Sea we had our first miracle and that in the very stanching of the flow of water and time the Prophet will replicate it—"

A redness had overtaken the Prophet's face. He stood.

"OK, I think we've done very good here today," Yehoshua said. "And I'm sure that Zeke will want to take some time to make notes while we prepare for prayer. Which is in an hour." Yehoshua got to his feet and ushered Zeke out of his trailer, Natan taking one last long pull on his vape pen.

BUDDING REALIZATION

Zeke was sitting in his car at the entrance to the Caves, biding time waiting for the Prophet, when he witnessed a curious scene. From his vantage he could see two separate visitors were dispatched from the entrance to the ummah, in two different ways. First, a late-'90s Toyota Camry pulled up. Inside, in front, were two teenagers. One got out of the car. Though there was a semicircle of armed Dönme standing watch, they did not seem troubled by the kid's presence. The kid came up to one and spoke to him in a low voice. He reached into his pocket, put his hand to one of the Dönme's hands, then put his hand back in his pocket. He got back in his car and drove away.

If Zeke were to have asked, Yehoshua Green would gladly have told him that in modern Hebrew there is a word for marijuana that is simply the transliteration for the word "marijuana," starting with a "mem" and ending with a "hay." The word for cannabis itself, in most accepted etymology, goes back to the Pentateuch, its origin in Exodus 30:23. While Hashem is giving a list of ways for the exiled Israelis to pray to him, including using myrrh, cinnamon, and others, he suggests that Moses include "sweet cane," in Hebrew "kaneh bosem." While there is no way to know for certain five thousand years later, it has been conjectured that among the spices God suggested to Moses that the Israelites use to pray to his holy name is weed. In Crown Heights, in Mea Shearim today, Hasidim roll fat blunts or pack pens as Natan of Flatbush does, and include smoking weed as part of their worship. The Hebrew for the spice itself goes back, after all, to Exodus. That's what makes it good, Yehoshua would have been happy to follow up on all this explanation. That's why we partake.

:::::

There was a lull of maybe five minutes, more than long enough for the Camry to have driven far free of the area. Now the sheriff's Dodge Viper pulled up. Its lights were not flashing. Earnest Shaw stepped out of his vehicle. He walked up to the armed believers, as well. This time Zeke had his window down further. The sheriff was not speaking in low tones. He was speaking more than loud enough for Zeke to hear him.

"He back?"

"He's back."

The sheriff nodded. As he turned to get back in his Dodge Viper, he glanced across the way and locked eyes with Zeke. At first Zeke put his head back down to his notebook as if to pretend he had been writing, but less than a second after doing so he understood that Shaw was still staring at him; he had been caught out looking at the man. So Zeke looked up. Of course the sheriff had his eyes locked on him.

"You do what you've got to do here today," Shaw said. "And when you come back to town, you come by to find me so I don't have to come find you."

SOMETHING REVEALED

When Zeke returned to the trailers, there was just one person waiting for him. He was not surprised to find Faiz Effendi, who had stared at him in rage inside Natan's trailer just an hour earlier.

"I believe it's time for us to talk," Faiz Effendi said.

"I feel like we've already talked a lot," Zeke said.

"Clever." There was a burning red in Faiz Effendi's cheeks, in his red-rimmed bloodshot eyes. "David Levin."

"Bucky Goldstein."

"Don't be cute, reporter. I know the Prophet has shared with you stories of the early days of the Caves. I know you've read stories about Yael, about the earliest settlers."

"Right," Zeke said. "So."

"So we need to talk."

Once again Zeke set out on a long walk through the thawing fields of the land Natan had settled twenty years earlier. Given that Zeke had now read all the prison notebooks, he had a new view of these fields, this land. For the first time since he arrived, he was able to imagine the development of the Caves more as a memory than as an event to be reported. It caused him to wonder what had shifted in the way Faiz Effendi saw it, walking next to him, in the years he had been bringing his family here. In the midst of a culture in which men seemed to grow old and lose their minds, Zeke for the first time started to wonder in what fashion Faiz Effendi had lost his.

"You think you know so much," Faiz Effendi said. They had arrived near the edge of the Sheep Meadow. "You think you understand a religion after reading, what, a handful of books? While these people have given their lives over to it. I recognize I haven't always acted in my life exactly as the maaminim demand, but I am trying. There was a time when I, like you, attempted to live my life by simply giving it all over to the demands of my secular endeavor. Do you know why they call a medical residency a residency? Because you live in hospital. The first four years of David's life passed and I barely saw him. But I was training to be a surgeon, and this was a training that took four years of secular university education, and four years of medical school, and four years of residency, and three years of fellowship. These were sacrifices Chana and I were willing to make.

"And we made them, together. We lived in Bexley and attended our Modern Orthodox shul when we could, and sent David to a Schechter school as we could, and while it wasn't quite our religion, we did it. We earned what we needed to be able to be where we are—"

"With all due respect," Zeke broke in, "you've told me all this before."

In the space before them the sheep were bleating. The red heifer lowed. There was a humidity to the air that seemed to draw them all together, something new in the air: smell. An animal smell, something like the smell of Natan and his original ummah arriving here.

"But have you listened," Faiz Effendi said. "In that time before we left to head south for Columbus, you can't quite imagine what we saw. I know you have stories of the losses the maaminim suffered. But to read about such a thing, and to have been here, to have witnessed it: two very, very different things."

Faiz Effendi stopped again. The farm smells were overwhelming, and they took a step back from the enclosure they were leaning on, walked a few paces back toward the creek.

"For so long Chana and I have been searching for a way to separate from the life that overcame us in Columbus. It's another of the things you can't understand, you can't imagine, until it's your life: the material effects, the things you must do to live as Natan and his maaminim live here. If we were going to live here again, we weren't just going to find a way for ourselves to live well. The entirety of the ummah have to live the same. Natan—Natan never really had a plan for that."

The lowing and the bleating were now distant enough to feel far off, far off in a way that sounds sometimes feel as if they are not coming just from a place far away, but from a time far away. Zeke looked at Faiz, looked hard at the crow's-feet next to his eyes, down to the softness of his surgeon's hands.

"You named David after yourself," Zeke said. "I thought Jews didn't name their kids after living relatives."

"This is exactly what I mean," Faiz Effendi said. "You keep misunderstanding. We made our choices as we made them. Some of us adopted Muslim names and some didn't. I had the chance to move away from Natan, so I took the name Faiz—I followed the commandments—and I moved away. The choices we make for our children are—they are different choices. After some initial difficulty we were embraced in shul in Bexley, and we gave our son a name to match that embrace. What greater way to allay any fears of my allegiances than to give our son the name of the king—"

"OK, fine," Zeke said. "But it all sounds so inconsistent. A set of contradictions."

He couldn't help but interrupt. He wanted to understand. He wanted to understand Faiz Effendi as a coherent whole, not as a series of conflicting facts. Which, even as he spoke, he recognized that this is what a person is. A complicated, sometimes incoherent series of conflicting facts.

"What consistency do you want from me? Different times in life, Zeke, we are different people. Change. We change, we adapt. This is how the Dönme have survived for four hundred years from the moment our prophet took the turban. This is how we survive. Not so different from all people. Instead of holding dogmatically to his outward Judaism, Shabbetai Tzvi immediately took the turban. Here we are, four hundred years later, still practicing, and thriving. That ability to change outwardly, while maintaining our beliefs within—that will save us. Same for the inherent antinomianism of the Dönme. This is what attracts so many of us—an orthodoxy about loving Hashem, fine. But the freedom from halakha? That is real freedom. What accompanies it is a responsibility to maintain the secrecy, the complication that remains. So you don't understand it all. You understand some. You understand enough to know we use our Muslim names in public, for the kafir—like you—and our Jewish names amid ourselves."

"So. Rabia, Chana," Zeke said.

"Slowly, slowly you begin to listen," Faiz Effendi said.

"David Levin, Faiz Effendi. But not Natan."

"Natan was Natan for too long after we got here to be any-thing other than Natan. Like Shabbetai Tzvi, he is the Prophet—Shabbetai stayed Shabbetai. Natan, Natan. Some of us, that was how it had to be—Yehoshua, Natan, some others."

"But you had a break," Zeke said. "Between David Levin and Faiz."

"Yes. What I left behind, I left behind. And what I've come back to, I'll claim for myself. When he returns after two decades, Faiz Effendi, David Levin. Still out in the world beyond, doing business to keep this community afloat. As attracted to the ummah Natan and I created because of what we can do as what we can't, and vice versa. Ready to do whatever it takes to protect this place. To protect them, and to protect them from themselves. To protect Natan in particular from himself. But the dream. The dream to one day be inside these boundaries, these borders, and at all times: David Levin."

THE SIN OFFERING

The air had taken on an aggressive springlike quality by the time Zeke returned from his conversation with Faiz Effendi by the Sheep Meadow, and at the quiet call for the first time since Zeke arrived of the muezzin, the entire ummah came to the space of prayer, the large open field just before the path Zeke had followed down to the frozen mikvah the day before. A day that felt epochs ago. It sliced a shiver into him. As each of the maaminim arrived, children and elderly in tow, the melting snow mushed in with the liquefied mud beneath, and prior to Natan even uttering a word, even setting foot at the front of the maaminim, the field was a mucky mess. It was hard to believe how many members of the community were here now. Where when he witnessed Faiz Effendi's call to prayer there were maybe a hundred, the ground was now packed with people, five hundred, maybe more. They must have arrived from Columbus, from Bexley, from whatever surrounding areas had come to join.

A murmur rose in the crowd as the door to Yehoshua's trailer opened. Many of the maaminim took out glass bowls, vape pens, tightly rolled Bob Marley–coned joints, and in the space of a minute the whole area smelled like the parking lot outside a Grateful Dead show. Zeke had a contact high before Natan even ascended the pulpit.

Natan was dressed in a ratty white Hanes T-shirt. Upon being passed a joint, he quietly demurred. He intoned a long prayer in Ladino. Then Natan spoke it in English:

> *We believe with perfect faith in the perfect vision of the mashiach, Shabbetai Tzvi, and in the perfect execution of his vision of the Ein Sof by his Prophet Natan of Flatbush, selah.*

This time the congregation repeated the selah with him at the end. Many were continuing to daven the Ladino version under their breaths as he continued:

> *We believe with perfect faith in the perfect fact that in his release from bondage, our Prophet will bring the teachings and the soul of the mashiach to the land of freedom.*

> *May it be pleasing before Thee, God of Truth, God of Israel and of the maaminim of Istanbul, of Ankara, and of Mt. Izmir, that these congregations may one day be reunited under the miracles to come. Amen.*

Once Natan had finished the prayer, a new recognition arose in the congregation. Faiz Effendi began a call and response prayer Natan did not immediately take up. It was a familiar Hebrew prayer:

Mi chamocha ba'eilim Adonai. Mi chamocha ba'eilim mashiach Natan.

They repeated it five, six, seven times, before Natan decided he would join in the call and response, "Mi chamocha ba'eilim mashiach Natan." It was the twisting of a prayer from the traditional liturgy. "Who is like you, God?" The second part was equally clear in its meaning:

"Who is like you, Natan, the messiah."

The call and response was followed immediately by a long period of private prayer. Many of the maaminim held tattered photocopied and stapled collections of the prayers they were to utter in this instance. Probably as many were able to recite Torah and Talmud from memory, bending at their knees and dipping forward and back on the balls and then the heels of their feet. The ground was muddy enough that it was hard to imagine any would be doing their bodily contortions and Jewish Islamic approximations of yoga. The davening continued. Natan raised his voice again:

"It is a great blessing of my life to have returned to Mt. Izmir out of my state of bondage! Never before have I prepared a sermon for so long. One year. One year of bondage awaiting this day with you here at the Caves."

There were murmurings of praise for the Prophet. Mostly they were silent, stoned, intent on listening. There was an elevated pitch to Natan's speech, hearing him aloud, that was in some new register for him.

"Today I prepare you for a new miracle, my greatest. Moshe leading the people from bondage in Egypt parted the Red Sea so that they might escape, and upon their escape he let the waters be. Tomorrow, when the sun is in its wane in the late-afternoon sky, I will call upon Hashem to dry the riverbed of the Bosperous Creek." A murmur arose within the ummah. "With the snow on the ground and the warmth of spring on our skin, the maaminim, our entire congregation, will cross the river, will together enter the Cave of the Dragon. When we have reached the other side, the waters will again fill the riverbed, and Natan of Flatbush will take his proper place as your Prophet, never again to leave you, free to lead you. Selah!"

There was less a cheer from the maaminim than a further murmuring. Faiz Effendi could sense a confusion, so he piped up from the front row: "Shema, Yisroel, Shabbetai Tzvi eloheinu, Shabbetai Tzvi echad!" The maaminim all repeated his prayer, and with a bit of a scowl on his face, Natan followed: "Shema, Yisroel, Shabbetai Tzvi eloheinu, Shabbetai Echad, and Natan of Flatbush is his Prophet!" With that tempering of the promise of a miracle, a reminder of the Prophet's place in the life of the Dönme here and abroad, there was general revelry until again Natan took the center.

"Today, as we have long promised, we will undertake the ritual of the sin offering." From down deep in the Sheep Meadow, Dave Effendi was pulling a wooden cart. In the cart was the carcass of the red heifer Zeke had seen in the manger along with the maaminim's sheep just hours before, during his conversation with Faiz Effendi. It had been butchered—could it possibly have been butchered in the short time since Zeke had heard it lowing? A pyre of logs and kindling piled close to the path they would follow the next day down to the mikvah.

"This ummah has had the great luck of being blessed with the first red heifer to appear in four hundred years," Natan said. "For whatever sins we have committed against each other, will commit, we say our prayer." As Natan entered into a long davening in

Ladino, Faiz and his namesake took the carcass of the red heifer and hoisted it onto the pyre. Effendi lit a long stick and put it to the dry kindling. Soon the pile was smoking. The whiff of burnt animal hair was followed by what could only be described as a barbecue, the burning of cow fat and flesh.

Then Natan pulled out what must have been two, three pounds of enormous buds. Maybe five thousand dollars' worth of weed. He dropped it atop the sin offering. Zeke had the instinct to look at Faiz Effendi, who was glaring at Natan, his lips quivering. Natan didn't look in his direction. He swept the last of the buds from his hands. As he did, Rabia and two other women with their heads covered came with fans and bellowed the smoke in the direction of the maaminim. Zeke inhaled the admixture of burning heifer and skunky pot smoke, a smell unlike anything he'd ever known. Dönme all around him came up to the burning pyre and cupped hands around their mouths, funneling smoke. They did just the same as Zeke, closing their eyes, opening them again. The entirety of the maaminim stood rapt, davening, witnessing a sin offering for the first time.

Natan waded into the smoke-filled congregation and proceeded to hug, to kiss, and to talk with every member of the congregation. The intimacy of his knowledge of each maamin, each child and family, was remarkable. A number of these conversations, particularly with the younger of them, were transacted in Yiddish. But when he spoke in English—and he knew each time to whom he might speak in English and to whom in Yiddish or Hebrew, its own trilingual and interpersonal feat—Zeke could hear the genuine warmth. "And I know that Moshe was liking the purple kush, but then shifted over to a sativa he preferred. The body high is good?" A woman obviously wearing a wig to cover her shaved head nodded and kissed his bearded cheek. "Ah, sweet Avram! You were barely a baby when I had to leave. Shaina punim!" Natan grabbed the child's fat cheeks. "Are you doing better with the lactose intolerance?" The kid didn't speak, but his father nodded, said that they'd found almond milk in the new health food section at the Kroger, like he suggested. In response there was also a clear concern and care from the maaminim for Natan as he was, above all, a grieving father. He did not hold himself back. When each member of the ummah came up to him and whispered in his ear, the privacy of their shared grief being too sacred to encroach upon, the anguish on Natan's face was open and obvious. He wept, wiped his face and his eyes with his arm, and moved on as each conversation—consolation—commiseration—found its natural ending point.

The sun was already halfway to the horizon by the time Natan finished kibitzing, crying and catching up with his maaminim for the first time in months. It was, above all, a clear display of a particular kind of leadership. Human warmth. Zeke assumed he'd say a goodbye and let Natan rest in advance of this miracle he'd promised for the next day. When Natan saw him still standing there, a light arrived in his eyes as if he'd just woken for the day.

"You've made it through the entire prayer and sermon, sin offering and all. I'm surprised with all you've been doing that you haven't returned to your cabin."

"I should say the same about you. You must've talked to seven hundred people in the last hour."

"Ah, these people, they are like a battery for me. I'm all charged again. A full year I was without this battery. Now it is here, charging me up. I'm so full of joy I could do it all again right now. To touch each member of the maaminim, to hear all about what

I have missed week upon week. Truly I could do it all again as we stand here.

"And yet," Natan continued, "if you're not too tired, there's something I'd like to show you. It will take an hour, if that."

He stood there, Natan, this Prophet all full of scripture, his tearstained face tinted black with the smoke of the sin offering, the carcass of a red heifer and a whole season of weed growing having wafted over him, the Prophet's face full of Torah and THC. If he had the energy to travel, so would Zeke.

A GROWING CONCERN

When they arrive at Zeke's car, he is surprised to find Natan pushing him out of the way to the driver-side door.

"Where we're going, it's too dangerous for you to drive," Natan says. "There are dangers too present, too consequential."

"Well, it is a rental," Zeke says. "But I mean, do you even have a license?"

"I do. And I do as I wish here in Mt. Izmir," Natan says. "*My* Mt. Izmir." So Zeke hands him the keys, gets in shotgun. Before Zeke has a chance to latch his buckle, Natan has executed a perfect three-point turn. Tight, fast, smooth. Natan throws the car into drive. "Between Footsteps and moving out here, I ran shipments for a guy I know. You know the history of Jack Johnson? He was the first stock car racing champion, like the predecessor to NASCAR. He learned to drive because before that, during Prohibition, he drove illegal shipments of alcohol from Canada down through Upstate New York. A hundred ten miles per hour, the lights off through the dark, just stars above to guide him."

The rented PT Cruiser is flying out of the Caves. The sun hangs just above the horizon in the earliest moments of the day's gloaming. The chalk-white moon hangs mid-sky, the first twinkle of the North Star. Natan jerks the car this way and that, lights off, and tears through the roads down below the Caves. He takes a left onto SR-36 and slows. Puts on his lights. Goes exactly forty-six miles per hour in a forty-five. It's unclear what he's up to, but as they drive out of the Caves and into Salonica, at the gas station at the town's center, he sees what Natan knows will be there. Sheriff Shaw in his Dodge Viper. Natan dips the MPH down to forty-three, crawls up the road a quarter mile, then a half mile from the sheriff. His eyes trained to the rearview, his neck not craned, nothing that would be discernible from a car outside theirs. He hits a half mile, three quarters of a mile, when Route 36 comes to a big ess in the road, maybe a forty-degree turn. As soon as he hugs the shoulder tight to the right, Natan flips off his headlights, throws back the sunroof, and floors it. Seventy-five, eighty, eighty-five, ninety.

Natan doesn't speak. Stalks of papery dead corn give way to a full darkening field of snow-frosted soy. They can see to the ridge across the way, atop which sits William James College. It occurs to Zeke for a flash that he needs to go talk with Declan Wren once more in the morning, but before he can think about it further, Natan has swung the car hard to the left, up a dirt road. Now their seats are rumbling like it's 1930 and they're Jack Johnson himself, taking the back roads in the dark of night. Another right and they're even deeper into the woods, now on a dirt road Natan expertly navigates, missing massive ditches in the brown dirt, tree stumps and grassy patches, until he makes another hard right. The night is deepening to a pure navy blue. The first stars in the late-winter sky flash impermanence above while Natan brings the rental car to a complete stop. They're at the edge of a soy field, all scraggly gray in the nighttime gray scale being revealed from the melting snow atop that's a near black in the early evening.

"Over there," Natan says. He unbuckles his seat belt. "What I want to show you." Across the field, maybe two hundred yards from where they're parked, sits a long metal barn. This one is longer, taller than those at the Caves, and in the early dark Natan flashes a tiny flashlight he's got in his hand three times toward the door. The door opens. Standing in a rectangle of light is a maamin—Zeke can tell by the boxy black suit and the outline of his shtreimel— with a rifle strapped across his chest.

"In there," Natan says. "Follow me—follow me close and quick." Natan begins tearing across the soy field on foot. It isn't apparent the man even could move that fast, scrawny and sinewy as he is. It takes all Zeke has to keep pace, the chalky moon glowing so bright it provides light against the grainy melting snow cover. When they reach the barn, the door is again closed. Natan again flashes his light three times. Again it opens. The maamin standing there immediately moves to block entry.

"He's with me," Natan says. The man moves his body to reveal a huge hangar-like space, maybe two thousand square feet of warehouse, concrete floors, and grow lamps all up and down the eaves. And on tables up and down the place, more mature marijuana plants than Zeke has ever seen in his long pot-smoking life.

"Oh," Zeke says. "Oh, OK."

"So you see why I wanted to show you. You see why I drove so we wouldn't be followed." Natan begins to walk up and down between the rows of plants. The smell is a combination of the musky strident smell that wafts from a cured prepped bud and something else, something dirty and fresh and alive.

"This whole row here is the strain that got us our toehold," Natan says. He's a well-trained and experienced docent at the curation of professionalized pot growing. "I named it myself: the Ein Sof. It's actually an indica-sativa hybrid, so it's not too much of a body high and not too much of a mind high, either. Just an entryway to the experience of direct contact with Hashem."

Natan walks a bit faster. There is a strangely familiar feeling to walking this way that takes a moment to identify—it's like trying to keep up with the cool girl in high school who won't deny you the opportunity to walk with her but isn't going to slow for you, either.

"Do you see the thin red hairs in the blossom on this plant? This is a new indica bud that will match the indoor plants that OH-High-Grow has begun to cultivate. We set out to call ours Heneini.

"Have you read about OH-High-Grow? No? But surely you saw the dispensary on 36 on your way in from the west."

Zeke reminds Natan that he flew in, flew in amid a blizzard, and was basically half conscious from his car accident the whole way up to Mt. Izmir after that.

"Well, you're a reporter, so you'll report on it later. They're set to make marijuana legal in Ohio. There is a single government grant to grow it. Over thirty million dumped into the first grow cycle! Does this contract come to the Dönme, who know best how to cultivate it, who would have a freedom of growth in our religious exemptions? No. The contract goes to a group of doctors and entrepreneurs who know them. Just as it always does in these situations. What will this mean for the livelihood of the maaminim? The legalized marijuana industry could cut prices of our crop by eighty percent. Eighty percent! It would put an end to our livelihood altogether. The way we've gotten by as a community for a decade. We can't accept such an outcome. Coming on twenty years building this community. We're not just going to watch it wither."

There's no benefit in telling Natan that of course this is all the first he's heard of any of it. Natan already knows.

"When we first arrived in Ohio, we came because we knew of the Effendis, the family Faiz took his adopted name from—real Dönme who were connected to the original group, to the Istanbul Yakubi. But those first winters. They were long and they were tough and we would have to find some better way to make a living for the community than what we did in Brooklyn. Our fathers when they maintained their homes in Monsey, in Crown Heights, in Williamsburg, all learned accounting, programming. That would get us nowhere in Central Ohio—and it was what we'd just escaped! We were not going to go straight back to building pyramids after escaping Egypt.

"So what did we have? We had what we still have—redemption through sin. This was the perfect solution. This plant, this natural growth, in our midst. We put a seed in the ground, in a pot of soil. We let it grow, see it form buds, cut them down, then, with the fire like the fire Elijah rained down on the followers of Baal, take it into our lungs.

"Not all the maaminim were on board with it. You've read my notebooks. I told Faiz Effendi it was time to talk with you, to make you understand when we first arrived, that it was him who didn't feel comfortable. But with time comes change. There were changes in Faiz's life from when he was still David Levin. There were changes in what the world thought—of religion, of the cannabis. I know you've spent a lot of time with Faiz—I know he's not always the easiest. He can be very rigid in his religious thinking, and ever changing in his way of acting in the wider world, and all I can say is: We don't choose our family. We grow up with them.

And ... and all men are a long series of contradictions. You. Me. Faiz. Every man. If we do not love them for their contradictions, we won't be capable of love. And, as we change, so might love.

"That's the inevitability, isn't it?

"One day, as Faiz Effendi, he showed up again. At the end of his previous time with us, Faiz had taken the name of the true followers of the Prophet. Had been using medical marijuana with patients. It turned out the religion of his youth, the friends of his youth, had acquired the skill and distribution lines to set him up for success. What a dream for Faiz Effendi! A dream for me, too, I suppose. To have my oldest friend back in the ummah. He was always skeptical that we could keep it secret long enough to let it pay off. He had been cultivating the connections with the state, with the businessmen I'd never be able to work with. Who would never take me seriously— but would take a doctor, a businessman ... seriously."

"And," Zeke says.

"And what."

"And you suspect ..."

"That my boy led the Dragons, those kids, to know where we were? Osman was the sweetest. He was ... everything about my boy was perfection. But he did like to tell tall tales. And Faiz told me, he told me many times we need to talk to him, to get him to ... to keep it to himself. Was it good, having Faiz's son and Osman in among the kafir? Obviously not. But did Osman deserve ... Could we have stopped the kafir from ... I have been alone, in prison, for some time. I have had more time to think than I would like."

Natan is quiet. They walk up and down among the plants, the high-pitched buzz of the grow lights the only sound in the place.

"What's the feeling of being high," Natan says. "A feeling of being just a step closer to the oneness. That feeling of 'Heneini,' here I am, part of one continuous whole with all the rest of the world, humanity, and here's the perfect tool to help us along. The Deuteronomist wanted everyone to drink wine and celebrate with Moshe. We want everyone to smoke and celebrate. What is smoking if not the perfect expression of Lurianic mysticism? The plant is the husk. Inside the husk, the qelippa—there we release the divine spark. When you light these buds, that's just what they do. You can feel it. The whole ummah can.

"Beyond that, you know, we weren't creating any Mitzvah buses or the proselytizing like we escaped back in Crown Heights, but it all fit in perfectly anyway.

"There was the bonus that we knew what we were doing. I'd grown hydroponics in my parents' house when I was fourteen. It was what got me kicked out. I mean it was probably what got half of us who came through Footsteps kicked out of our communities, smoking blunts on our stoops. That was what we had in common after we got free—we were leaving because we were tattooed, or we loved other men, not other women, or other women, not men, or both women and men, or because we just needed to get out. We grew up in a time when smoking weed was barely even a transgression, let alone a crime. We all knew. We started growing. At first we sold quiet and local—waiters at restaurants we went to in Mt. Izmir. Then the kids on the Dragons teams, long before our boys were old enough. By the time Osman and his friends were old enough for high school, they'd been slinging eighths in Mt. Izmir, in nearby towns, down in German Village, to the OSU frats, for years.

"When DYS came and said the boys needed to start attending school, what else could we do? Of course we wanted to keep them in the ummah. But it would be far worse if these people started interrogating our finances, our business. We'd kept it all so quiet, so separate from the Caves and the maaminim. And then all at once suddenly coming around the corner was legalized weed. Medicinal. An opportunity to legitimize it all, and as I say, Faiz Effendi to smooth it all through, make it legit. Like the Chabadniks with their properties in Williamsburg. They could rent their secular apartments, and we could sell our sacred weed. We could support ourselves and do so free of the incursion of law enforcement.

"Then the contract went to this OH-High-Grow group, a group Faiz had worked with earlier on. Probably we should've known that's where it would go. And they tried to cut us all out—they cut out Shaw, they cut out half of Columbus, they tried to cut out all of us. What will any of this be worth with the market flooded with dank, cheap legal indoor weed? No one knows. No dispensary has opened yet. Our only real hope all along has been having Faiz Effendi on the inside, working to keep us in. And now. Now. What hope do we have."

The words hang in the misty air of the barn. Zeke walks along a table of plants behind him. They are all juvenile, the dainty green telltale leaves just flopping their way up into the world.

"What's this strain?"

"Some plain old OG kush. We grow traditional strains along with our specialties. Weed like you used to smoke when you were fifteen, probably, and bought it in eighty-dollar eighths." Zeke doesn't have the heart to tell him he would've killed for an eighth of that, but in the suburbs where he lived at the time, he couldn't even have gotten a whiff.

"So you think maybe there's a chance that instead of the teenagers, maybe some part of Shaw's group attacked Osman, then?" Zeke says. He's been so taken with the story Natan has been telling he's almost forgotten their reason for being there, the weight of Natan's freedom right then.

"I don't know," Natan says. "Like I said. I've been in prison alone, a long time. I do not know." Tears are rolling down Natan's face. "I know how useful it would be for the world to think I did it. That I strangled my own son. It's easier to think that, than to think . . . How distracting it would be for everyone except for OH-High-Grow."

Zeke says that he can't believe it. He's sorry for ever doubting him. That he'll do what he can to help uncover the truth.

"That's just the thing," Natan says. "You can't do any of that. We can't do any of that. This whole thing?" Natan lifts his arms to the fluorescent grow lights high above their heads. Where in Johanna's apartment the stickers of false stars glowed, now above them are the lights of a dozen false suns. It is still late winter, and here they are inside, the power of a generator outside this barn given over to these lights that will trick plants into believing they are lifting their heliotropic arms toward a sun that does not exist. Much as Zeke has found himself walking across the Caves here in late winter only to perceive it is spring, or early summer, only to look closer to find snow across the ground. Across the humid space there must be a couple million dollars' worth of plants. Off to the back of the space, four female maaminim are sitting at a table, heads covered, trimming and cultivating buds the size of a man's fist, packaging them, vacuum-sealing them in plastic. "It's not legal. Weed will be legal, sure. As the Prophet, I can tell my maaminim that Hashem will come closer to us when we smoke. But if Faiz Effendi isn't able to keep us in the project. Or who knows—even if he does, and Shaw finds out he's been cut out—who knows. You have come here to report on the story of the maamin losing its son. I fear you do not know what you set eyes upon here. Do you?"

"Do I what?"

"Know what you see here."

"I don't know," Zeke says. "Like . . . two million dollars' worth of mature pot plants."

"That. Yes. But I also fear you see the path to my martyrdom. The altar for the massacre of an entire ummah. I hope it is not so. I will do my part not to let it be so. If there is a martyrdom, let it be mine alone. But theirs is a real present danger here now. The sheriff, his boys, whomever he deploys—they suspect such a harvest has existed, does exist, will exist. Even Faiz Effendi didn't know until I was taken to jail *where* it is. We have been exceptionally careful to keep it well hidden. Should they discover it—well, Osman did not survive their search."

As the reality of Natan's statement hangs in the air, Zeke looks back to that table where the buds are being pruned. The women look up at him, narrow their eyes, and then get back down to the tedious work of clipping green leaves off buds the size of your fist. One woman is standing back behind them.

She looks at Zeke, knows him of course, then sits down at the table and begins trimming two large buds, probably a half an ounce each. She does not look back up. Clearly they do not want him in there, or any closer.

The last thing Zeke sees before he rejoins Natan at the front of the barn is, by the table where the burka-clad women are trimming weed, a long line of metal suitcases. Small cases, with stippled black faces and chromium trim, like the case his delivery guy uses in his neighborhood back in Brooklyn. He can only assume that these will be filled with the pot the Dönme will bring out into Central Ohio when the time comes for them to unload their crop.

THE LAST PHILOSOPHER

Zeke is alone in his Airbnb cabin. He opens his computer and looks back over his email correspondence with Natan of Flatbush. It occurs to him now, for the first time in a different light, with a different valence, that at no point has Natan of Flatbush wavered in his denial that it wasn't he who killed Osman. The emails tell another story—one that suggests some kind of conspiracy, a conspiracy that looked far-fetched in the past. A conspiratorial thinking that Johanna dismisses out of hand if it's even hinted at, sticking to the facts offered to her. There is another strain, as well, a theoretical claim of a divine right to protect the maaminim that can sound like a confession.

As he's finishing reading over these communications, looking back for a moment at some of Natan's writings, there is a knock at the door. Each time that door has been knocked upon, it has brought worse and more dangerous news than the last. Whoever is there does, in fact, go away. Zeke opens Slack on his phone and lets his boss know he'll be in on Monday, that the story has deepened but not clarified itself yet entirely. He lies back to watch some mindless videos on his phone. He does so for an hour before another knock comes at his door. Ignoring the last was so successful, he doesn't even give a thought to answering this time. But the knocking continues, after it a muffled voice. It is Declan Wren.

Declan is alone. He wears a puffy Patagonia down vest over his Carhartt sweater, a pair of rust-colored Carhartt pants: the local uniform. His old friend, now an esteemed professor, has learned to assimilate to this culture.

"You . . . you don't look great," Declan says. "Your nose! Jesus. What happened."

"Nothing that cannot be undone by time and the right poultice," Zeke says.

"O . . . K. Well, I'm glad to see you. Sounds like it's been an eventful couple of days since we saw each other. Just from reading the *Dispatch,* that is."

"It has been. But an experience, as well, and not from reading the *Dispatch.* Suffice it to say I've got more firsthand knowledge to add to this piece than I could have imagined."

"Apparently. Well. You can tell me all about it. I know you will. Meantime. Have you come any further in your conjecture about the murder itself."

"I . . . have learned a lot of things since I saw you last."

"Like."

"Did you know that Mt. Izmir's sheriff, Sheriff Shaw, went to William James with us?"

Declan sits on the edge of the bed.

"Well, not *with* us, exactly," Declan says. "He was a super senior when we were freshmen, I think. But I. We. Folks at the college keep pretty well clear of them. The police. Billy is on the Dragons with his kid, but that's it. I've said hi to him a couple times. Town-gown relations, you know. They've . . . they've gotten very, very bad since we were students. It's not a good idea to interact at all, really."

"Well. Huh. Well. To answer your initial question: I am firmly of the belief that while I do not know who killed Osman in specific, I have a far better idea of the circumstances of his death. It couldn't have been Natan. I mean, if anything . . . I think there's a chance it might have been Shaw."

"Well then!" Declan says, betraying nothing of his own thoughts on the matter. "I'd love to hear what brought you to that conclusion." Zeke proceeds from further back than probably he should—he spends a long time describing his experience in the frozen mik-vah, his vision, Johanna bringing him back around when he came home, the experience of watching Natan with his maaminim.

"And surely just watching him with these people was not enough. But what was enough . . . did you know that the Dönme grow their own weed? And sell it?"

"I did."

"And you didn't want to tell me?"

"Well, you're a reporter. I'm a . . . member of the larger community here. A community that's soon to have legal weed. What you just told me . . . is as much rumor as it is fact—I mean, if you were to ask me, 'Professor Wren, have you yourself ever purchased a bag of THC-saturated weed from a neo-Hasid,' my official answer would, of course, be: 'Fuck no!' Even on deep background. But now that you're doing your investigative best, and since we're not even on deep background, I hardly know anyone who hasn't at one time or another bought a bag off a neo-Hasid. I mean, not from Natan himself, of course. And when we heard that the legal grow facility was going to be established up here—and read in the paper that doctors at Ohio State were involved in overseeing it—well, lots of people putting two and two and two and two together. While still steering clear of the Caves, only with more purpose."

"There's no judgment of them as a result?"

"I'm not sure how you mean it."

"When there was a murder in their midst, there wasn't an immediate prejudice that although weed has been mostly decriminalized by a majority of states, if this community was making money off black market drug trade, it would seem not shocking to learn there was a murder in their midst?"

"I see," Declan says. "Not sure I've thought about it in those terms before. But no, no, I don't think so. Not entirely. I think it's more that there's always been a healthy skepticism of just how religious the Dönme really are."

"They're religious."

"And slinging bags of perfect weed, like they did back in Brooklyn."

"Actually they didn't start until they got here to Ohio."

"OK. But."

"I'm not sure those two don't still go more hand in hand than you're assuming. I mean of course there's the obvious examples of Jamaican Rastafarians, or of Utes out West eating peyote. But then there are far more mundane examples."

"Such as?"

"Deck, I have drunk more than my share of Belgian Trappist quads with you over the years. I don't think anyone's expecting Dostoyevskian murders in the midst of abbey monks because they brew some of the world's finest beer."

There's silence. Zeke stops. He and Declan are very quiet.

"Point taken," Declan says. "I guess the real question I care about at this point is, if you really think a crooked cop killed this kid, what do you think you're going to do about it?"

"Well, there's not much I can or would do. I mean, if it's true, it means that even Johanna doesn't know about it. There are, of course, limits to what she can know in her position—especially if she's being intentionally misled by police. Whatever would reveal it was outside the realm of what she knew. Knows. In which case it's either below her pay grade—or way above it. Either way—sketchy, and dangerous for her. As for me . . . I'm a reporter, a writer. So I'll finish my reporting, then I'll write."

"How can I help you then."

"With some insight. Do you think your boy and his friends are in danger?"

"From the Dönme?"

"No," Zeke says. "From Shaw."

"Whose first name is Earnest. Like, a living character from a Hawthorne story. You're asking me if I think my son and the son of the sheriff himself are in danger."

"I get it sounds out of character."

"Out of character? If you want to know the honest truth, my friend, it sounds batshit. Have you interviewed Ernie in person?"

"I have."

"You've seen that he's basically just a dude like you or me under the hat and the uniform and all. Is an alum of the very same college you and I attended. Where I now teach and where I am raising my family. Is doing what he can for his family."

"You feel these are facts that would put him out of the running for doing damage in the world."

"Dude. Zeke. I think you're getting a little too involved in all of this, if you want my honest opinion. You're a journalist—an editor—not a member of a religious cult. Stick to what you're here to do. What more reporting do you have to do?" Declan says. He's looking a little more serious. He's looking down at his hands again.

"Tomorrow, after dinner, Natan plans to perform a miracle."

They are quiet. Zeke moves over, sits down on the bed next to his old friend. They let the claim sit in the air between them.

"He says he'll be making the water in the creek stop long enough for the entire ummah to cross to the Cave of the Dragon, dry as bone."

Declan is still looking down at his hands, as if studying them for lines of scripture. Zeke does not drop his eyes to the floor. He continues to look right into the eyes of his old friend.

"So . . . you're trying to tell me you think such a miracle is, like, empirically a thing this charlatan can do."

"I . . . I don't know, Deck. I don't know anything about any of this anymore."

"Well then, I can tell you—next time I'll bring a recorder so I can play it back, and you can hear how crazy you sound."

"There's an excellent voice recorder right there on your iPhone, Declan. You don't even need to download an app. Use it right now if you like. I know what I've seen. I love you, buddy, and I care more for your son's safety, and the safety of his friends, and the safety of the folks up in the Caves, than I do about how I might *sound* to you."

"Well, you *sound* to me like a fucking true believer. You should do what you need to do with it."

They let Declan's words sit in the space between them. Then there's a loud knocking at the door. Declan moves as if to stand, and Zeke places his first finger of his left hand stridently across his lips. Motions for Declan to sit again. There's another loud knock, then another.

Then it's quiet again.

When another minute has passed, Zeke stands.

"I think you should go now."

"That kind of cop knock a regular occurrence here at the lovely cabin you've rented along the river in Mt. Izmir? Or perhaps the Lord has come to reclaim his firstborn before he returns to the world of sin and capitalism in New York City."

"Like I said," Zeke says, "I think it would be safest for you to go."

ESTABLISHMENT CLAUSE

"So listen, I know you think you know what you're doing," Johanna said. "You don't. You don't have any idea of what you've gotten yourself into."

"Don't you think you're being a little condescending?"

Zeke stared up at the ceiling of his cabin. Of course it was Johanna with the cop knock while Declan and he were talking. She didn't want to get involved with a conversation between the two of them. Thank the Lord she stuck around long enough to knock again. "I mean I am, after all, an experienced reporter."

"Who has gotten himself in way, way over his head. What do you think will happen tomorrow night when the Dönme all discover that the miracle doesn't happen? That there's no such thing as miracles."

"What do you think I'll think when I discover that there are."

"Come the fuck on, Zeke. Honestly."

They lie in bed looking upward. A thin patina of light from the moon makes it so that just enough of Johanna's expression is visible to make her meaning comprehensible.

"So in all the forensics, the state police never uncovered any other illegal activity from Natan, or anyone associated with him."

"If you mean did I know he and his group sometimes grew and sold pot—yeah, dude, come the fuck on. I'm good at my job."

"But the police never found their grow lab."

"I'm not sure they ever looked that hard. I mean, legalization is basically upon us. I suspect federal legalization isn't that far behind. OH-High-Grow is growing more plants, like a hundred miles from where we're lying right now, than the Dönme could possibly have imagined."

"You never pursued whether that might have something to do with a murder in their midst. Of a teenager who could be caught up in a drug deal or something."

"Of course we did. Nothing came up. It was not a fruitful avenue."

"Fruitful Avenue. Worst name for a jam band ever." Johanna turned her back to Zeke and pulled the covers onto her. His left leg was left uncovered, and he tugged back. "I know it can seem like weed's kind of harmless now that it's being legalized. But from the business perspective. From the side these folks at the Caves are on. It's like business business now. Real money. In a way it seems like it's most dangerous of all right now."

"Maybe. Maybe it is. But. I know what you want, and there is exactly zero possibility of my coming to another dinner with you now that Fritzman is free. My job at this point is to help get the false prophet *back* into jail, not compromise myself by seeing him while he somehow roams free. Establishment Clause or no Establishment

Clause, that guy has no business being anywhere but in federal prison."

"I'm happy to simply disagree with you on that point. And yes. I get it. I know you're not coming tomorrow. It's fine."

They lay next to each other with the ruse that they were both asleep. Both knowing the other was awake. So when Johanna spoke again, it was really no surprise to either of them.

"So after you witness the not-a-miracle, that'll be it. You'll head back to Brooklyn and write your story."

"I'll head back to Brooklyn and write my story."

"And."

"And."

The loud exhale of the heater in the corner of the room was the only sound.

"You could come visit me. As I understand it, there are a lot of things to see in New York City. I hear it's a lovely place to visit."

"I get two weeks of vacation a year. During which I mostly sleep off the previous fifty."

"I hear New York City has like four or maybe even five boroughs. Each has a DA's office."

"I like my job, Zeke."

"I know you like your job. And I like mine. But just hear me out: I know you'll never believe it, but I think there are way more people on your side of the wall who know more about what's been happening at the Caves, what happened with Osman, than you could even know."

"This is starting to sound a little mansplainy."

"I know," Zeke said. "I know. But just hear me out. If it turns out this is worse than it even appears—would you think about coming to New York? In principle."

Johanna stood and turned on the light. Two o'clock in the morning. They each put a shirt on.

"You're being serious now," Johanna said. She was looking Zeke right in the eyes.

"That New York is a teeming metropolis, rife with good-paying legal jobs?"

"Stop fucking around. I'm being serious. You be serious, too. Like you were."

"OK. Yes. Yes, I'm very into you. I think that we could be very good together. And I get it sounds selfish, intractable, inflexible, for me to be saying New York, not Columbus. But. That is what I'm saying, if only because I'm growing a little worried that the parts of this state that aren't Columbus aren't exactly what you think they are."

"Hmmm," Johanna said. "I'm willing to strike from the record the last part of your statement, and return to the part where you said you think we could be very good together."

"I do," Zeke said. "I really do . . . still love you."

They kissed a good long kiss. They didn't talk any further, but they were that rarest of things, particularly amid the chaos surrounding them: they were happy. Together.

Johanna got up and went into the small bathroom. The sound of water running. The toilet flushing. Light so bright Zeke pulled the covers over his head, against his wishes and his better judgment, with the pure exhaustion that washed over him, alone in this bed for the first time in days, and fell asleep.

SOME KIND OF MIRACLE

When Zeke woke, Johanna was gone. Light of day so bright it must already be ten, maybe even eleven o'clock. A glance at the digital alarm clock revealed it was already two in the afternoon. Two. Two P.M. He'd slept more than twelve hours. He could hardly believe it, and he was gripped with a panic—the dinner would start at four P.M. The iPhone was awash in messages from Declan, from Johanna, but he ignored texts, opened Slack, gave a quick update to his boss, who he was now beginning to think of as his editor. He'd achieved that, at least: thinking of himself as doing what he'd set out to do here, reporting. He let his editor know he would spend one last night at the Caves tonight—Natan was going to perform his miracle, after all—and that he'd set up to fly out from Columbus International the next morning.

:::::

Security at the gates to the Caves was again heavy. It looked like every rifle the Dönme owned was strapped to the back of a black-hatted or shtreimel-wearing maamin. There must have been thirty of them. It was warmer still today. The snow on the ground outside the entrance to the community was starting to melt in earnest, and it was not lost on Zeke for a second that this snow-melt would all be seeping into the ground, moving with gravity downhill, and rolling into Bosperous Creek. The creek would be running its hardest, current the strongest it had been since he arrived, perhaps even since last fall, with the added volume from the melting snow.

Inside the gates Yehoshua Green was waiting.

"Welcome, welcome!" Yehoshua said. He was carrying in his left hand a big cone spliff. He handed over the lit joint. "Enjoy." Zeke took a pull off what he now knew was the mellow strain he'd been smoking with Yehoshua every time they saw each other—Ein Sof. He'd learned from Natan the day before it was the bud that had put them on the map when they started selling here in Mt. Izmir a decade ago.

"I hope you brought a mighty appetite," Yehoshua said. "The whole community has been working on our meal since prayer ended yesterday."

"Honestly, I woke up like an hour ago, so yeah. I can't even re-member the last time I ate a meal. I'm fucking starving."

"That's my boy."

The main fields of the Caves were for the most part empty, as the majority of the Dönme had already begun making their way to the metal barns back near the Sheep Meadow for the meal. For a mo-ment Zeke felt a hollowness in his chest thinking about Johanna. He really did like her a lot. Love. He did love her. He did, after all, want her to come to New York with him. That wasn't realistic, he knew—having her hop a flight with him on a day's notice. But. Honesty was what had come to him here in Ohio, and if he was being honest, that's what he would have liked most. He hadn't even said goodbye to her when she left last night. But he was here for this night, he needed to focus, and he let the wave of feeling pass.

Yehoshua led the way up the hill toward the meadow. This was the third time he'd marched this way. The first, the two Effendis, young and old, showed him the deeper levels of what they had built here in the Caves. The second he'd come along with Johanna for the tish, and it was much later that night before he realized they'd been eating a rather large meal that if you selected right could have provided tons of edibles—and now that made a whole lot more sense, now that he'd seen their grow facility. It took almost nothing away from their harvest to make ganja butter out of smaller buds, shake, and leftovers from a harvest of the size he saw in that metal barn nearby, a barn Natan had driven him to so fast and up and down so many dirt roads he wouldn't have been able to find it again if he tried. How many more of these maaminim even knew about it? Leaders like Yehoshua must have been in on it. And of course the women whose job it was to trim and clean the buds. Beyond that, not many of the nearly eight hundred likely knew what funded them, even if they knew Faiz Effendi's return had put them in a position of greater ease. They must have assumed what he had assumed: a doctor, a businessman, had come in and righted the business side of things. That he had had their best interests in mind, not his—that this was what good, successful men did. Not give in to corruption, to their own needs. But help the community. Because they were successful. Surely Faiz was more competent than, say, Natan. How many people, upon setting foot in a traditional shul, all ugly stone and stained glass, likely thought about what the size of an endowment was that could keep such a place going?

Yehoshua grabbed his elbow.

"Let's pick up the pace," he said. "We gotta get up there before the meal begins. I suspect the pizzas the women have made will go fast."

They hauled themselves up the path toward the metal barn. To their left the rolling fields of the Sheep Meadow had begun to slough their snow, large brown and green spots the size of pitchers' mounds now opening up so wide with their irregular boundaries that many were beginning to touch each other. It was sunny, the touch of a ray a bit hot and physical on Zeke's cheek, like the smallest reminder of the physicality of the Ein Sof. The edges of those muddy patches appeared to be visibly warming snowmelt. The temperature was pushing seventy. The sheep themselves were shorn, to the animal, and glad to be so, their pen roomier with the red heifer gone. They rutted in the small patches of mud uncovered in their pen.

Up ahead the hut showed itself again in the newly blue sky. The entire community was already there. There must have been twice as many Dönme there since the tish, a more varied group. There were the black-hatted twenty- and thirty-something men and burka-ed women. But there was a whole new group, as well—well-dressed men and women in their sixties and seventies, clearly Orthodox Jews from Bexley who'd come to see what they could make of the miracle Natan of Flatbush was offering in this newly enriched encampment—the Dönme had been doing some impromptu recruitment online and down in synagogues. There were dozens of young people, probably close to a hundred, young skater and hippie kids who all appeared to be some iteration of Dave Effendi, in among the crowd. They milled and chatted, took clandestine hits off vape pens or openly toked large blunts and joints. Edibles were apparently too subtle for such an occasion.

"OK, let's get you a seat at the table," Yehoshua said. They pushed through the crowd until they'd reached the same picnic table where they had eaten a week before. A place setting had the name "Baruch" beside it in Hebrew.

"Looks like the last seat's taken," Zeke said. "I'm fine to stand."

"No," Yehoshua said. "It's yours."

Not far from the table, Natan was holding forth to a group of young men. He looked over.

"I will say very little today, dear maaminim!" Natan said. He was shouting into the wireless mic they had connected to the PA set up in back, and his voice boomed across the barn, echoed across the fields and down to the creek and out across the property. "I have told you as of yesterday what today's miracle will reveal. We'll eat our dinner, and you'll follow me down to the Bosperous Creek when we've all finished, and there at the bank's brown edge I will walk you all across to the Cave of the Dragon, where, untouched by parted waters, we'll warm ourselves in the glow of the Prophet, the Prophet of the mashiach, Shabbetai Tzvi. In the meantime: Ha motzi lechem min haaretz!"

Natan lifted the loaf of bread above his head, tore a small piece of it, and put it in his mouth. It was an unusual challah, shot through with wiry sticklike filler. The entire ummah intoned, "Amen," and Natan said back to them, "Selah!" Now he chewed deliberately, a grin across his face, and swallowed hard. "And with it the tea brewed for the occasion." Natan said the hagafen over the tea, odd given it was just tea, not wine. One of the women came over to Natan, brought him a piping hot pot of steeping tea. She poured a small cup, like one they'd use to serve a cup of sake at a sushi bar. Natan spoke in Ladino, many heads going down in the learned solemnity of a religious voice they could not understand, couldn't possibly access, and when Natan finished with "Selah" they picked up their heads. He repeated in English, then Hebrew:

> *Let it be pleasing to you, O Lord our God, host of hosts of the people of the mashiach Shabbetai Tzvi, and his Prophet Natan of Flatbush, and the Scribe of the Prophet Baruch, that we take this tea and think of thee, that in the time of our miracle we might see what others do not. Selah!*

> *Baruch atah Adonai, eloheinu melech haolam, borei pri hagafen! Amen.*

The meal began in earnest.

: : : : :

When the teapot came around, each member of the ummah poured a healthy portion in their cup. Where the last time he was here, there was a robust meal of fish and lamb, vegetables and the rest, this time it was far simpler. There were loaves of the challah that Natan had used for his motzi, and there were pizzas. Pizzas pizzas pizzas of all kinds, topped with sardines and tomatoes, mozzarella and basil. They were more what restaurants would call flatbreads than pizzas, thin and covered in toppings. There were Greek-style flatbreads with eggs baked into their tops, meats and green peppers and yellow peppers, feta and pineapple. It all looked delicious. It all *looked* delicious. As it was passed before his nose, each loaf of challah and loaded flatbread passed by him, there was a strange after-aroma, one oddly hard to place. Yehoshua said, "You don't like anchovy and garlic? It's not a problem. Just pass it along and wait for the next." He took the pie from him with a bit of a side-glance, like he was growing suspicious of something.

On the next flatbread to come along, a traditional Margherita, Zeke began to eat. He took three large thin pieces and put them on his plate. No sooner had they hit the plate than he began eating. He looked around while he took his second and third bites and noticed that there was little conversation, given how many people were there. Just the sound of plates being passed, and people digging into this monumental feast made to precede Natan's miracle. Natan himself was busy slowly, deliberately eating his own flatbread.

As Zeke chewed on the three bites in his mouth, he felt something new—for some reason there was a response in his throat not to swallow. An actual gag reflex. It was tied to that smell, not entirely to his immediate Ein Sofistic response to the food as to a sense memory accompanying it. The pizza had a *flavor* of whatever that smell was he'd smelled—on the bread, on the pizzas, even in the tea. Zeke turned to the maybe sixty-year-old woman sitting next to him, her head uncovered.

"You liking your meal?" he said.

"Very much. We came for the miracle"—she laughed as if she was unsure if she meant it in earnest, or in irony—"but did not expect such a miraculously elaborate meal."

"There's a flavor in it I just can't place."

"My husband used to work as a sommelier. I've developed a decent nose myself." She stopped, chewed deliberately. He could see that she seemed to have almost the same gag reflex Zeke had, but as a matter of decorum she suppressed it, aware Zeke was looking, the way you might on the first bite of a pungent Camembert that mellowed after its initial taste. "It is cardamom? And something more pungent. Like an unpasteurized cheese—bleu cheese? Goat's milk?"

How reasonable it sounded. There were two dozen sheep just

down the hill from where they were sitting. It made perfect sense some of the gaminess of their milk, or even their meat, would find its way into the food.

"Or sheep's milk," Zeke said. They went back to eating. All around the place, more like Odysseus and his men than Moses's flock, the group ate. Zeke finished the flatbread in front of him, two slices, and sipped his tea, when his stomach was overcome by a familiar odd feeling. A prickle, like a hundred tiny needles poking at his gut in all directions, and now the smell, the prickle, and a buoyant throbbing hit him all at once.

"Shrooms," Zeke said.

"What's that, sweetie," the woman next to him said.

"It's mushrooms."

"Oh, I don't think so. Shiitake? Or morel? I think I'd recognize those. Portobellos would be so big you'd see them."

Zeke pushed back from the table, stood, and began to look for Yehoshua. A quick scan of the place turned him up quickly, at a table to the rear. Zeke walked right back to him, tapped him on the shoulder.

"Dude, we need to talk," Zeke said. Yehoshua was in the midst of what appeared to be an intense conversation with a teenager next to him.

"Just give me a sec—"

"No," Zeke said. "Now." They were barely out of the hut. "There's shrooms in all this food."

"There's what now . . ." Yehoshua said.

"Don't fuck around with me. You dosed the pizza."

"Well . . . Yeah. Yes. I mean. There's a miracle to be performed here tonight. And the maaminim, they know how miracles can be assisted."

"Well, I didn't fucking know."

"Now you do. Have you tried psychedelics before?"

"Yeah. Yes. When I was younger. Way, way younger. And I always knew it. I always fucking knew what I was doing."

"Then keep in mind—a healthy Ein Sofistic attitude will help you enjoy your experience. Coolo tov."

There was a prickling deep in his bowels—Jesus, how much had he eaten between the challah and the flatbread and the tea, you could never really tell with tea how much you were taking, an eighth? a quarter? had he eaten half an ounce of shrooms?—and now his head went, *Wow wow wow.* There was a feeling not only of starting to trip, but zooming back in time and entering the last trip. That feeling you could only feel when you were back to eating these drugs—a feeling of *Oh, right,* this *again.* There was another space you entered when you ate psilocybin or ate acid, you entered the last trip you'd had, all over again in a massive collapsing of time—which was, to be honest, all the more reason to go with what Yehoshua had said. Maintain the joy. It always started with the ears, a sound like both ears were held up to conch shells. But today, not only that but a splashing sound off to the side of the barn where a couple of older maaminim were vomiting.

Memories were all a lot, all at once. The trip was senior year of college, right here in Central Ohio, when a weird thing had happened where a number of friends fell when they ate mushrooms, fell just when they started tripping. That was it: they'd black out for a second. Once it had passed, after the initial hit, they were fine, had fun, tripped their faces off.

There wasn't a blackout this time. Yehoshua had given him a vape pen, and, fuck it, he was taking a long draw off of it. Quickly he was kind of tripping his eyeballs off. *Wow wow wow wow* in his ears.

He stood back up and looked out to where all the maaminim were standing now. Now. Standing. It sounded like a wow wow wow in his ears, just saying those words. Thinking. Thinking. Those words.

::::::

Off in what must have been the longest of long distances, Natan was speaking over the PA system again, not words, just a whirr whirr whirr of the Prophet's very knowable and affable intonation, and now a girl next to Zeke who was very beautiful was putting something cold and hard in his hand.: He looked down and couldn't really tell for a second what it was.: He looked at her dark face, the black spots all along it, and she put her thumb and forefinger together and put them to her mouth and looked down at the hard cold thing, it grew apparent it was a vape pen, he put it to his mouth, his lungs felt filled with Ein Sof, releasing the divine sparks, discarding the husks, his whole body had a warm glow all over, starting at his shoulders and up in the sides of his neck:: There was a tickling in his inner ears and the wow wow wow was in his deeper ears again, now he was walking.: They were all walking.: So many people walking! It was a hundred, a thousand people walking in a kind of exodus, while they were walking at the same time it was so so hot:: There was snow on the ground still and sun in the sky bodily it was so fucking hot! Up ahead three, four, eighteen thousand of the people were starting to take off their coats, then their sweaters, the girl with the vape pen was taking off her shirt, she was just wearing a bra, which was white against the very brown of her bare torso:: How do you do away with hot skin! You take clothes off.: You . . . was that out loud, that "How do you do away with hot skin?" Was he speaking it to the girl who was now in front of him? Who walked, she walks in front of him, the whole Ein Sofistic world coming forth at once::

To the right the sheep are braying in their pen.: Each time what was once supernal snow now clearly is not snow but brown ground.: Brown ground.: "Brown ground," it's definitely in his mouth now, in his head brown ground round mound confound, and he's sure he didn't say that last part but the girl hands him the vape pen and they stop while the influx of the mass of the masses of maaminim file past them so they can take another toke.: The girl looks at him and she's laughing so hard there are tears coming from her eyes there are tears coming from eyes so watery the world is indecipherable and the girl says with her mouth all exaggerated "Brown ground":: He hands her back the toke machine he thinks of it now as the toke machine:: He says out loud he knows he's saying out loud "Immonna call it the toke machine because it's the toke machine" and they keep walking and the girl's saying "toke machine, smoke machine, everybody's gonna have to choke machine" in a hard-to-place tune, they're way past the sheep they're way down the path, the heaviest of the supernal wow wow wow has subsided with the warmth on skin and they're down into a declivity they're up into the blue sky down into the woods::

They will be walking past a wood with the circle in the wood a familiar one, the circle in the wood makes his stomach prickle and movement stops pushes clear of the crowd moving in waves all around and puke comes up past his feet and the hot hot neck stops it stops but the girl is gone:: Then a flash of her white bra and "Are you OK" she says it, it's clear what she means so he wipes his mouth and spits and wipes his mouth again and says "Yeah" and she hands over a white round thing, puts it in his mouth the burning sensation is all around the inside of his mouth mind says "mint" mouth says "thank you" with the burning sensation around it: They are so far past the circle in the wood:: time but there is no time and the sound of the rush of water and isn't the water supposed to stop but now the people move to the sides along the bank of the creek they're at the banks of the creek and it seems they're all there, every one of them, while there is a man next to him still in a black suit black hat dipping his body back and forth and back and forth there is no sweat on him.: Most of the people are not in clothes anymore:: Even the elders with their pachyderm skin hanging off like entropy has decided to allow them the freedom of the Ein Sofistic world with skin that does not so much distinguish them from those around them as they have before and.: Down to his thighs there are still boxer briefs on.: They feel scratchy against hips but tugging at them he doesn't take them off:: pink spots on girls' chests show they are in the shapes where they no longer wear clothes and along with them lined tubular penises he does not want his penis to hang down like that because there is comfort in the way the brief is scratchy on his hips but keeps his right now shriveled inward-hiding cold penis in place with the cold on his feet even though his neck sweats::

Now there's a wow wow wow again people making all kinds of bass sounds because the Prophet is standing up to his naked waist in creek:: He is in the water but the water is not moving around him:: It takes time though there is no time to hear it but Natan is saying it over and over again, "As you move through the creek, the water will part around you! As you move through the creek, the water will part around you.: As you move through the creek, the water will part around you.: Move through the river! The water will part around you!"

All at once there is movement back way back in the line of people, bodies knocking into each other and rushing by:: Natan is turning, he is beginning to move through the creek bed he cannot tell if it has dried since sprays of cold cold water are lifting up in a mist but there are bodies mostly naked moley backs but also black suits white shirts they are all moving.: The girl is still standing near again:: She says, "one more toke machine before we choke machine" she hands over the vape pen:: Smoke in and smoke out and an older woman has been knocked down by a current still drawing down, a man next to her is struggling to pick her up out of creek water.: There's a sickly feeling like when they walked through the circle back in the wood but the girl is in front she turns around she smiles says "As you walk through the water it will part around you"::

In the creek bed around legs now instead of hot, the cold of dragons' teeth up all over legs:: There is memory, there is the cold the freezing cold from the time before but it resounds again and again:: as you walk through the water it will part around you, all the splashing, all the maaminim bounding up to their chests in the water that will part around you and the surprising thing about the cold is that it is up to your neck if you fall to your right you will feel the current tugging so hard you could give in, head all the way downriver but just as you do there is a hand a strong hand the strong hand of the host of hosts on your hand pulling you up up up onto the shore:: There you can feel off to your right there is cold under your feet there is off to the right that heat, that heat that comes from the cave, there are so many huddled by them:: Now there is someone who has turned to face him, someone in front it's not the girl it's Josh he says, "You made it, dude, you're across, the waters parted for you, my dude" wrapping a blanket around him.: He's wrapping a blanket now though it's so wet so cold so shivering shivering shivering the wow wow wow is gone, the girl in the now-wet-against-her bra with pink hard shapes under it walks over and she hands over the machine again she says, "As you walked through the creek the water parted around you, toke machine coke machine everybody gone broke machine":: He grabs the cold hard metal from her hand puts it to his lips sucks in in in there is a sense of coolo tov there is there is a sense of everybody in the cave everybody is warm they are all there together in the warmth of the cave and it could go on it could it could go on forever::

: : : : :

The inkblack night is thick as inkblack night. There have been so many pulls on the toke machine how many pulls. Somehow there's a loose white button-down and it smells of body sweat. Somehow in the cold, a black suit coat. He's a forty regular, he remembers that, this must be like a fifty. Maybe long. Long. Weird word for a suit coat, loooong. David Byrne in this is not your wife this is not your car and the days go by huge gray suit, Chris Farley fat-guy-in-a-little-coating, of a Roth story where a guy ends up in a Hasid's coat and hat but he pushes that away and he's back to same as it ever was, same as it ever was, same as it ever was, same as it ever was.

He hears it come from his mouth aloud: "Same as it ever was, same as it ever was," expecting to be handed the coke machine toke machine everybody hokeypoke machine from the girl with the white bra but now there's just a guy with a big old Hasid's beard sitting there. The guy is wearing Zeke's Patagonia fleece, rubbing his hands together. He gives a blank blank blank blank stare at the Talking Heads coming from Zeke's toke hole. The feeling of laughter in the inkblack night and the wow wow wow is back but then from across the fire they're sitting around the sound of "This is not your life. This is not your beautiful wife"—it's the girl again. She's wearing the shtreimel that goes with the black suit coat he's got on:: She's radiant in the radiant inkblack.

Under the cast of the dark black sky something feels physical against the back of his neck, a blue in the corner of his eye, then a red, then the whole of the circle of maybe a dozen maaminim.

Now the whole world turns blue.

Then back to inkblack.

Then red.

The red on the girl's face brings out the crimson moles across her face and she's both much more beautiful than was previously apparent and much much much much younger. Maybe more eighteen than twenty. At least she's shirted now. He feels an itching on his head that has been bothering him longer than he could remember, puts his hand to his head: he's wearing a black Hasid's hat, he doesn't like it, tosses it on the fire, before the "hey hey hey what the fuck" arises they're all moving in different directions. Half the group running back into the snowy wood. The other half moving slowly in the opposite direction, the direction of the parking the entrance to the Caves. They move slowly in that direction; they turn blue as ice.

Black as night.

Red as supernal sun.

Zeke could stand then, he could turn around to see what's happening behind him, but he takes one more pull off the toke machine, not knowing just what's coming next, puts it in his pocket but it's infernal hot against his thigh so he takes it out holds it in his hand. The beard next to him has pulled the hat from the fire is stepping out the sparks on its rim.

Zeke turns around he does not hear what's happening.

The red and the blue and the black and the red and the blue is the whirling lights of the sheriff's Dodge Viper.

The car has pulled right up in front of a white trailer, which now turns blue and then black and then red itself.

This trailer is familiar. Yehoshua's trailer. Most of the maaminim have scattered now. Natan the Prophet is standing in front of Yehoshua's trailer: he's saying something. He appears to be shouting. The big black pupils at the center of Natan's eyes are visible because they've been visible all night, ubiquitous like memory though it was only hours ago he was sitting by the again raging creek Natan talked of the success of his miracle—"The maaminim have crossed the dry creek. The water has parted around them, the miracle performed"—while he and the now very young girl and so many of the maaminim whooped and wow wow wowed.

Now the driver-side door to the police vehicle opens. Up stands a man, a very familiar man. Zeke has talked to this man. He knows more than he knew when he talked to him, having learned what he's learned about OH-High-Grow from Faiz Effendi.

Sheriff Earnest Shaw. That's the man.

No other police officer with him. His hand is hovering over his sidearm. That's what they call it in the police shows—a sidearm, someone should kind of be writing because this is the kind of scene that people like to read in a magazine article, maybe later in a book expanded adapted from a magazine article, maybe if there was a scribe in a scripture, letting the days go by letting the water hold me down letting the days go by under the silent water this is more like what he should be thinking than what he is thinking.

"Wow wow wow," the sheriff says.

"Wow wow wow wow," the Prophet says. Now the two of them aren't alone, another of the maaminim has joined them. This is very familiar too like a story he's read too many times before. He is short and stocky and officious and he is Faiz Effendi who Zeke has spoken to before as well. He has come in to join the conversation and now here it is, maybe this is team OH-High-Grow together all together. Faiz Effendi is speaking in a low tone now too from just far away enough it's like "Wow wow wow wow wow wow wow."

It is very very deep in the night. Natan is exercised and talking loudly wow wow. He is laughing. It's been a good night. He is waving his arms around in a kind of dance, a same as it ever was same as it ever was kind of dance, some wow wow wow coming from the folks around him. The maaminim, that's what they call it! The maaminim baaminim ohlalaminim there's all that laughing again. It's not loud laughing this is what happens, just all the laughing the unstoppable laughter of Sarah. No one has noticed. Tries to make the laugh laugh low. Some wow wow wow, for a second it breaks through that the girl is talking.

"Fuck, he's gonna get himself arrested again," she's saying. "Think we should do something? Can we? Can we do something?"

"Oh, I don't think we can *do* anything," Zeke says. Says but also so much laughing. "I'm sposed-ta *write* something. Not *do* something. I'm not really a doer-of-things kind of person to be *honest*. And there's things you don't know things I don't know. They don't *arrest* a Natan like Natan. They might *martyr* a Natan but they don't arrest no they do do do not." Wow wow wow.

The girl looks up at him he can see she can see he can't, he can't do something. Even if he was the kind of person who could or would or did or will do something he is not that kind of person now. He is a laughing dancing walking-through-dry-riverbed shrooming kind of person. They stand. Look up. Natan is dancing his dance again the sheriff has one of his hands, now he has him spinning around. Natan does not dance. There's some wow wow wow around him again now he can hear that it's more of a Baruch atah Adonai, the tall beard who they were around the fire with saying, "Shabbetai Tzvi, esparamos a ti! Natan of Flatbush, esparamos a ti!" But this time Faiz Effendi does not say it along with him. Natan is the only one praying.

There are many more maaminim surrounding the scene, what feels like dozens, maybe hundreds, maybe all of the Dönme who exist still on this property moving back toward the scene where they have now seen there are not multiple squad cars or DEA agents or paddy wagons but just the one, the sheriff arriving as he has arrived so many times before to meet Natan and Faiz Effendi, among them there is a wow wow wow there is a wow wow wow there is a mi chamocha ba'elim Adonai and a Shema Yisroel Adonai eloheinu Adonai Natan there is a kadosh kadosh kadosh shemo: there is shame as it ever was shame as it ever was letting the days go by let the water hold me down under the silent water and a take me to the river drop me in the water holding me holding me down.

Natan does not hear any of it. He's turning. His body has slowed. It looks so slow in the slow blue then slow inkblack then the slow red of the lights that keep flashing on Natan, flashing on Faiz Effendi, in each slow shift of the slow color it is as if the color is drawing them all together, bringing them into supernal Ein Sofistic singular whole. It's there. You can. You can feel something low and sad in your chest as you realize it at just the moment now when Natan has given himself over:: His hands behind his back:: His head dipping below the roof of the squad car and the door closing, putting an end to their view of Natan of Flatbush, Prophet of Shabbetai Tzvi:: Selah!::

RETURN TO THE HUSKS

When he awoke in the morning, Zeke was shivering uncontrollably. He was lying on a couch. It took him a moment to comprehend that he was once more in Yehoshua Green's trailer. The smell of weed and vomit. The smell of burning wool and man sweat. A rough blanket like a sisal rug draped over him. Looking down, he saw he was wearing the white button-down shirt and the extra-large black suit jacket from the end of the night. On the table next to him, a big black hat with its brim singed from fire. On the couch across the room from him, a girl, maybe twenty years old, probably younger, with dark moles on her face. The girl from last night when. Oh, God. Oh, Jesus. Last night they were tripping their faces off, stoned out of their heads, and it was still a little wow wow wow from the night before, whether from memory or continued tripping, who knows. Laughter. Laughter was here again. The laughing from the night before was still lodged in there. Head like it was filled with some kind of sickly thick syrup it would take days to drain.

Somehow on the table in front of him were Zeke's actual shirt and Patagonia fleece, and in a moment of the return of responsibility to his brain, he reached for his left jeans pocket and felt for his phone. Phew. What luck. He pulled off the suit pants, pulled on his own jeans and his own shirt and his own fleece, and quiet, so as not to wake the girl, he slid out of the trailer into the sun-searing morning in Central Ohio. Stab of cold returned to the air, dry and sharp. The Allman Brothers yellows of the space had returned to the field. Most of the snow was gone, only three days since it blanketed the ground, and the mud of the night before was mucked up from hundreds of feet all dancing and walking and miracling. Even the thick tracks of the sheriff's cruiser were clear in the mud. Shaw. Shaw had been there, Shaw and Faiz Effendi.

Zeke walked back toward the solitude of the woods. He pulled his phone from his pocket. It was all green and gray with text messages. He briefly opened Slack to see if there was anything from his editor—there were more messages than he could take in all at once, but he could tell they were mostly just, "MIRACLE WAS THERE A MIRACLE WHAT WAS THE MIRACLE WAS THERE ONE." There was. He didn't have the wherewithal to write back and say so just yet. But the texts from Johanna he would answer. He called her instead of writing.

"Didn't hear from you last night," Johanna said. Her voice was exceptionally flat.

"It was a . . . long night. There was . . . a miracle. There was. If you walk in the water, the water will part around you." And while he was talking, there was that uncontrollable laughter again. Wow wow wow still a little.

"The sheriff called to say he saw you in quite a . . . state."

"As I say it was a long night. But trust me. It wasn't what that sounds like, however he painted it. It wasn't salacious. It wasn't erotic. It was more . . . religious."

"Redemption through sin."

"Exactly."

"The Dimming of the Candles."

"Not exactly."

"Well, I'm sure you know that now there will just be a deep uncertainty."

The conversation was growing too oblique for addled morning-after brain. Things were going to need to go a bit more direct.

"Well, what uncertainty. I'm sure Shaw told you he came to pick Natan up again. So I guess that's it? He'll just be back in prison until the appeal is over. All the battle over his future for nothing."

"Wait—what are you talking about. The sheriff's department has an APB out on Natan. He wasn't there."

"What do you mean he wasn't there?"

"Shaw reported directly to our office this morning. There's a written report. He came to the Caves last night and discovered a wild orgy. There was no Fritzman. We're working under the assumption that whatever the community was up to last night must have been some kind of subterfuge to allow him his flight while the police were distracted."

There was silence on the line. Zeke didn't sober up, exactly, but a lightning strike of reality shot through his brain to retain some sense of purchase on the fallen world, the ability to perceive empirical facts.

"Hold on. No way. I was stoned, but I know what I saw for certain early this morning. Before sunrise. I watched Shaw put Natan into the car myself. Natan and Faiz Effendi. I saw it. Me and like seventeen dozen other Islamic Jews. Jewish Muslims. He even did that thing where he tied his hands up with the plastic twisty tie or whatever. The clichéd putting his hand on the Prophet's head so he couldn't hit it on the roof of the car."

"I don't know what you think you saw last night."

"A miracle."

"A miracle."

"The parting of the waters."

"What drugs were involved with your believing in this miracle."

"Well, there was . . . hmmm. Uh."

"I'm gonna need more than that, Zeke. We have a full report from Shaw. Came to the Caves, had the forbearance not to arrest anyone—though there was evidence of ample illicit drug use. Potentially by minors. And there was over a million dollars in community cash missing. With Natan. As you know, he's business partners with Faiz Effendi now, and Effendi wanted out. So they left."

"So they left."

"I mean, from a purely Occam's razor perspective, this is how it was always going to go, wasn't it? Drugs, a big crazy cultish party, and Nathan Fritzman in the wind. I mean, if anything, you're lucky it was whatever drugs you took, and not Kool-Aid. Stop. Before you say it, Flavor Aid. Whatever."

"There's another razor," Zeke said.

"Now you're really not making sense."

"Just listen, though. You've sobered me up here. Think about it. Another Occam's razor: I was wrong about Earnest Shaw. Or not entirely right. It's him *and* Effendi. Trying to cut Natan out of whatever growing deal they've got."

"That doesn't make sense, Zeke—to take that kind of risk—"

"But that's just it," Zeke said. "Don't you see it now? I see it now.

The risk *was* Natan. The messiness of the community, the religion, all of it. They got their connection to Natan's grow lab, they quieted Osman when he was too great a liability at just the wrong moment. Whatever Effendi wanted from the start, this is what he wants now. And now."

For the first time in many conversations, Johanna was quiet for some time.

"I wouldn't say that's a simple explanation," Johanna said. "But I can see how you've come to that conclusion. And. You know. If it's between you and a small-town sheriff, you know who I'm inclined to go with. But. Thing is, if that's the case, they're smart enough to know that there are now also two people who could put it together. I mean, maybe Shaw would think the word of whatever drugged-up Jewish Islamists wouldn't carry much weight. But. He knows yours does. Which would put you in a very dangerous position right now. And. Who else."

"You," Zeke said.

"Don't undersell yourself here, reporter," Johanna said. "You're the one with the conjecture. Well . . . I have to see Shaw no matter what the truth is. I still have to be a professional. I still have to do my job. I'll play it safe. You do the same for now. I don't—I don't know what to think, Zeke. I honestly picked up the phone so confused I kind of assumed I was ready to wash my hands of all of this. I need to think. To do a little poking around."

"I can see why," Zeke said. "I mean, none of this is certain. It's just. How it's looking. I love you. And I do need you to believe me. I saw what I saw last night. You of all people know. Eating too many mushrooms can skew a lot of your thinking inking twiddly dinking. But it can't make you see what I saw." And then he started laughing a little from the leftover effects of the mushrooms. Held the phone from his mouth so she wouldn't have to hear.

Johanna ended the call. The black inscrutable face of the iPhone was inscrutable. Black. Zeke still had a flight to catch later that day. A story to write. A psychedelic hangover to nurse. An editor to call, a simply trashed Airbnb cabin to clean up. He was a believer now, but in what, he most certainly could not say in words yet.

So being still a professional, even after a night that was not what you would call professional, Zeke opened his phone and looked to his email to find, of all things, he had a final note from Natan of Flatbush. Attached to their reply chain, in a note that contained no message but just an attachment, Zeke found a final installment of Natan's prison notebooks, the *Shivhei ha-Natan*. The email was time-stamped, sent at nine in the morning, day before, while Zeke was still sleeping in the rented cabin. Long before he arrived at the Caves. It was another entry in the prison journal. It was long. There wasn't going to be time to read through it now. There was a lot to do in a short time.

WORDS OF THE PROPHET
HIDDEN IN YOUR POCKET

Back at the Airbnb, things were worse than he'd even imagined. Clearly someone had been there again that night looking for him. The door was now hanging on just one hinge, just the slightest movement still built in like a perpetual motion machine. Inside it wasn't just that his belongings were strewn about—someone had been in his place looking for something, tearing open couches and pillows and punching holes in drywall. He was not going to get a great Airbnb rating for this stay.

A sound behind him. Zeke swung around.

"Not going to get a great Airbnb rating for this one," Johanna said.

"I was literally thinking the same thing."

Zeke's heart banged in his temples, a psychedelic hangover beginning to seep like sap from his head. But here she was. Johanna. She was not meeting with Shaw. She was here.

"This does kind of confirm both our fears, doesn't it."

"How?" Zeke said.

"There's really only one thing they could be looking for, one potentially incriminating document that we didn't have at trial, that you're the only one to have seen."

"The *Shivhei ha-Natan*. Natan's prison notebooks. But they're mostly filled with religious writings, and the history of the sect."

"Right," Johanna said. "You know that. You've told me that. If you were Faiz Effendi, on this massive cleanup gig now ahead of legalization, a thirty-million-dollar deal, would you leave that to chance? Fuck, Zeke. The things that didn't arise in discovery in this case. Or more likely were suppressed at discovery. What a total shit show."

The words echoed around the place. Zeke began to clean up, and Johanna helped. At some point amid packing his bags, she sat down and started thumbing her phone. Asked him again what time his flight was, on what airline. He told her, told her he didn't think missing the flight was the biggest concern right now.

"I mean my biggest concern right now is you. Your safety," Zeke said. "What it comes down to is: Do you want to believe in me?" Finally he was packed. "Either way, I guess this is it. I can still make this flight. I mean, I'd ask once more if you're sure you don't want to join me in New York, but to bang my head against the same wall again and again—"

"I got a seat on the flight. It's an aisle. Not next to you. But three rows back."

"Say again?" Zeke said.

"I always get set up for plan B, Zeke. Didn't mean at first I'd have to use it. But I did some poking around before I went to see Shaw. There wasn't anything in his name, as there hasn't been all along. But his son. His son has some gigantic accounts with Bank of America. Dave Effendi, too. Neither of those teens must know about it. But if Shaw and Effendi are laundering through their sons—and if they really did come after Natan like you say, risking being seen by members of the Dönme. I mean, where does that mean Natan is now? He hasn't been seen. And Shaw claims not to have seen him, which means he needs to be able to convince me of that long-term. Which. Fuck. Who knows what could come next. And for me it would mean. Well. Well, oh me, oh my, oh, fuck off forever, Ohio. Or at least fuck off for now."

"Don't you need to pack or—"

"Do I look like a person who does not have two go bags in the back of her Prius? Let's get the fuck out of here."

THE SUPERNAL PRESENT

The Final Chapter of *Shivhei ha-Natan*, the Prison Notebooks of Natan of Flatbush

Natan the Prophet rises to lead his people to the banks of the Bosperous Creek. Alongside him are Yehoshua on his right hand, Zeke on his left. Down the path they walk in the highest spirits—a miracle is to occur! On this very day!

They walk down the pathway singing praises and singing out of the sheer joy of the day, of the activity, of the anticipation of impending miracle. This is the reason they study Kabbalah, the reason they have followed all along: to interact directly with the host of hosts::

As each of the hundreds in the maaminim approaches the Bosperous Creek, Natan awaits them on the other side. Guiding them. The cold of the frozen mikvah will be nothing when the waters part around them, and the parting is something different from what they expected. Rather than the water parting side to side, a dry riverbed to walk across, the waters part in orbit around their bodies. The miracle in the midst of the Ein Sofistic present is the separation from the mass around them. The curse of the individu-ated individual. The evil. The waters rage. The current is so strong it could pull them downriver and drown them, but each member of the maaminim walks across the creek in joy, water parted around them::

: : : : :

Get above it and see it! See Ezekiel, see Yehoshua, see David Ef-fendi.: See the son of the Prophet, Osman, his sixteen-year-old body bare against the water. In a swirling semicircle around each of them, a spark-thin dry boundary keeping the river water off. The elation—it is on their faces as one by one they cross the river, exalt their Prophet, and with selahs and amens and Adonai echads they cross the river, dry in the Cave of the Dragon::

"It is good," Yehoshua says to the Prophet when the last of the maaminim crosses. "It is very, very good"::

"It is a thing of joy"::

: : : : :

The rite that follows is the kind of ritual they have always wanted. They smoke their vape pens and toke from their glass. Those with guitars take them out and sing psalms in the words of David and laments in the words of Jeremiah, extol Jerusalem city of gold, cry holy to the Lord and songs of redemption. Extol the stone that the builder refused, the gospel plow. It is a thing of pure joy. It is the thing the Prophet has longed for. He has done his duty. And he suspects that he will have no choice now but to proceed into his martyrdom::

: : : : :

When the police car shows up it comes as no surprise. Natan feels half resignation and half elation at the merging of past and present, at the meeting of all the days that have come and all the days to come. He sees the Law step out of his vehicle alone. He will spare the maaminim from seeing anything further so he dances a dance of joy:: Coolo tov::

Joy quickly stops. He sees, off to his right, approaching him not Yehoshua, not Ezekiel, but David Levin. His oldest friend, the maamin he has missed most, has been happiest to have back, even if it is on whatever terms of Moloch he has worked out with the sheriff, with his business partners. And as David Levin walks up, the Prophet sees he is now only Faiz Effendi. There's barely a drop of David Levin left in him. What Natan has suspected for a time grows clear in every dark line on Faiz Effendi's face. He is entirely husk. Qelippa. No raising of the sparks can save him, no confession, no repentance. There is evil in the world, the kind of evil that would both kill a child for having broken the 12th commandment—and the kind of evil that would simultaneously be engaged in breaking the 12th commandment for his own material good. It's the secret of the husk and the spark. They are one. One rests inside the other::

Natan says to the Law:: "Take me."

"Oh, I'm gonna take you all right," the Law says::

In the car Natan begins to believe he is on his way back to prison. The Law takes a left, then a right. Faiz Effendi is in the shotgun seat, says nothing. Natan's hands are tied behind his back in the back seat. When he gets out to the state route, and past the downtown, Sheriff Shaw turns his high beams off and he drives slow. And then not he but Faiz Effendi turns to Natan::

"I know you think we have no idea where your grow lab is. You were careful for so long. What I would've done to have found you out ten years ago. To have spared Osman this. To have spared you. And now, with so much on the line—on the line for you! For your friend! You still thought you could keep it to yourself." The Law does not join in the cajoling, just stares forward into the long black night::

Natan does not speak. He accepts what is to come, whatever it may be, just as he accepts what has passed. That does not mean he needs to be affable in it. He looks out. To be a tzaddik is to put one's body out to the ummah. To put one's body out to the ummah is to risk husk for spark. Faiz Effendi. Husk all through. Qelippa. The night is inkblack, stars so prominent in the sky it is as if the creator has put each there to guide his eyes away from the impermanent world below. Natan knows trees pass by outside his window but the ink of the black night has blotted each out.: There is only a single dark Ein Sofistic mass that passes outside his window: He can picture them: He can picture each branch, each leaf, each small green dot of chlorophyll throbbing with the knowledge that the heliotrope will arise to grant life, the oxygen they emit entering his lungs, one single living breathing mass—

"If you don't want to be a part of this," Faiz Effendi says to the Law, "you don't have to be. I can let you out at the edge of the property and leave you at your car and meet up after"::

No sooner has Faiz Effendi, David Levin, spoken than the Law has fled to his vehicle wanting no part in what is to come.

Faiz Effendi now turns to Natan:

"You don't need to tell me where to take you. I know now." The car judders left and juts right. They pass through darkness. Natan can see where they're going. It's not a secret. No one but select members of the maaminim have even been here. Not one of them could get here on their own but Yehoshua. Maybe Rabia. Rabia. But Rabia.

The lights cast searching beams across the dirt, strike upon the long barn. No one is there tonight but Natan and Faiz Effendi. They are all back at the Caves celebrating the miracle::

Faiz Effendi exits the vehicle. Opens Natan's door. Natan is not reluctant. He gets out.

"Unlock it," Effendi says. Natan looks at him. "You know the code, so unlock it." It occurs to Effendi what Natan is waiting for. So Natan turns around. Effendi takes a survival knife out from his side pocket. Natan has his back to him. Perhaps this will be it. Maybe this is the moment he will see the chariot and the throne as Ezekiel did, the cherubim with their animal faces and their wheels within wheels. He will enter the Merkabah and find the infinite rooms to come, the rooms with infinite corners.

He feels a tugging at the plastic around his wrists, the pain of them cutting into his skin, then his hands are free. He shakes feeling back into them. He punches the numbers into the lock on door. Six. One. Three::

"Now turn some lights on"::

All at once the light casts upon the hundreds of plants. The mushrooms all gone, pounds of them, into the bodies of the maaminim. Faiz Effendi wants him to talk, he can see it, but this is the one thing he will deny him. Shabbetai Tzvi took the turban. He accepted the exchange.: becoming outwardly Muslim so he could keep his head.: No such deal is in the offing here:: There will be no apostasy:: No further word with the qelippa embodied::

Before he can hear another word, he turns toward Effendi. He sees his oldest friend has a pistol pointing at him. Effendi does not speak. There is the shock of the sound. The feeling like he has been punched by a steam locomotive in his chest. He is thrown back. He can only briefly feel the smack against his forehead—

There is no chariot::

There is no throne::

There is a room like the room where he and Yael first lived when they left Fort Greene. By all reasonable measures it was squalor. Just one third of the third floor of a brownstone. Outside their window the sounds of cars shouting horns at each other as they entered and exited the BQE. Yael is not here now but Natan searches the corners. He exits the room—he is able to enter and exit through the walls, not the doors—upon exiting he is in another room. He reenters the room. In one corner he sees a pile of ash, too tall to climb or sweep. This is not the corner. He looks to the second corner: there is nothing, just a corner. He looks to the third corner: there is the oven they never used, only opened to keep their old siddurim, copies of the Talmud and Torah and Natan's own writings::

In the fourth corner stands the angel Metatron, face wild with rage and recompense. Natan turns from this corner as fast as he is able, moving to the next corner and the next, infinite corners in this infinite room, looking forever for Yael, for Osman, not finding them there and never knowing if at some point he will again find the corner containing Metatron, the thousand wild eyes, the face of the lion the lamb the leopard and the man, raining fire like Elijah on the followers of Baal upon all the land in the face of the supernal forever:: Where forever means to search only for those you love most knowing only love exists outside of time::::

THE LAST HUSKS

Sitting in the chairs of the United terminal of the Columbus International Airport is Sheriff Earnest Shaw. He is in full uniform, brown shirt and hat and all. Zeke rolls his roller bag with its broken wheels and dirty contents up to the gate. A21. Sits. Johanna is still in the Starbucks grabbing coffee.

"Officer," Zeke says.

"There's what you think you saw, and there's what you saw. I know what you think of this place. I can see the disdain. I get that you've got a story to write. I can tell you this right now—every word you think you can quote from me, from my son, is off the record. I am off the record. Whatever you think you know is off the record. Whatever you think you saw at any point while you were here did not happen. Did. Not. I will dispute the living shit out of it to your editor, to your publisher, to whomever."

"Whomever. Nicely grammatical."

Shaw stands. He does not put a hand on Zeke, but obviously he could. Would. The people in seats around them shift. Some stand and walk away. The gate agent is looking over at them. Just as they're nose to nose, Johanna walks up.

"Earnest," Johanna says. She hands Zeke a caramel macchiato. "Your caramel macchiato, Zeke."

"Jesus, I don't want this sweet—"

Johanna looks at him. He takes the coffee.

Sheriff Shaw sits.

"I don't hate people who believe things," Shaw says, still talking to Zeke, though keenly aware Johanna is now listening, as well. "I don't have any hatred for that community. You know that." He pauses. "You both know that. But there's a danger posed by people who believe too much, too hard, too much too hard. A pliability, a malleability, and a danger. A hope, even a utility, but also a danger. And there sure as shit is a danger to believing too much too hard in a single person. A leader."

"So it was you then," Zeke says.

Shaw looks at him again. Then he looks at Johanna.

"I uncovered what's in the bank accounts," she says. "Your son's, that is."

"Unconnected," Shaw says. "Unrelated to the events. And totally outside your purview to be looking into me like that. I think you should see by now that it's you who will be fucked, not me, if you stay around. Do more searching on this front."

"As you can tell," Johanna says, "I'm out. But I'm out with you knowing that I know what I know."

"You don't know fuck all," Shaw says.

"Well, you were just saying how much you respect people who believe things," Zeke said. "So. She believes what she believes."

"Fuck off," Shaw says. Now he's turned back to Zeke. "Anyway, since this is all above the water now—I might as well say thanks for leading us to the grow lab. We knew it existed, it was close by, for years. Never could find it, and it was putting some real trouble in our final negotiations. Hard to become the main supplier for a newly legal state if you can't present to your partners *where* the supply is, you know, *coming from.* We're not Humboldt County, but the dirt roads out there, they can be a maze even to me. The Prophet was wily with his movements. But I knew—I did—it'd be too much for him not to show you once you were here. Almost lost me, but never entirely. I guess I can thank you. And I'll say thanks in advance for not publishing what you've got."

Shaw looks Zeke deep in his eyes, must be able to see the tears welling there. This is it. He's right. Shaw has the upper hand. There are stories that get written and find readers, stories that get written and find followers, stories that get written and expand with each pair of eyes traversing the page—and there are stories that get killed because they cannot be verified, cannot be fact-checked, cannot be supported by the magazine's legal department. Stories that could put those who didn't realize they were compromised, but just want out, in legal jeopardy. Stories that an editor might even want a writer to keep pursuing, but which have become too complicated to keep telling, to tell.

Stories like this one.

Probably he should have known from the day he first heard of Natan of Flatbush that this would be one of those stories. Really never had a chance. That's what he wanted to tell all along. There was one more chapter on his phone, and not a word he could say to Earnest Shaw that would help him or his friend.

"OK, then," Zeke says. "You win."

"Stand up," the sheriff says. Nothing happens. "I said, stand up, one last time, Fake News. Stand up."

He stands. He looks around. Just about every pair of eyes at gate A21 is on them. Shaw knows it, too. Loudly, too loudly, he says, "Always good to see an old college friend out here in Columbus." Then he drops his voice, and so only Zeke can hear it, he says, "Now get the fuck out of the great state of Ohio. Forever. Selah."

: : : : :

With the sheriff gone, Zeke and Johanna have their first moment alone at the airport. Johanna sits staring straight ahead. Zeke reaches for her hand, and she clutches his so hard his fingers burn.

"I would ask you if you're still sure you want to do this—but I'm not going to insult you like that."

"I might not have been entirely sure on my way here," Johanna says. "I am now."

The thin piped-in air-conditioning of the airport blows down at them. People walk briskly as they do in airports, leaving for places that are not Central Ohio.

"The thing that I saw in the end with Natan," Zeke says, "was not necessarily his belief. It wasn't his intelligence, all that. It was . . . he might not have been a prophet, but he was a leader. A leader who loved people. Actually loved them. Was a real tzaddik. And the way he showed them love was with time. He gave to them his time. Shared. He allowed them to rethink time. He gave them his own time spent alone in prison." Zeke stops again. "To give the gift of time . . . it's the gift of being human. To see time, and to see how it's given."

"You're starting to sound a little prophetic yourself," Johanna says, and immediately sees the happiness on Zeke's face drop. "And I love that in you," she says.

Whether she means it or not, it is just the right thing to say in the moments before they board the plane to head back to New

York together, every aspect of the days ahead uncertain but for their renewed love for each other. That would be real mysticism, real convening with the Lord. Knowing one person enough to see His image in them, fully, totally. To comprehend that the body is the body, the husk, but that it's what's inside the body that brings you to them. That the boundary between what is truly inside them and outside them is not so finite. Inside. The spark. No husk. Zeke could not know if what they were about to do was smart, would keep either of them safe. He would have to believe. It was a move he could only make on faith. Belief. Selah.

ACKNOWLEDGMENTS

In this space, in normal times, I would go through and thank by name the people from the Jewish mystical sects depicted in this book who helped me during four years of research and writing, and the experts who walked me through it all. But these are not normal times. Autocratic rule in Turkey has placed members of the Dönme in Istanbul in more immediate danger than usual; and they are not usually out of danger. Simply accusing any Turkish official of being a "secret Jew" could put their public life into turmoil. So here I'll simply say: thank you so much to those who took the time, care, and patience to talk with me, to read the sacred texts with me, and to help along the way. You know who you are.

Also, as ever: Hugest thanks to my agent, Brettne Bloom, partner in crime. And to my editor, George Witte, who is the most thoughtful and incisive reader I've ever encountered.